# Black Hat Butte

*Also by John D. Nesbitt
in Large Print:*

Black Diamond Rendezvous
Coyote Trail
Man from Wolf River
One-Eyed Cowboy Wild
Wild Rose of Ruby Canyon
North of Cheyenne

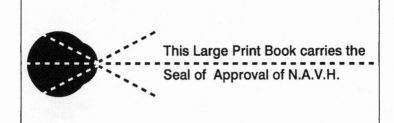

This Large Print Book carries the
Seal of Approval of N.A.V.H.

# Black Hat Butte

## John D. Nesbitt

Thorndike Press • Waterville, Maine

Published in 2004 by arrangement with Leisure Books,
a division of Dorchester Publishing Co., Inc.

Thorndike Press® Large Print Western.

The tree indicium is a trademark of Thorndike Press.

The text of this Large Print edition is unabridged.
Other aspects of the book may vary from the original edition.

Set in 16 pt. Plantin by Minnie B. Raven.

Printed in the United States on permanent paper.

**Library of Congress Cataloging-in-Publication Data**

Nesbitt, John D.
    Black Hat Butte / John D. Nesbitt.
        p. cm.
    ISBN 0-7862-6445-4 (lg. print : hc : alk. paper)
    1. Ranch life — Fiction.   2. Wyoming — Fiction.
    3. Large type books.   I. Title.
    PS3564.E76B584 2004
    813′.54—dc22                                    2004043991

For Cathy,
who deserves to be free.

As the Founder/CEO of NAVH, the only national health agency solely devoted to those who, although not totally blind, have an eye disease which could lead to serious visual impairment, I am pleased to recognize Thorndike Press* as one of the leading publishers in the large print field.

Founded in 1954 in San Francisco to prepare large print textbooks for partially seeing children, NAVH became the pioneer and standard setting agency in the preparation of large type.

Today, those publishers who meet our standards carry the prestigious "Seal of Approval" indicating high quality large print. We are delighted that Thorndike Press is one of the publishers whose titles meet these standards. We are also pleased to recognize the significant contribution Thorndike Press is making in this important and growing field.

Lorraine H. Marchi, L.H.D.
Founder/CEO
NAVH

* Thorndike Press encompasses the following imprints: Thorndike, Wheeler, Walker and Large Print Press.

# Chapter One

Black Hat Butte sat raven-dark on the landscape, its shadow like a hat brim pressed against the plain. When he had been looking at it straight-on, Braden had not seen it as anything more than a butte, dark in its own afternoon shadow. But half turned now in the saddle, glancing in back of him and then looking forward again, he saw its resemblance to a hat. He wondered if, like a lot of hats, it was clamped down tight to keep things from getting out.

Braden gave a quick shake to his head, settled back to his normal position in the saddle, and gave rein to his horse. As the bay picked up its step, its black mane bounced in the afternoon sunlight. Braden looked at the ground as it moved beneath the horse's hooves. Then he lifted his gaze and took in the country around him.

Off to his right a couple of hundred yards, where the land fell away and then rose again, a lone buck antelope stood watching. The tan body and dark horns made a contrast with the green hillside, and the animal gave the impression, as antelope so often did, that it had materialized out of the folds of the rolling plain. The buck stood motionless in the calm afternoon, a pale profile with its black notch of horns and brow turned toward the horse and rider. Braden knew the dark brow held a pair of bulging eyes that suited the animal to life in the open, broad reaches of this country; he knew it gave the antelope comfort to have a liberal space between itself and a foreigner. Even from a man's point of view, the keeping of distance made for pleasant company.

Braden looked ahead again, thinking he would ride around the left side of the butte. The land lay a little higher there and would give him a better view of the country beyond. Anything a man saw might turn out to be important, but at the present his main lookout was for horses — ranch horses with the Seven Arrow brand. Braden's thought flickered back to the corral at headquarters and the thirty-five horses he and the other boys had brought in. Gundry said there should be as many as a dozen more, scattered out on the open range where they had roamed all winter, and he sent the boys back out. Braden wondered how they were going to squeeze another dozen horses out of this country. He had seen saddle stock today, along with cattle and deer and antelope and a couple of mules, but he had not seen a single horse carrying the brand of an upright seven with an arrow running crosswise through its shaft.

The bay picked its way up the slope toward the south side of the butte. Braden thought that if he could bring even one horse back to camp, he would feel better about his day's work. It stretched the mind to try to place a dozen horses out amid a thousand dips and rises, buttes and gulches.

The grass had greened up fine, and now in mid-May the carpet flowers were out. On the ground beneath his stirrups, Braden could see the little, white, five-petaled flowers called phlox. Here and there he saw little yellow flowers, also with five petals, that he didn't know a name for, and in one small indentation he saw a clump of bluebells. Prettiest to his eye were the white phlox, which bloomed in low-lying clusters and reminded him, by their color, of the slender-petaled sand lily that had already made its show and was now but a trace in memory.

Lifting his gaze once again, Braden felt a

quick surprise at the sight of a pale horse and rider angling their way from the north end of the butte. The rider held up his hand, so Braden did likewise, stopping the bay. As the oncoming horse covered the ground with its easy gait, Braden wondered how he had missed seeing the pair sooner. He did not think he had been gazing at the flowers for that long, but the horse and rider were out in the open and must have come from somewhere. Unless they had emerged from a cleft in the butte — or arisen from the grass, as antelope seemed to do — they had been in plain sight for several minutes. Yet he had not seen them. Braden shrugged and decided he would just wait to see if the man seemed to be up to something.

As the dun horse came closer and gave a left-side view, Braden noted the features of the rider. He had long, rope-colored hair and a matching mustache that drooped past the corners of his mouth. He wore a sackcloth jacket and corduroy trousers, which, like his hat, were the color of jute — a pale brown like winter grass. The fellow had a cheerful air about him as the horse sauntered in for the last twenty yards and stopped.

"Shappo nwar," said the rider, tipping

his head backward toward the butte.

Braden wondered if the man was a foreigner, maybe a Swiss or a lean Swede. "Didn't catch that," he said.

The man's light brown eyes twinkled as he raised his right hand to his hat brim. Then he opened his hand, passed his palm downward in front of his face, turned the hand and made a circular motion with his index finger pointing upward, and pointed his thumb backward over his right shoulder toward the butte. Then he said something that sounded like "Santa Fe wren." He gave a sideways shake to his head, passed the reins from his left hand to his right, and looked Braden square in the eye. He held out his left hand, half closed, and rotated it to point at himself with his thumb. "My name's Rove."

Braden gathered that the man did some of his speaking with his hands, even if it wasn't in a sign language that anyone else knew. The mannerism struck Braden as peculiar but not troubling.

"Oh, uh-huh. Pleased to meet you. Mine's Braden. Noel Braden. I work for the Seven Arrow. Run by a fellow named Gundry." He motioned with his head back toward the east.

"Good."

11

Braden wondered what might be good about that, or bad about anything else, but he just said, "Out huntin' horses. Have you seen any with the Seven Arrow brand?"

Rove's eyebrows went together. "Not that I know of, unless you're riding one." He pointed with his chin, as if to indicate the off side of the bay horse.

Braden laughed and nodded. "Fact is, I am. But we're lookin' for a few others, to make up the rest of our roundup herd."

"Well, that's work."

"Sure is." Braden flicked a broad glance at Rove and the dun horse. The man didn't look like a saddle tramp, and he sure didn't look like a hired gun. "Do you ride for someone?"

Rove's light brown eyes twinkled again as the corners of his mouth lifted in a smile. "Not yit," he said, in a voice that sounded like an imitation of a high-pitched Texan.

Braden wondered if everything was a game to this fellow. It wasn't polite to be inquisitive, so instead of asking any more personal questions, he said, "Nice country."

"The best." Rove smiled. "Then you go someplace else, and it's the best, too."

"Well, I've been here a few years, and if

they don't run me off, I might be here a few years longer."

"That can be work, too."

"How's that?"

Rove shrugged. "Just staying clear."

"I don't follow you."

"Old story."

"I don't know if I've heard it."

"They say if you hadn't been with the crows, you wouldn'ta been shot at. But they'll shoot a meadowlark just for singing."

Braden felt a chill creep across his shoulders. "I don't know anything about that."

Rove gave a rolling motion with his arm off to the east and north. "I'm talkin' about *them*, you know."

Braden wasn't sure that he did know, but he said, "I see."

Rove seemed to be settling back into himself after a brief flight. "But you're right. It's a good country. And a man can do well in it."

"I try."

Rove had a half-smile. "So do I."

Braden nodded. "Well, I guess I'd better get back to huntin' horses."

"Hope you find some. If I see any, I'll just whistle."

Braden gave him a close look. "You

know where our camp is, then?"

Rove turned down the corners of his mouth and shook his head. "No, but I like to whistle."

Braden laughed. "Good enough, Rove. It's been good meetin' you." He moved his horse sideways, held out his hand, and shook Rove's.

"Been a pleasure, Braden. We'll see you again."

As Rove turned his horse to the left, Braden saw the right side of his outfit. The man had a grass rope tied to the front of his saddle, and a rifle butt poked out of a scabbard behind his leg. All in all, Braden sensed nothing to cause alarm, even though Rove had some quirks.

Braden topped the rise on the left side of the butte and looked at the plain that spread out to the west. About a mile away lay a homestead site consisting of a house, a couple of sheds, and a windmill. He had thought he might ride over there under the general business of looking for Seven Arrow horses, but now as he took a broad look he had his doubts. Across the plain from the southwest came another Seven Arrow rider. He was nearly a mile away, but Braden recognized the high-crowned dark hat and the blocky brown horse. It was Greaves, leading a gray horse on the end of his rope, with a smaller mouse-colored horse tagging along free beside the gray.

Good enough, Braden thought. If Greaves had two horses, and if the other riders had any at all, they would have something to show for their day's work. Greaves was riding straight toward him now, so Braden waved and dismounted. He watched as the darksome rider came across the flat and then let the horses trot up the slope.

The horses came to a stop, snuffling and snorting, in a small cloud of dust. Greaves got down from his horse and stepped forward, the rope and the reins all in his right hand.

"Found two," he said.

"Looks like it."

Greaves held his right hand forward. "How would you like to hold 'em for a minute, while I roll me a smoke?"

Braden nodded as he took the rope and reins. He looked over the two animals, both of which still had a few tufts of winter coat. He remembered the horses, though neither had been in his string.

Greaves rolled his cigarette and lit it, tipped back his dark hat, and looked over the country he had ridden across. When he turned back to Braden, his brown eyes were hard-set, and he had a grim look on his face.

"Well, you found two more than I did."

Greaves nodded. "Such as they are. Neither of 'em is a top horse, but they'll fill out a string." He took a drag from his cigarette and let out a cloud of smoke. "Did you not see anything?"

Braden shook his head. "Nothin' to speak of. Met a fellow back over here, just a little while ago. Said his name was Rove. Rides a dun horse."

Greaves frowned, then wagged his head. "Don't know him."

"Nice fellow, it seemed. Maybe a bit of a queer bird, but he didn't seem to be up to anything."

"Uh-huh. Does he ride for someone?"

"Not according to him."

"Huh. Just passin' through, then."

"Well, he didn't say that, either."

Greaves raised his eyebrows and took another drag. He was quiet for a moment after he blew away the smoke, and then he said, "I saw someone."

"Oh?"

"Yeah. Wyndham and Farnsworth."

"That shouldn't be much of a surprise.

I'd imagine they're out doin' the same thing."

Greaves shrugged. "I don't know. Seemed to me they didn't have anything better to do than to check on me."

"Were they watching you?"

"It seemed like they waited for me, then rode up on me. They took a good look at the brands on the horses."

"Well, if they're lookin' for horses too, you could expect 'em to be interested. I suppose it's all in the way they do it."

Greaves fixed his brown eyes on Braden and nodded, then took another pull on his cigarette. "It was nothin' friendly."

"Did they act like you were up to somethin' shady?"

Greaves shook his head. "Not really. It was like they had a grudge against me. I didn't like the looks they gave me."

"I wonder what's eatin' on 'em. The way their boss is buddy-buddy with anyone that's got more than a hundred head, you'd think they'd at least act the part."

"You'd think." Greaves took another look out across the country, raised his cigarette halfway to his lips, then paused and turned back to Braden. "They got a bug in their ass, you see." Then he took a drag.

Braden absorbed the comment. Whatever the problem was, Greaves wanted him to know about it. "Uh-huh," he said.

Greaves took off his hat with his left hand and dragged his cuff across his forehead. His wavy brown hair shone in the sunlight until he put the dark hat back in place. "You know," he said, "for the most part, you try to mind your own business and not know any more than you should."

Braden nodded.

"You see someone brandin' a stray calf, or you see where someone killed a beef real careful, and you try not to know or care."

Braden nodded again. "That's generally the best way. It all comes out even, it seems."

"Uh-huh. And even if you know it was a few head of cattle and not just one, you still try to shrug it off. You know?"

"I think so. And if it was a few head of cattle, it probably took a couple of fellows to do it."

Greaves took a last long pull on his cigarette, dropped the stub on the ground, and squashed it with a twist of his boot. "Not to mention any names, or to make you know anything more than you care to, but I don't like the looks they gave me." He looked straight at Braden again.

Braden met his gaze. "Given the circumstances, it sounds like somethin' another person should probably know about."

"Sort of what I thought." Greaves took a deep breath and exhaled. "I don't think they did it on their own."

"You mean they're in cahoots with someone?" Braden felt a small pulse of worry.

"No, I mean they did it for their boss. About a dozen head of mixed brands. They drove 'em up north and sold 'em, unrecorded, to the fellow who has the meat contract for the railroad crew. Then he took 'em over west to Shawnee, where he butchered 'em."

Braden felt another ripple of worry. He wondered how Greaves came to know so much, but he couldn't come right out and ask. So he said, "Just the two of 'em did it, then?"

"The actual movin' of the cattle, yes. But they did it for their boss, and a couple of fellows in town set up the deal. Probably not the first such deal, or the last."

Braden paused for a moment and then said, "That sure is more than a person would like to know."

Greaves gave him a straight look again. "It's not somethin' I went out of my way to find out, but from the looks they gave me,

I figured I should tell someone."

"Well, you sure want to be careful. I take it they didn't say anything about this thing in particular."

"Oh, hell no. But it hung in the air like a rotten smell."

"And you think they're afraid you'll tell someone."

"Well, I just did, didn't I?"

"Yeah. But I mean someone who would do something."

"I don't know if they think I would tell someone, or if they're just tryin' to warn me not to, if you see the difference."

"I think I do. Well, like I said, you've got to be careful. And that makes two of us."

Greaves shrugged. "I don't see how. You don't know a damn thing."

"Never did."

They mounted up and headed back east in the direction of their camp, Greaves with his rope still around the neck of the gray horse, and the mouse-colored horse trotting alongside. It was a calm afternoon, and Braden could feel a light breeze in his face as he rode along. With no sounds except the drumming of horse hooves and the creak of saddle leather, he fell into his own thoughts.

He did not like the import of what

Greaves had told him. It sounded like bad blood where there was no need. Braden could picture Wyndham and Farnsworth's boss, Vinch Forbes, the man with a smile and a ready handshake. He was new to the country, had been here a little over a year, and had made friends with anyone who seemed to have influence. Braden figured it was just the way some people did things, and it made no matter to him. But this development of ill will on one side was bound to complicate things. If Forbes was going to be great friends with the other cattlemen, including Patrick Gundry, the boss of the Seven Arrow, he ought to watch his p's and q's and have his men do the same. He should keep things clean, if only on the surface, and not risk losing the support that he was making such an effort to gain.

Braden shook his head. He didn't really know Forbes. Maybe the man was the type who couldn't do things straight even if it was easier. He didn't know, but he would have to be on the lookout.

The sun was still warm on Braden's back when he saw the clump of trees that marked the campsite. He looked at Greaves, who nodded.

They were the first ones back to camp.

After letting all the horses drink at the creek, they ran a picket line between a couple of trees and tied the two range horses to it. Then they staked their saddle horses out a ways from camp, where they could graze.

Beaumont was the next man into camp, riding a sorrel horse and leading a blue roan.

Braden stood up from where he had been kneeling to build the campfire. "Hello, Wes."

"Howdy." Beaumont's smile gleamed.

Greaves walked over to look at the horse on Beaumont's rope. "Of all the horses to find, you had to bring in that son of a bitch. He was in my string last year, and I didn't care if I ever saw him again."

Beaumont got down from his horse. "Catch as catch can. It was the only one I found all day."

"No matter," said Greaves. "At least you got one."

"Looks like you fellas got two."

"Ed got 'em both," said Braden. "I didn't find a one."

Beaumont smiled. "You spend the day at a road ranch?"

Braden shook his head. "Might as well have."

Beaumont turned to put away the horses, and Greaves went back to sorting out halters.

Braden knelt again to work on the fire, setting twigs on a nest of dry grass and then laying thin branches on top. With his first match he got a blaze going; then he blew on it and fanned it with his hat. A little flame leaped up, and he had a fire.

He sat back with his heels on the ground. There was something satisfactory about cooking grub on a fire. Some punchers didn't care, just ate everything out of a can, but Braden never minded the effort it took to build a fire, wait for the food to cook, and clean up afterward.

Beaumont came back and sat down with his hands around his knees and his boots sticking out forward. "Long day," he said. He took off his hat and set it upside down on the ground next to him. His dark, wavy hair lay matted where the hat had ridden, and the upper part of his forehead showed pale. His dark eyes, no longer in the shadow of his hat brim, sparkled. "Three horses," he said, "and the boss wants a dozen. I wonder where in the hell he thinks we'll find 'em."

Braden leaned forward to feed some larger branches onto the fire. "I suppose he's leavin' that up to us."

Beaumont laughed. "I guess so."

Braden went about slicing salt pork and was laying the pieces in the skillet when Slack came in, riding a sorrel and leading another.

Beaumont's voice sang out. "Howdy-do. Whatcha got there?"

"One for your string, if I remember right."

"Looks like my little crow-hoppin' pal. I don't suppose you just rode up to him and dropped a loop on him."

Slack swung down from his horse. He was a lean rider, of medium height, but no horse was too tall for him. "No, we played stop-and-go most of the afternoon."

Beaumont smiled. "Grand total of four today."

Slack gave a shrug. "Could be worse."

Braden looked at him. Slack had bushy dark brown hair and mustache, and a pair of deep, dark eyes. He had a habit of tossing off casual comments, but now, as always, Braden had the impression that he didn't wind down very far.

Greaves came up to the fire, carrying a halter and a lead rope. "Braden's got grub on the way," he said. "I'll help you put 'em away."

It didn't take long to fry the meat, and it took even less to put it away, along with a dozen cold biscuits they had brought from the ranch. The first wisps of steam were coming out of the spout of the coffeepot when Beaumont took the stack of tin plates to the stream.

Braden poked at the fire while Greaves and Slack rolled cigarettes. Greaves lifted a stick from the fire, held the glowing tip to the end of his cigarette, and then handed the branch to Slack. Braden watched as the expression on Slack's face narrowed. Then came a puff of smoke, and Slack tossed the stick into the fire.

"Sing us a song, Ed."

Greaves shook his head. "I sing like a tomcat. We'll wait till Wes comes back."

Slack took another intense drag on his cigarette. "I've heard you sing plenty."

"Maybe so, when I'm off on my own. But we'll wait for Wes."

Beaumont came back to the fire just as Slack was smoking the last of his quirly down to his fingertips.

Braden looked up at him. "The boys want you to sing, Wes."

"Everybody wants somethin'. I want more money, the boss wants more horses. There's no end to it."

Slack tossed the last of his cigarette into the fire. "Let's have a song or two, Wes.

Why don't you sing the one you sang the other night?"

"The one I sang in the bunkhouse? The one about my sunshine girl?"

"Yeah, that one."

Braden chimed in. "I'd like to hear it again, too. And so would Ed."

"Well, let me get settled here." Beaumont let himself down and sat as before, with his knees up in front of him. "Let me see if I remember it all." He cleared his throat and hummed a few bars. Then his voice came out mellow and clear.

"Out on the wide prairie in broad
    sunny grasslands,
Or back in a canyon 'midst cottonwood
    trees,
Wherever the wildflowers bloom in
    the springtime,
You'll hear this sweet song on the soft
    evening breeze:

"*Yoodle-ooh, yoodle-ooh-hoo, so sings
    a lone cowboy,
Who with the wild roses wants you to
    be free.*

"This hand that I offer is yours now
    and always,

Please take it, my darling, step into
    the light
The darkness and clouds you can leave
    there behind you
As forward you move into fields warm
    and bright.

*"Yoodle-ooh, yoodle-ooh-hoo, so sings*
    *a lone cowboy,*
*Who with the wild roses wants you to*
    *be free.*

"I offer you sunshine and flowers,
    my darling,
A few simple things from a country
    boy's world,
Please come to my arms now and let me
    protect you,
Please come to Wyoming to be
    my sweet girl.

*"Yoodle-ooh, yoodle-ooh-hoo, so sings*
    *a lone cowboy,*
*Who with the wild roses wants you to*
    *be free.*

"We've seen how our lives have grown
    into each other,
We know that together we're destined
    to be,

So please let me help you ward off the
dark shadows,
Please come to Wyoming, to sunlight
and me.

*"Yoodle-ooh, yoodle-ooh-hoo, so sings
a lone cowboy,
Who with the wild roses wants you to
be free.*

*"Yoodle-ooh, yoodle-ooh-hoo, so sings
a lone cowboy,
Who with the wild roses wants you to
be free."*

As the last notes of the song trailed away,
the other three punchers gave a light round
of applause.

"That's a hell of a good song," said
Greaves. "The only thing is, it makes us
want to hear another."

Beaumont smiled, and the firelight made
a contrast between his white teeth and his
dark hair. "Well, let's not make me do all
the work. Let's sing one we all know."

They went on to sing a few trail songs,
including "The Little Black Steer," "The
Cowboy's Lament," and "Lorena." By then
the coffee was ready.

Beaumont said he had had enough of

mournful songs, so the talk turned to other things, including the next day's work.

Greaves finished his coffee first and said he was going to go check on the horses. As Beaumont talked on about the likely places to find Seven Arrow horses, Braden could hear Greaves singing the chorus of Beaumont's song about sunshine and shadows. The larksong notes of "Yoodle-ooh, yoodle-ooh-hoo" carried on the evening air.

Later on, as Braden settled into his bed on the ground, he could still hear the chorus of the song running through his head. He thought about Greaves, and he thought about the girl in the song. Maybe everybody had dark clouds at one time or another — even cheerful Beaumont, who had to know something to make up that song. It was a pretty tune, and a haunting one as well. Braden thought it was good to remember there were pretty girls out there, even if some of them were sad.

# Chapter Two

For breakfast the next morning, Slack served leaden flapjacks. As near as Braden came to the process, he gathered that the cakes consisted of nothing more than a paste of flour and water, fried a gob at a time in the greasy skillet set aside the night before. To make the mess more palatable, Slack brought out four cans of peaches, which he opened with his jackknife in what seemed like a gesture of elegance. As each hotcake came off the skillet, one of the men would receive it in his tin plate, then dump the can of peaches on top and dig in.

"Not bad grub," said Beaumont, first served and first finished, now lifting his nose toward the coffeepot.

"Sticks to yer ribs." Slack was using his index finger to scrape the last of the dough off the mixing spoon and into the skillet. "Gives a cowpunch' somethin' to ride on."

Braden separated a bite-sized piece from the center of his plate and spooned juice onto it. He thought the coffee would help quite a bit. "Sure does," he said.

No one else said anything for a few minutes. Braden felt he had observed the general rule of not complaining about the grub and had thrown in a lukewarm compliment on top of that, so all that was left was to get breakfast done with and go to work.

Greaves, who had offered to stay in camp and see to it that the horses got a chance to graze, said, "I hope we bring in a few more."

"If they're out there, we'll git 'em," said Beaumont.

The sun had just cleared the eastern horizon when the three men saddled up and rode out of camp. Beaumont went south, Slack rode north, and Braden headed west. He thought he would pick up where he left off the day before, although he realized at the same time that horses could have moved into the area he had already combed.

He found the world around him calm and quiet, with no surprises. Sometimes in the morning a fellow might ride up closer than usual on a big deer or a feasting coyote, but this morning he saw nothing but cattle, and none of them up close. When he came to Black Hat Butte, he thought he might see the antelope he had seen before, but he didn't. He realized it was a kind of superstition; when he saw a memorable animal in a place he could mark in his mind, he half expected to see it there again.

He rode up the slope to the south side of the butte, as he had done the day before, and drew rein to take a look around. A broad expanse of country lay spread out around him. Off to the southwest, almost in a line and a few miles apart from one another, stood three buttes. The closest one looked like a pyramid or a cone, with a little nipple on top that earned it the nickname of Little Sister. Second in line stood a broader butte, about the same height but with a narrow, flat top that looked like a hog nose. Braden did not know a name for it. Last in the line, at a distance of about ten miles, loomed Castle Butte with its dark ramparts.

Moving his gaze to the right, still a little south of due west, Braden could see the Laramie Mountains, dark blue and hazy, more than a day's ride away. Below him and beyond him, to the northwest and north, the land rose and fell. It was big country, with distances always farther than they seemed. A rider covering the country would find, tucked among the hills and rises, an endless series of wide draws, little valleys, and surprise canyons. Almost all of it, as far as the eye could see, was good grassland.

Having taken the wide view, he looked now at the little homestead he had thought to visit the day before. It lay about a mile away, but the features stood out in the clear morning air. He saw no movement in the yard, and even the blades of the windmill were still. He might have thought that the place was uninhabited, or that the occupants were asleep, except for a wisp of smoke rising from a stovepipe sticking out of the roof.

The wonder of early morning still lay upon the land as Braden rode down the slope. The little white and yellow carpet flowers bloomed on this side of the butte as on the other. Braden heard a meadowlark sing and another answer, notes tinkling as from a silver flute. A cottontail rabbit started up from behind a growth of sagebrush, bolted, turned, and darted into another clump of cover. A hundred yards to the northwest, a magpie lifted from the ground, zigzagged twice, and flew on. The bay horse snuffled and the saddle leather creaked. Braden felt the energy flowing out from his center, across his chest and into his shoulders and arms. He recalled how, half an hour earlier, his breakfast had felt like a lump of dough in his stomach. Now the good energy of life, some of it no doubt from the starch and sugar, was flowing in his veins.

Quiet prevailed as he rode into the yard between the house, which faced south, and the two sheds. He imagined someone in the house would hear the hoofbeats. If the door didn't open in a minute or so, he could call out. As a matter of habit he turned to look in back of him. A mile away, Black Hat Butte stood dark in its morning shadow. Off to the left, closer to the homestead but still more than half a mile away, sat a longer, lower formation that looked like a sugarloaf. Seeing nothing but landscape, Braden turned back around and brought his horse to a stop in front of the house.

The door opened in a combination of soft sound and shadowy movement. A person appeared in the doorway — a young, smiling, sandy-haired person in a work shirt and trousers.

"Well, hello there," came the cheerful, girlish voice.

"Mornin', Birdie. I hope I didn't wake anybody up."

"No, we're up. Come on in."

Braden swung down, loosened the front cinch, and tied the horse to the hitching rail. He paused long enough to pull a scrap of grass out of the black mane, and then he walked to the door of the house.

Birdie was turning back from having looked inside the house to say something. Then she turned and smiled at Braden. "Come on in, stranger," she said. Her brown eyes were open and friendly, and her face had a smooth tan. Her sandy-colored hair, not much longer than a boy's, was cut in bangs across her forehead and hung straight along the sides to cover her ears.

Braden winked at her. "Don't mean to be such a stranger," he said. "I was on my way here yesterday, but I didn't quite make it."

Birdie moved back to let him into the house. "Beryl has some coffee goin', so it looks like you timed it right."

As Braden took off his hat and stepped into the front room, he caught the aroma of fresh-brewed coffee. An instant later, as his eyes adjusted to the interior of the house, he saw Beryl standing with her back to the kitchen table. Her long, dark hair fell to her shoulders, and her womanly shape was evident even in her work clothes. The first sight was worth the visit; his pulse told him so.

"Hello," she said. "You're just in time for coffee."

Braden smiled. "So I understand. It would be bad manners to turn it down, I suppose."

She smiled back, an even smile that lit up her face. "We could sit outside," she said, "and enjoy the morning."

Birdie glanced at Beryl. "I'm goin' to take care of the critters." Looking at Braden, she wrinkled her nose and said, "I really don't drink much coffee."

Braden smiled at the girl and resisted the temptation to rumple her hair. "Plenty of time for that." He nodded to her, and she ducked out the door. Then he looked back at Beryl, whose appearance quickened his pulse again. "Sure," he said. "It's a nice morning."

She turned to the kitchen and a moment later came back into the front room carrying a coffeepot and two cups. Braden stood aside to let her go out first.

"Go ahead," she said.

"You can go first," he answered. "You've got your hands full."

She handed him the two crockery cups.

"Here. You go ahead. This door doesn't shut right unless you lift it just so."

Braden put on his hat, then took the cups and stepped outside. He had to admire Beryl for her tact. If she didn't want to have a man inside her house, or even closing her door behind her, she had a graceful way of letting him know.

He looked around for Birdie. She was probably in one of the sheds, or in back of them, tending to a horse or a cow or a goat. Birdie was a good girl, all right — old enough to know when other folks might want a minute or two to themselves, but not old enough to want to try things out for herself. He didn't know that she would be that flirtatious even when she got older. She was probably fourteen or fifteen now, and she didn't seem to care for much more than critters.

He glanced back at Beryl, who was pulling the door shut.

"There's a bench over here on the east end," she said. "Birdie and I like to sit there in the shade on a warm afternoon. If the sun isn't too bright, we could sit there now."

"Sounds fine."

They went around to the east end of the house, where a bench about five feet long sat a couple of feet out from the building. Braden set the cups in the middle, and Beryl poured the coffee and set the pot next to the cups. She sat at the far end of the bench, at an angle, with her back to the house, while he sat on the near end at a parallel angle, with his knees pointed at the building. The coffeepot and cups sat on the bench between them.

Beryl looked at him and smiled. He thought she had a fine presence — relaxed and self-assured — as she sat upright with her coffee cup in both hands on her lap. Her gray-green eyes had a clear, friendly look to them, but her expression seemed guarded. "It's been a little while since you dropped by," she said. "I imagine work is picking up now."

"That it is," he said, sipping on his coffee. "I was going to drop by yesterday afternoon, but then I ran into one thing and another. So I thought I'd stop in this morning while I had a chance. We're out tryin' to find the rest of our horse herd. Seems like they got pretty scattered over the winter."

"Oh, uh-huh." After a pause she said, "So, you must be about ready to go out on the roundup."

"Probably in about a week." He took another sip of coffee.

She nodded, and her countenance seemed to soften a little. "So you'll most likely be out on the range for six weeks or so."

"About that."

"Well, I hope everything goes well for you."

Braden interpreted that to mean that she hoped he didn't get thrown from a horse and break his neck. "Oh, yeah. No worry. But thanks." Then after a short moment he said, "How about yourself?"

She looked at her cup and back up at him. "Oh, not much. You know I sold what cattle I had left, so I don't have anything to look out for. Other than taking care of things around the place here, there's not much to it."

"That makes it easy for the time being, even if you don't have anything comin' in."

"Well, I have enough to get by for a while. As time goes on, we'll see what we want to do next." She looked out across the country.

Braden followed her gaze around. "Do you ever think of fencing in your quarter-section?" He didn't like fences, but he knew homesteaders needed them.

She raised her eyebrows. "I suppose I should if I wanted to keep everyone else's cattle off it. But for right now, Birdie keeps an eye on the few animals we've got, and she brings them in each night."

Braden glanced at the shed and back at Beryl. "Well, you know, if you ever need a hand at anything, just whistle." Then as an afterthought he said, "Just say the word."

"Well, thank you. I don't have anything pressing right now, but it's nice to know the offer is there." She gave him the clear, guarded look.

"It's been there." He sat holding his cup with his right hand and resting it in his left.

Her look softened again. "I know." Then she smiled and raised her cup to drink.

He drank at the same time. "By the way," he said, "the coffee is good. I would even go so far as to say it tastes better than the stuff Slack boiled up on the fire this morning."

She laughed. "Well, thank you. I can almost imagine."

Braden smiled back. "I think it might have something to do with the kind of cup you drink it from, too." He paused. "And the company, if I'm not stepping too far."

Her head was tilted toward her mug, so she gave him an upward glance. "Not yet."

A smile played on her face and then disappeared.

They sat without saying anything for a few minutes. Braden finished his coffee and set his cup on the bench. "Well, I probably should be moving along."

She looked up. "So soon? You just sat down."

"I know, but I really should be out lookin' for horses. I didn't find a single one yesterday, which wasn't my fault, I don't think, but I wouldn't want it to happen two days in a row."

"Well, like they say, come again when you can stay longer."

"I know," he said. He felt a smile come to his face. "I won't be a stranger. Say good-bye to Birdie for me. And thanks for the coffee." His eyes met hers. "And I meant it. It was good." He stood up.

She stood up as well, and they faced each other with the bench still between them. Braden reached out his hand, palm up, and Beryl laid hers palm down on his. He pressed the back of her fingers with his thumb, and the hands separated.

"Thanks again," he said.

"Thanks for stopping by."

He touched his hat and turned away, going to his horse and snugging the cinch

41

without looking back. As he gathered his reins and swung into the saddle, he saw her standing by the corner of the house. He didn't know why, but as he raised his hand to wave good-bye, he laid his index finger against his cheek, just below the cheekbone. She broke into a smile. Then he waved, and she waved, and he was riding westward out of her yard.

Beyond the sheds he looked off to his left and saw a small procession headed southwest. Birdie was riding a palomino horse, bareback and without a bridle or halter. A dark horse ambled alongside, and behind them walked a cow and two brindle goats. Braden took off his hat and waved. The motion must have caught Birdie's eye, because she turned and waved.

Braden put his hat back on his head and touched his spurs to his horse. The bay picked up its pace, and Braden settled back into his morning ride. Within a few minutes he fell into the routine of scanning the country, varying his direction as he went down hills and up, pausing on the high points to gaze out over the land. Looking for horses called for attention, but it also left him free to think about a thing or two.

Waving good-bye to Birdie had made a

nice close to the visit. She was a good girl, maybe a little bit of a tomboy, but innocent and wholesome. She was a kind of girl he had seen often, the kind that loved animals and lived close to them. He had also sensed that she was something of a sheepdog, whose presence made it feasible for Beryl to live on a place with her husband gone.

Where her husband was — or if she really even had one any more — was a bit of a mystery to Braden. The most he had been able to get out of anybody else was that she was a grass widow, which could mean either of a couple of things. It could mean she had a baby with no father, which wasn't the case, what with Birdie being no more than ten or twelve years her junior. It could also mean that her husband was gone, which by all indications was the case; but under what circumstances, Braden was yet to learn. Beryl had a polite way of being sociable, but conversation with her had not yet come around to the topic of what her status was. Braden thought that was good enough for the time being. He had the feeling that whatever the case was, it would probably not be all bad news when the knowledge came his way. As principled as he saw her, she would not be even as open as she was if she were more attached. He recalled the way she had smiled when he touched his cheek. That had been a good close to the main part of his visit. He smiled to himself at the thought. Whatever the story might be about the missing husband — last name of Camber, now that he thought of it — it would come in its own good time.

He turned back east a ways, rode north for a couple of miles, and then veered west, zigzagging from one high spot to another, until he came to a place he had well fixed in his mind. The layout itself had no special features — just grassland that rolled and rumpled away on all sides. Off to the west lay a stretch of broken country, a network of gouges and breaks that drained southward toward the Platte. Beyond the broken country several miles farther, maybe halfway from here to the mountains, the river ran in a southeasterly direction until it curved more eastward and flowed, a good twenty-five miles south of here, through the North Platte Valley and on to Nebraska. Around to the north, the land stretched away the same as where he now sat looking across the ears of his horse.

Only in the farthest distance did any

landmarks rise above the swells of the plain. If there was a line of demarcation for him in that direction, it was the railroad, with whistle-stop towns every ten or twenty miles. Off to the east, at a distance of a half-dozen miles, a line of hills a little darker than the grassland ran north and south. Parallel to the hills ran a well-traveled road, which Braden had in his mind as a sort of intermediate boundary. Up against those hills, almost due east from this spot, would be the Seven Arrow headquarters. On the other side of those hills, at a distance of another eight to ten miles, lay the Rawhide Buttes, dark and rugged, and on the other side of them he pictured a main road, the old Cheyenne–Black Hills stage route. He turned in the saddle and looked south, where he saw Black Hat Butte in plain view. It was not a huge formation, but for him it was a major landmark. He had had a clear view of it from as far away as ten or twelve miles north.

The place where he sat, from the point of view of a wandering traveler who had strayed from a main road, would be the middle of nowhere. The land stretched away forever. To Braden, he was more or less in the middle of a huge tract of land bounded on the south and west by the North Platte, on the north by the railroad, and on the east by the old Cheyenne-to-Deadwood road. Those were the boundaries he pictured as he sat on the bay horse on a calm May morning, here on the one hundred and sixty acres he had claimed. This place, common and undistinguished from the surrounding range, with Black Hat Butte in clear view, was the center of the world for him.

Just a quarter-section of grass — it wouldn't make a living for a man trying to make it on his own, but it was something. Possession of land was something new to Braden, as he had just filed on this piece during the winter. Before the year was out he would prove up on it — build a shack, dig a well, mark his boundaries — and then think about what came next. For right now, just having the liberty to bask in the sunlight on his own land, with the world stretching out in all directions, gave him the feeling that life held promise.

It would have suited him to snag a Seven Arrow horse on his parcel, but a short ride around the high points showed him no animal life at all. Horses, cattle, antelope, jackrabbits — none of them knew boundaries on the open range, but they all just happened to be somewhere else. Braden looked at the sun, which had made a fast climb, and he decided to keep riding north.

On he rode as before, with the sun warming his back, then his right cheek, then his right shoulder, then his back as he varied his direction. On a hunch he turned west, where he knew the land fell away into a grassy bowl. He always found cattle there during roundup, and he thought he might find a horse or two there this morning.

He stopped the bay a few yards short of the crest, before he could see down into the bowl. Then he stood in the stirrups and caught a quick glance below. He saw animals. He edged the horse closer and rose again. Out of ingrained habit he counted the cattle — seven cows and five calves — but his main interest fell on a strawberry roan horse that was grazing a few yards off from the cattle.

Braden sat back down and untied his rope. He thought he knew the horse as a Seven Arrow mount, but he would have to ride close enough to read the brand before he could rope the animal anyway. He nodded to himself, then turned his horse around, went down the slope a ways, curved around to the left, and dropped into the bowl.

Before he came within a hundred yards, the cattle started running, setting up a rumble of hoofbeats and a cloud of dust. As the bay horse took out after them, Braden saw that there were six calves. No matter there, he thought. He turned the bay to go after the roan, which had bolted off to the left when the cattle broke. Now the roan stopped and looked back to its left, showing the Seven Arrow brand. Braden slowed the bay to a trot and then a walk, edging up to the left side of the roan. He swung his rope three times, thinking the roan would break again, but it didn't. He dropped the loop, and that was it. It was almost too easy.

As Braden gave the rope a couple of turns around his saddle horn, he watched to see if the roan was going to put up a fight. Still no trouble. Braden turned the bay to the left, and the roan fell right into line.

Coming back up out of the bowl with the sun in his face, Braden gave a thought to where he was. The ranch was several miles east and a couple of miles south. Horse camp was farther south but not quite so far east. For all the difference between them, he might as well take the horse to camp, and Greaves could add one to the tally. He fixed the point in his mind and headed the bay southeast. The roan trotted right along.

Braden relaxed now. He thought that if he saw another horse he would figure his odds on whether he could turn the roan loose, catch the new horse, and hope the roan would follow. As easy as the roan was, he could come back for it if he had to. Braden smiled at himself. He had ridden all day the day before without finding a single horse, and here he was thinking about how he could double up.

His ride across country presented no challenges. Twice he rode up on Seven Arrow cattle, which ran off, but no other large animals came into view. The sun rose higher in the sky, and a few clouds began to gather on the mountaintops in the west.

When Black Hat Butte was on his right and the Seven Arrow headquarters would be back to his left, he saw two horsemen headed at a right angle to the direction he was taking. He sat up straight now, estimating the point at which their paths would cross. It would be almost a mile ahead. He could see the two riders, and he could see the probable junction. Unless the two men wanted to avoid him, they would meet.

The other riders disappeared in the landscape, but a few minutes later they came back into view. Braden thought they looked like his own boss, Gundry, and the latecomer Forbes. It could well be. Forbes might have gone to the Seven Arrow, and Gundry might have ridden out with him on an errand. What that errand was, or might be, did not concern Braden. If the men chose to recognize him, he would show his catch and move on.

After several more minutes, Braden could see that the meeting would take place. Forbes and Gundry had slowed to a stop and were waiting a couple of hundred yards ahead. Both wore brown hats and rode sorrel horses, and their faces were in shadow, so they looked like a matched pair at this distance.

Drawing closer, Braden could see the differences he already knew. Forbes had reddish-blond hair and a beard the same color, while Gundry had nondescript brown hair and went clean-shaven except for a trimmed mustache. Closer yet, Braden saw the early silver streaks in Forbes's beard, then his blue eyes, then the plain brown eyes of Gundry. Both men were looking in Braden's direction but with no great intensity.

"Good morning," he said as he brought the bay to a halt.

The other two returned the greeting, in cheerful tones.

"Caught one, huh?" said Gundry.

"Sure did," said Braden. "We got four yesterday, was all, and we hope to do better today. Depending on how the others do, we might all go over to the breaks tomorrow, or even after dinner today, and work them together."

"You might have tried that first."

Braden shrugged. "Didn't think of it, I guess."

"Oh, well, I doubt that it matters. As long as you get them in."

"We'll give it our best try."

Forbes let out a short, high laugh and then said in his light voice, "That's the best you can do, isn't it?"

Braden gave him a half-smile. "I guess so."

Gundry spoke again. "Well, you men know how to do your work. But I think it would be a good idea to take the ones you've got so far and get them back to the corrals, and then all of you go over and work the breaks." Then he added, "Do it the best way you know how."

Braden nodded. "I'll tell the boys."

Gundry looked at the roan. "That one looks like he's in pretty good shape. Almost fat."

"Uh-huh. Doesn't look like he's been runnin' with a band. I found him pokin' along with some cattle."

Forbes's high laugh came out again. "Just likes a little company, doesn't he?"

"Seems like it."

Gundry lifted his reins with his left hand. "Well, we're goin' to be on our way. Go on about your work, and don't let us get in your way."

"Will do."

Forbes touched the edge of his hat brim in what seemed like a gesture of politeness. "Say hello to all the boys for me, Braden. How many of you are there, now?"

"Four of us."

"Well, say hello, and I hope you find plenty of horses."

"Thank you."

Forbes and Gundry rode off in the direction of the butte, and Braden pushed on toward camp. He glanced at the two men and then looked back at the country ahead of him. Gundry was not a bad boss, for all that; he just liked to be boss. As for Forbes, he always seemed a little too light and friendly. Braden figured that was natural for a fellow who had a thing or two to keep in the dark. And what did it matter how many of them were out hunting horses? Braden shrugged. Forbes probably wanted to make sure he was sending four helpings of goodwill. Maybe that was the way a fellow thought he had to act when he lifted a few head of cattle now and then.

# Chapter Three

Braden relaxed on his bunk, sock-footed, with his hands behind his head. As any puncher soon learned, he took his rest when he could get it. After three full days of rounding up stray horses, he and the others had come back to the ranch, where each man worked with his string and helped get all the equipment ready for roundup.

All the horses had to be combed and curried. Some took shoes, and they all had to have their hooves trimmed. Each day, a man tried to get a saddle on every horse in his string. Some horses needed to be bucked out, some needed to be run, and some just needed to be reminded of what the saddle and bridle meant.

In the meanwhile, the men had also cleaned and greased the two wagons — the chuck wagon and the bed wagon — and they had inspected the harness, the axles, the tongues, the singletrees, the tarps, and the poles they carried along. They had cleaned and caulked the water barrels, ground and double-bagged the coffee, and stocked the chuck wagon with canned goods, dried fruit, flour, rice, and beans. Lum, the bunkhouse and wagon cook, oversaw every detail pertaining to the wagons. In two days the crew would roll out, and Lum didn't want a spoon out of place.

Braden had some apprehensions about the coming season. Gundry had announced that Forbes and his riders would be joining the pool, which in the last couple of years had consisted of the Seven Arrow and two other outfits. Now there would be a fourth. A few more riders and their horses didn't make much difference, as reps from other outfits came and went as the roundup moved across the country. But Braden had a queasy feeling about sharing the company of Forbes and his two riders Wyndham and Farnsworth, when he knew what Greaves had told him. And he imagined Greaves liked it even less.

From all appearances, Greaves had told no one else. The subject had not come up again, even with Braden, but the names of Forbes and his riders had come up now and then in conversation. Greaves didn't bring them up, and Braden didn't, but Beaumont and Slack tossed in a comment here and there that suggested no awareness of what Greaves knew. Now lying on his bunk, staring at the cobwebbed rafters, Braden found it worrisome to think about having to be always on his guard, having to wonder if Forbes knew that Greaves knew, or if Forbes guessed that Greaves had told someone. For all of Forbes's good-fellowship, Braden knew that some of them on roundup would feel the strain.

He tried to brush aside those thoughts and think of more pleasant ones — of a little homestead on the other side of Black Hat Butte, for instance. He recalled Birdie and her critters, free spirits at ease out on the prairie. With a feeling that ran deeper he thought of Beryl, clear and firm and poised, but soft in a moment. Even if there were things he didn't know, she had not given him cause for an ounce of dread.

His thoughts traveled to another locale, a couple of miles north of the butte. From his place he could see the landmark, just as she could. It was as if he could go out of himself, across the country, and meet with her in a common spot. He was glad he had stopped by at his claim a few days earlier; he was glad to renew contact with a place that gave him a feeling of optimism. It helped him stay with his plan, to keep setting money back for improvements and for a few head of cattle of his own. It gave him a sense of pride, having earned something for himself. It wasn't a subject he talked about very much with the other hands, or that he had talked about yet with Beryl or any other woman. It was enough to be able to look at himself and feel solid about it.

He sat up on the bunk, turned, and put his feet on the floor. Beaumont was shuffling the cards and calling for a game of rummy.

"Come on, boys. Step right up. Won't cost you a dime. Just for fun. Not a single dime. Save yer money for the big top."

Chairs scraped on the floorboards as Slack and Greaves took their places. Braden walked over to the remaining chair.

"Come on, young feller," said Beaumont, still in his imitation of a sharper. "Just for fun."

The next day being Saturday, the four men ate a quick supper and got scrubbed up to go to town. The wagons were scheduled to roll out on Monday morning, so this would be their last little fling at fun for a while. The town of Carlin lay eleven miles north, where the road that ran along the base of the hills met the railroad. Braden wished they could have gotten an earlier start, but he knew they could sleep in on Sunday if they got back way late.

The sun had set and darkness had settled in when the four riders reached the town, all of which lay on the north side of the tracks. Where the road coming into town crossed the main street, two buildings had lights shining — on the left, the Lucky Chance saloon, and on the right, the Aster hotel and restaurant. Both of them faced the railroad. The other businesses, such as the general store, the livery stable, the blacksmith shop, and the coal chute, would have closed up a few hours earlier. Their outlines were visible, as were the church and the dozen or so houses, some of which showed lamplight in the windows. Not a sound issued from the stock pens on the west edge of town, and except for the low mutter of sounds coming out the front door of the saloon, the town was quiet.

Saddle horses stood tied to the hitchracks all along the side of the street that the saloon occupied. Braden imagined that most of the cowpunchers for miles around were doing the same as he and his pals were doing. Once inside the saloon, he saw how right he had guessed. Two of the first few men he saw were Wyndham and

Farnsworth. Forbes's place on Antler Creek was south and west of the Seven Arrow, so these two men would have ridden in on the same road ahead of Braden and the others.

Braden had never cared all that much for either Wyndham or Farnsworth. They had worked for a couple of other outfits, first separately and then together, before they took up with Forbes. Of the two, Wyndham seemed to be the leader. A little taller than average, with a full build, he had dark hair that was graying even though the man wasn't very far into his thirties. His blue eyes took in the Seven Arrow boys as they walked past him.

Braden also caught a glance from the dark, beady eyes of Farnsworth, who stood on the other side of Wyndham as the men came into the saloon. Farnsworth was small and wiry, below average height, with mouse-colored hair that was always mashed down and never looked clean. Braden thought he had a shifty glance, as if he didn't want anyone to see what he might be holding back. Up until the last few days, Braden had thought it was the guilty habit of someone who often had a hangover and didn't want anyone looking into him.

As Beaumont ordered the first round for his group of four, Braden took another look at Farnsworth, who had continued watching them but now turned around when Braden looked at him. The small man was an average sort of cowhand, who had let it be known that he would like to get into detective work. For that reason, among others, Braden supposed, he had attached himself to his partner. Wyndham made occasional mention of having done some sort of police work down in the Indian nations, and he spoke with an accent from that part of the country. Braden had heard him say on a couple of occasions in this very saloon that he would like to go back into a comfortable line of work such as he had had before, perhaps in a larger town such as Omaha or Denver. From that, anyone at the bar could project that the big man was going to help his little buddy ease into the detective ranks. Braden looked at the two of them together. Maybe that would be a good place for them — a big city far away.

Beaumont handed out the drinks, and with a "Here's how" the four glasses clicked in a toast. The bar was packed elbow-to-elbow with cowpunchers and railroad workers, and the tables in the saloon had men in chairs crowded around them, so the four young men stood and drank in place, one or another of them shifting to let another man pass by. Between sips, Braden got a look at the crowd.

At the back of the saloon he saw the crib girls but did not try to keep track of them. There were three or four of them, and they came and went as their favors were requested. Braden liked girls well enough, but he didn't care for the ones who worked near a railroad, not any more than the ones who worked near an army post. It was the company they kept in those places — swaggering men who carried the clap from one spot to another. Braden noticed that Greaves and Slack were both looking at the girls; that was their business. He cast his glance around the crowd again, and to his surprise he saw Forbes.

The light-haired, light-bearded man was making his way through the mass, pausing here and there to pat a shoulder or shake a hand. Braden figured he must have been somewhere in the back part of the saloon, blocked out by the crowd. He was working his way to the front, in no apparent hurry. He paused to pat Beaumont and Braden on the shoulder, one with each hand, and moved on. After a brief exchange with his two men, he walked out the front door.

Greaves and Slack, meanwhile, gravitated toward the back of the saloon. Greaves was making talk with a voluptuous yellow-haired girl, and Slack had his head lifted in conversation with a redhead. Braden looked away, and when his gaze traveled back, he noticed that Greaves and the yellow-haired girl were gone. A few minutes later, Slack and the redhead had also disappeared.

Time passed, and Braden went to the bar to buy drinks for Beaumont and himself. Connors, the barkeep, said hello and served the drinks. Braden went back to stand near Beaumont. Not long after that, Slack appeared again in the saloon and without a comment took his place in company with his two pards. Beaumont fell into talking with another cowpuncher, while Slack, who as a rule did not talk a great deal anyway, drew into himself. Braden imagined he was in the afterglow of a trip to the room, trying to get more out of the five minutes by reliving them. For Braden, there wasn't much to do except stand around, exchange greetings with other men, and make a drink last as long as he could.

At about eleven o'clock, three men came

into the saloon. They looked a little out of place among the cowhands and railroad workers, but they had the air of feeling quite at home in the Lucky Chance. Braden recognized all three as men who worked in town.

First in line was Norman Dace, a lean fellow in his forties who always reminded Braden of the phrase "chicken neck." He had a thin neck with striations and wrinkles, and on top of it sat a head that seemed just a bit large for the narrow body. He looked undernourished, or, as people said, like a cat that had been eating lizards. He carried his head, with its medium-brown hair and medium-blue eyes, tilted back just enough to give the impression that he didn't recognize everyone he knew. Braden thought he was a little high-hatted for a hotel clerk, but he did have friends.

One of those friends, Ben Varlett, followed next in line, palming his straight-stem pipe and puffing out smoke. Like Dace, he was dressed in a jacket, vest, and collared shirt. He had dull blond hair and a receding hairline, and beneath the broad forehead he had a pair of large brown eyes. Owing to a slight curve in his shoulders, not so pronounced as to be called a hunchback, he carried his head forward, which caused him to turn his head in an odd way when he looked to the side. Braden thought he must have learned to compensate for the effect by giving a person a steady look when he said hello or paused to talk. Varlett was in charge of the restaurant part of the Aster, just as Dace ran the hotel. Unlike Dace, Varlett was friendly. He said hello to everyone, and he was something of a toucher, especially with women. Braden had noticed in the café that Varlett was given to touching waitresses and female customers on the arm, elbow, and shoulder. Braden had the impression that Varlett said hello to men as a way of assuring the world that he was equally outgoing to everyone.

Dace and Varlett's companion was a fat man named Shadwell, who helped out on both sides of the Aster. He strolled along behind the other two, smoking a cigar as if he didn't have a care in the world, but he had a jaundiced tone to his complexion and a generally unhealthy look to his whole person. He had thin blond hair, almost white, sparse across the top and unkempt around the sides. His pale blue eyes were usually bleary and often bloodshot, and his upper cheeks showed a few broken blood vessels. Despite his jowls and soft mouth, he had an affable smile. Beaumont said he had been a jailer somewhere in Nebraska, which Braden had heard from others as well. Beaumont also said he got fat by eating all the pies that came in, to make sure no one smuggled files to the prisoners. Braden thought that was Beaumont's embellishment.

With the appearance of these three men, Braden figured the Aster had closed for the evening. Anyone who wanted a room would either know to look for Dace in the saloon or would go there to ask, as it was the only place in town still open. In his way, Braden thought, Dace was a true company man, who took his work with him.

Varlett made his way to the bar, and in a couple of minutes he turned back in his rigid, semihunched way to hand a glass of whiskey to Dace and a mug of beer to Shadwell. Then he fetched his own drink, also a glass of whiskey, and joined his cronies.

Braden twisted his mouth to keep from speaking or laughing. He thought that down a ways from the surface there was something absurd about the trio, something less tangible than Varlett palming his pipe or Shadwell jingling the coins in his pocket. It was the air of importance they assumed, the demeanor of men who thought they carried weight in the affairs of Carlin and its surroundings. Influential cattlemen did stay at the Aster and eat in the café, and Braden had seen Dace, who often sat at a table by himself reading a newspaper, pull his chair around and give a few sage nods. On like occasions he had seen Varlett, wielding a roasting fork or carrying a coffeepot, pause at the cattlemen's table and put himself on a conversational plain with them. Even Shadwell seemed to consider himself a notch above the cowpunchers and section hands, as if on the coattails of his two associates he had made himself sociable with men of prestige.

As the night wore on, the crowd at the Lucky Chance began to thin a little. At some point between eleven and twelve, Braden noticed Forbes come back into the saloon, pause to speak to his two hired hands, spend a few moments of merriment with the trio from the Aster, and leave again. Braden wondered where in town a man might have gone to at this time of night, but then he shrugged off the question as none of his business. When Wyndham and Farnsworth left a few minutes later, Braden figured they were headed back to the ranch with their boss.

Two men moved down the bar to their right to occupy the space just left by Forbes's men and to hurl genial comments at two men standing at the end of the bar near the door. The movement left space in the middle of the bar, and after exchanging gestures, Beaumont and Braden moved to the available space, with Slack standing by. Now they had a place to set their drinks as they waited for Greaves, who had still not returned from the back regions.

Connors, the barkeep, paused as he gave a routine swipe to the top of the bar. "Hello again. Are you all right on drinks?"

Braden looked at their glasses. "I think so, Lex. But, say, you wouldn't have any idea of what happened to Greaves, would you? He went in back with a girl over an hour ago."

Connors raised his eyebrows. He had a full head of ripply gray hair, combed back on all sides, and a pair of dark, coffee-colored eyes, so the gesture showed expression. "Must be gettin' his money's worth."

"I hope so. I hope he's not just passed out."

"It's been known to happen. But he didn't have all that much to drink, did he?"

Braden shook his head. "Just one drink. Did he take a bottle back there with him?"

Connors drew his face into a frown. The wrinkles on his forehead, along with the blotches on his upper cheeks, gave him a thoughtful look that Braden had seen before. Connors was an educated man and was known to have a few books in his room. Sometimes a simple question or comment brought on that studious look, which ran deeper than the topic of the moment. "No," he said. "Not that I recall. I let out a couple of bottles at that end of the bar, but not any to him."

"Let's not worry about him," said Beaumont. "It's probably been a while since he saw a pretty set of toenails, and he's makin' the most of it."

Connors nodded. "I'd give him a while longer. No one has ever gotten fleeced back there, not for as long as I've been here, anyway." He tapped the bar with his folded rag, as if in reassurance, and moved away to tend to his other patrons.

Braden looked at Beaumont, who shrugged, and they each took a drink. It wouldn't do to worry too much about a fellow puncher, who would take it as a suggestion that he needed looking after. Braden glanced at Slack, who had focused all of his attention into rolling a cigarette.

When Connors drifted back again, Braden decided to bring up another subject. "Say, Lex," he said. "I've got a question."

Connors stood and turned. "Uh-huh. What is it?"

"I heard a fellow say something funny the other day, and I was wondering if you could tell me what it meant."

Connors gave a clever smile. "I don't know if I can explain someone else's joke."

"It wasn't really a joke, just something he said."

"Well, give it a try."

"It was a little odd. I'd never met this fellow before, and out of the blue he said something that sounded like 'shappo nwar.' "

"Say it again?"

"Shappo nwar."

Connors's lips moved as he made the sound for himself. "You know, I think it might be *chapeau noir*. It's French. Means 'black hat.' "

"Oh, sure. That's got to be it. We were out by the butte when I ran into him."

"Well, it seems to fit, but I can see where it might be a funny thing to say without any explanation."

"This fellow was a little strange, but not bad. And now that I think of it, he said something else like that. It was something that sounded like 'Santa Fe wren.' But Santa Fe would be Spanish."

Connors shook his head. "You've got me on that one. And I do know a little Spanish, too."

"I couldn't make sense of it either. But that's what it sounded like."

" 'Santa Fe wren,' huh?" Connors went to turn away, and then he paused. "Hell, I bet that's some more of that trapper French."

"He didn't look like a trapper."

"No, but people like to throw around the lingo, repeat things they've heard."

"Uh-huh."

"There's a phrase in French that goes *Ça ne fait rien*. It means 'That doesn't matter.' "

Braden let out a sigh and shook his head. "Just small talk, then. Fooling around, most likely." He recalled Rove's playful manner, and he laughed.

Beaumont had been following the conversation but did not say anything. When Connors walked away, he looked at Braden. "Some kind of joker?"

"I bumped into this fellow the other day,

name of Rove. It was out by the butte, just before I met up with Greaves. Nice enough fellow, really. He just said a couple of funny things, was all."

"Some people talk funny."

"I guess they do."

As the conversation fell back into a lull, Braden became aware of movement to his right. The men who had been standing there had left, and the three men from the Aster had moved up to the bar. Shadwell stood at Braden's right, then Varlett in the middle, and Dace on the other side.

Dace said something that Braden didn't hear, followed by a comment from Varlett.

"I've heard several cattlemen say it, and Forbes said it again just a little while ago. Not much winter loss, and a good calf crop. Should be a good year for everyone." Varlett held a match to his pipe.

Braden felt himself being irritated by the authoritative tone. He didn't care to eavesdrop on other conversations anyway, and when Dace muttered another comment, he was glad not to hear it. He was trying to think of another topic to open up with Beaumont and Slack, when he felt a nudge at his right elbow. He turned to get a full look at Shadwell's face, which had a friendly expression that a person would like to see on the face of a benevolent uncle.

"Is that the way it is out your way, too?"

"What's that?"

"Not much winter kill, and plenty of calves?"

Braden shrugged. "I don't know for sure. We'll know more as the roundup moves along."

Shadwell smiled, exposing a row of stubby lower teeth. "It's what everybody is sayin', sounds like to me."

"Well, let's hope it turns out that way."

"Should be good for everyone."

"We can hope it is."

"Did you ship a lot last fall? I heard 'most everyone did."

Braden pursed his lips and then spoke. "I don't remember the exact count. I think it was normal."

"Your boss Gundry — of course, you'd know better than I would — said it was a good year."

"I suppose it was, especially if he said so. It paid all the same to the rest of us."

"Oh, uh-huh. Well, it looks like there'll be plenty of work this year. Not like some years, where they have to lay off hands in the middle of the season."

"Let's hope so."

"Of course, they wouldn't let the better ones like you go first, anyway."

"Hard to tell."

"Well, that's just what I heard."

*You heard a lot,* Braden thought, but he said nothing. He thought the conversation might die away, but he knew it was just a hope when he felt another nudge at his elbow. He turned to see the smiling uncle again.

"Did anyone ever tell you, you look like an Indian?"

"A couple of times." In reality, Braden had heard it more than a couple of times. He could see it himself in the mirror behind the bar — the dark hair, dark eyes, and prominent cheekbones. For all he knew, there might be some Indian blood somewhere back in the family, but he didn't see where it mattered, most of all to Shadwell.

"Didn't mean anything by that, you understand. It's just that when you turn your head a certain way —"

"Think nothing of it."

"Well, really. I didn't mean anything."

"I know."

At that moment, Braden was thankful to hear Beaumont's voice.

"Well, here comes Greaves, at long last."

Braden turned to face Beaumont and the back of the saloon. Greaves, with a foggy look about him, was making his way forward. When he joined his friends, Beaumont clapped him on the shoulder.

"A few more hours and we would've started worrying about you."

Greaves shook his head. "I think I passed out."

Slack gave him a close look. "Did she put something in your drink?"

"I don't know. I've still got all my money, except what I gave her, you know."

Beaumont grinned. "Well, at least you got your wick trimmed."

Greaves took a deep breath and exhaled. "I guess I did. But I really don't remember."

Slack made a hissing sound with his tongue and teeth. "If you gave her some money, I hope you did more than just sit around and talk."

# Chapter Four

Lum set a platter of fried potatoes and another of fried beef on the table. "This is the best kind of grub to pull you boys back into shape after bein' out all night," he said. Half a minute later he came back with a tin plate of biscuits and the coffeepot. "Eat up," he said, "but take your time and enjoy it. The wagon rolls tomorrow."

Braden waited his turn and then served himself. He glanced across the table at Greaves, who had a morose look on his face. Braden could tell he wasn't just sick from having had too much to drink. Maybe a day off would do him good.

Braden dug into his meal and thought about the coming week. As Lum said, the wagon would roll on Monday morning. In truth, two wagons would roll, but everyone spoke of "the wagon" as the center of activity during roundup. The Seven Arrow was providing both wagons and the cook, plus four riders and Gundry himself. Another cattleman, Davis, was contributing five riders including himself, plus a day wrangler. The third outfit, the MT, which was owned by an eastern partnership, was putting in four riders and the night wrangler. Forbes, with his two men, did not seem to be supplying anything additional, but it was understood that even though his part was smaller, he would provide every fourth beef they butchered for camp meat. Braden saw some irony in that arrangement. He thought it was like a fellow buying a round of drinks for the poker table after he had cheated everyone out of a pot. Nevertheless, Forbes and his men would take part in the roundup, and to some appearances Forbes would be on an equal footing with the other outfits.

Gundry would be the roundup boss. He contributed more men and equipment — perhaps, as Braden thought, to give him more authority — and he had a natural talent for laying out work and giving orders. Braden could see why Forbes had cultivated Gundry's friendship, and he thought he understood why Gundry went along with so little reservation. It gave him more power, as men who formed these alliances shared power among them. It also gave Gundry more of a base — not only for his current authority, which left him at the peak of a pyramid of four outfits instead of three, but also for any other ambitions he might have. It was common wisdom among the cowhands, Seven Arrow and otherwise, that Gundry had his eye set on Cheyenne and the track that led through the state legislature and beyond.

Gundry was still young for the world of politics — in his early forties, by Braden's estimate. He spent part of each winter in Cheyenne, where the cattlemen hobnobbed and the elite among them ran the legislature. Back home, he seemed to be practicing up — forming his base of support and building a reputation as a man who took charge and got things done. Today he was holed up in the ranch house, no doubt reviewing all of the details of men, horses, supplies, camps, and reps. If he was going to do something like boss a roundup, he was going to do it well. And, in a gesture that didn't cost him much to look good, he was giving his men the day off.

As Braden did not have a hangover to nurse, he thought he might squeeze in a visit to the homestead on the other side of Black Hat Butte. When breakfast came to a close, he said he thought he would go out on a ride. The others nodded, in the circumspect way they all practiced, and he got up and left the bunkhouse.

He picked out the bay horse and brushed it down. As he was adjusting the saddle on its back, Greaves came out of the bunkhouse and headed his way. The dark hat cast a shadow on Greaves's features.

Braden reached under the horse, brought up the cinch, and slipped the latigo through the ring. "What do you think, Ed? Are you feelin' any better?"

"I guess so." Greaves paused, then said, "Would it bother you if I rode out with you a ways?"

Braden paused in his task of snugging up the cinch. He saw a troubled look on Greaves's face. "No, not at all. Go ahead and get your horse. I'm in no hurry."

It was a clear morning, with a breeze coming from the northwest, as they rode out of the ranch headquarters and onto the prairie. When the buildings were half a mile behind, Braden looked across to his right at his fellow puncher.

"Have you got something on your mind, Ed?"

"I guess so. I just don't know what the hell happened last night."

"Well, sometimes when a fella drinks way too much, he blacks out. But you weren't that far gone to begin with."

"That's right. And that's what's got me worried. I think someone was tryin' to get to me."

Braden looked at him again. "Oh, really?"

"I can't say for sure, but here's how I'm piecin' it together. This part didn't come to me until later, but I remember when me and Slack first went back to talk to them girls. Forbes was movin' away from 'em, like he had just been talkin' to 'em, or had even been to the room with one of 'em. As I go back to put it together, I think there was somethin' between him and Emily."

"Is that the girl you were with?"

"Yeah."

Braden raised his eyebrows. "Well, that could be. But it's hard to see where he could have done anything, like give her something to put in your drink after you went to the room with her."

"I know. It seems like I'm stretchin' it. Some things add up, and some don't. But you know, lookin' back, it seems like she latched on to me. You don't see it that way at the moment, of course."

"Uh-huh." Braden knew the feeling. A woman could make a man feel like it was all his doing, if she was good at it.

"So I don't know."

Braden thought for a moment to phrase his question. "How much of it do you remember, once you were in the room?"

"Not much, really."

"I suppose there were times when you didn't have your drink in both hands."

"Well, of course. Once I was in the room and I gave her the money, I set my drink on her dresser while I took off my hat and boots. She had her back to me then, while she was facin' the dresser, and I figured she was stashin' the money like they do."

Braden had a picture of that. "Uh-huh."

"And then she said she'd be back in a minute."

"You think she went to get something to put in your drink?"

"No, I think she already did it. She just left me there alone, sittin' on the bed waitin', so I drank up the rest of my drink. When she came back I was pretty woozy, and she was teasin' me an' all, an' gettin' me into bed, but I don't remember doin' anything."

"Do you remember anything at all after that?"

"It was like a bad dream. I don't know how much of it was a dream and how much of it, if any of it, happened. But everything was dark, and it seemed like someone else was there in the room, trying to get me to answer questions."

"What kind of questions?"

"I don't know. Just questions that I didn't know how to answer."

"Can you remember the voice?"

Greaves shook his head. "Not really, but it wasn't her voice. It was some man's voice."

Braden looked at the surrounding country. There was no one in sight for miles. "You think it was Forbes, then? He's got a yellow-daisy voice you'd remember."

"That's a part that doesn't add up. I don't think it was his voice." Greaves gave him a look. "But you think he could have done it?"

"Well, I don't want to feed the fire, but he did go out the front door of the place and come back a while later."

"It could have been. I don't know. There could have been two of 'em in the room, and he was just listenin'. It just sounds so preposterous to say it out loud, but I know somethin' happened in there. I didn't get drunk and pass out on one drink, I know that."

"Sure sounds like it."

Greaves was quiet for a minute or so, and then he spoke again. "What did he do when he came back in?"

"Oh, he just said something to his two men. They were there when we walked in, you remember. And then he went over and said hello to Dace and his two pals. They had come in in the meanwhile."

"Oh, so those three were there? Old hear-no-evil, see-no-evil, speak-no-evil."

"I think it's their second home when the Aster closes up."

"Well, they're real thick with him."

"Now that I think of it, maybe he went over there to the Aster to see them for a while. Well, no, that doesn't make complete sense, either. He would have come back ahead of them or at the same time. And he acted like it was the first time he'd seen them that evening."

"Yeah, they're a fine bunch. All four of 'em. Two-faced bastards, they belong together."

"Well, he didn't stay around and talk to them for very long."

"He didn't have to. I'm sure he talks to 'em often enough."

Braden looked down to see how his horse was stepping. "Oh, how's that?"

Greaves spit off to his right. "I think they're the ones that set up these crooked deals for him. Shadwell knows the railroad bunch, so between him and Dace and Varlett, they serve as the go-between. Then Forbes gets someone else to do the work, and he keeps his hands clean."

Braden let out a long breath. "Sounds like quite a little setup."

"I guess they've done it enough to make it worthwhile."

The two men rode on for a ways in silence. Braden still had a thought nagging at him since the first time Greaves had brought up this subject, and he thought it was time to ask.

"I'll tell you, Ed. I think it's a good idea you mention something like this to someone. But when you tell 'em this much, I guess there's a little more they need to know."

Greaves made a frown. "I don't know what I left out."

"Well, I don't want you to take this wrong, but it would give me a clearer view of things if I knew how you came by all of this."

"Oh, hell, that's nothin' to hide. I heard it from a little girl there in Shawnee. She heard it from a couple of the railroaders, and from the way things have gone since then, I imagine there's somethin' to it."

"Sure sounds like it. Too bad she talks so

much. She probably told the section hands that she spilled the beans with you, and then they shuttled the word back over this way."

"That's probably about the way it went. I sure haven't said anything to anyone but you." Greaves spit again. "Too bad. She's a sweet little thing, but once she told me that, I quit goin' there."

Braden looked again at the landscape around them. "Well, what's done is done, I guess."

"No changin' it, that's for sure."

Braden lapsed into his own thoughts as the two men rode on in silence. Some of what Greaves had set forth was easy enough to believe — that Forbes was a petty crook, that he was in cahoots with the three men from the Aster, and even that he had some degree of confidence with the yellow-haired girl Emily. But the other part, with Forbes as the evil mastermind, slipping knockout drugs to a crib girl and staging ghostly interrogations, was harder to take even though it wasn't impossible. As Greaves said, some things added up, and some didn't.

It did seem as if Forbes had gone too far. The general code of the ranch country was to not pry into someone else's affairs. As a matter of principle, almost no one ate his own beef, and there were plenty of jokes about the custom. But that was one beef at a time, most often a distant or stray brand when it presented itself. It was nothing personal, and it evened out in the long run. The same went for branding a maverick calf now and then, if it was a true maverick and not one that was forcefully separated from its mother. Again, it was something a man did on his own, one head at a time. No one looked too close or dug too deep, and things came out even across the range.

But Forbes had taken it too far, and it seemed as if he was counting on support if any of his irregularities came to light. That might be his mistake.

"You know," said Braden, "I think the cure for this would be to just turn him in, for as much as someone would hate to be the one to do it. But it would be a big thing to do, and you'd want to make sure you had all the proof you needed."

"It would be hard. A fella would be stickin' his neck out."

"Well, if you had to, you could, especially if you had some proof."

"It would still be hard, I think. You know how these big shots all stick together."

Braden had an image of Forbes and Gundry riding across the prairie. "That's true. But I don't think they'd stick to some newcomer over something like this."

"I hope you're right, but I also hope it doesn't come to that."

"Same here, but if it does, I think you've got the hole card."

"I don't know. I wasn't goin' to do anything anyway, so nothing's changed. And like you say, what's done is done."

"The good thing is, you told someone. It's not goin' anywhere, but at least you don't have it locked up inside you."

"Well, that much is true. And I thank you for that."

Braden looked at him and nodded.

They rode on for a while longer. Braden had not said where he was going, but he imagined Greaves had a fair idea. The butte was still a few miles away, prominent and visible, when Greaves thanked Braden again and took his leave, the dark, high-crowned hat moving up and down as the horse jogged away to the north.

Braden rode on by himself, trying to think of the visit ahead but having to brush away remnants of the conversation he had just had. Greaves had stumbled into an ugly mess, all right, but Braden knew that no amount of worrying on his part was going to do any good. He hoped things would blow over, and if they didn't, it would be fair measure if Forbes were held accountable for his dealings.

Braden shrugged and rode on. Black Hat Butte still loomed ahead of him. For the first few miles since he left the bunkhouse, it did not seem to get any closer, but then in the last couple of miles the shortened distance became more noticeable. All the while, Braden kept his eye out for stray horses, as there were a couple still unaccounted for. He also watched, as always, for signs of other riders and for changes in the weather. At one point the bay horse was startled by a big jackrabbit that got up from behind a clump of sagebrush and ran, with its black-tipped ears aloft, in a zigzagging dash over the next rise. He also saw a band of antelope, all does and fawns, appear and disappear in the swells of the grassland.

The bay was making a gradual climb now, toward the base of the butte. Braden could see out to the west and northwest, on the right side of the butte, where off in the distance the land rolled away in a thousand hills and draws. The bay did not need much directing as it headed for the left side of the butte. A movement overhead caught Braden's attention, and he looked up to see a red-tailed hawk gliding in the air currents. Admiring the grace of the bird, he wondered if it had the power to kill an animal as large as the jackrabbit he had seen. He imagined so, although he had not seen a hawk feeding on anything larger than a snake or a cottontail rabbit.

Bringing his gaze back to earth, he saw a figure he recognized. It was Rove, appearing again as if out of nowhere on the dun horse. The pale rider raised his right hand in greeting, so Braden drew rein and waited for him to come near. As the dun came forward, Braden saw that Rove was dressed as before, in burlap-colored hat, coat, and trousers. With the first two fingers of his right hand he was smoothing a long strand of hair that hung over his ear.

Braden spoke first. "Hello again."

"Good morning, friend. Are you still looking for horses?"

"Not at the moment. I think we found as many as we were going to find." Then, thinking it might interest the other man, Braden added, "The roundup starts tomorrow, so this country'll be crawlin' with riders for the next few weeks."

"All the same to me. Like honeybees."

"How do you mean?"

"They don't bother me, and I don't bother them." Rove made a horizontal roll with his right hand as he spoke.

"It's a good way to be."

"That it is." Rove wagged his eyebrows. "This is the time they come out."

"The honeybees?"

"Them, and the narrow fellow with no legs, and the warty one that sleeps in the daytime." Rove ran his finger along the drooping end of his rope-colored mustache.

Braden took a look at the man. He doubted that Rove was some kind of a naturalist or field scientist, but he asked, "Do you study 'em?"

Rove smiled, and a shine came into his light brown eyes. "No more than I have to. Leave that to the beekeepers and bughunters."

It would not do to come right out and ask the man his business, no more than it would do to ask him where he came from. But Braden thought that if he sounded him out, something might come forth. Wondering if he could speak Rove's language, he gave a roll with his right index finger. "What's best to study, then?"

"Maggot pies, choughs, and rooks."

"Magpies?"

"The same."

"And rooks, you said."

"Rooks and daws." Rove smiled, and his fingers waved. "All our black cousins."

Braden recalled the conversation from their earlier meeting. "Crows, you mean?"

Rove winked. "Go to a village with trees, and they tell on a man who comes sneaking in at daybreak."

Still remembering, Braden said, "And do they sing as well?"

Rove's eyes looked glazed. "They sing like a thirty-thirty."

Braden felt a slight chill. "Plenty to study, then."

Rove smiled and held his hands apart, as if he were showing the size of a large rock. "More than enough."

Braden pointed upward with his index finger, as he had seen Rove do on that earlier occasion, and made a circular motion. "Even here?"

Rove nodded. "Ask the mistress in the dell."

Braden glanced at the crest of the hill, then back at Rove. "Do you know her?"

Rove shook his head. "Not at all. I just know what I see."

Braden felt his temper rise all of an instant, and he fell into his own language. "What do you do, then? Spy on people?"

"Friend of the gentle." The man seemed unruffled. He made a back-and-forth motion with his right hand held palm downward. "Fear not. I mind my distance and keep to my own trail." He turned his hand palm upward and gave an earnest nod. "She's more for you to know, if there's any measure at all."

Braden felt himself simmering down. For all his babble, Rove seemed to have a lucid streak, and a fellow might be able to get some sense out of him. Braden gave him a close look and tried to work back into his language to form a skeptical question. "Friend of the gentle, but cousin of the crow?"

"The meadowlark is cousin to the crow. So is the dove. I'm the last one you would have to worry about." Rove waved his index finger back and forth about a foot in front of his nose, then put out his hand for Braden to shake. "Here's a man's word on it."

Braden moved his horse closer and reached out his hand. As he looked the strange man in the eye, he did not see a glassy stare or an excited shine anymore.

He saw the calm eyes of a man who could have been his brother if he had one. The man could well be a lunatic, or he could have the jolt of a thunderbolt coursing in his arm, but Braden trusted him and shook his hand. "A man's word," he said, and then they drew apart.

As Braden rode up the slope, he did not look back to see what became of the pale stranger. Rather, he thought of his interest that lay ahead of him, down in the dell. He smiled at the quaint phrase. Rove had picked up a thing or two somewhere, even if it all seemed to run into a strange soup.

Braden looked over the crest, taking in the country below. The real world seemed to come back together for him as he saw the familiar landmarks of Little Sister, the hog-nosed butte, Castle Butte, and the mountains far beyond. The world was spread out in its proper order, beneath a sunny sky.

He figured it was at least nine in the morning by now — not too early to call, even on a Sunday morning. As he descended the slope and looked across the land, he saw Birdie's little menagerie of critters off to his left, southeast of the homestead site. But he did not see the girl. Maybe she had turned out the animals and had gone back to the house. He looked to his right, downslope to the sugarloaf formation, and then out of habit he looked back around toward Black Hat Butte. There, standing in the morning shadow of the butte about two hundred yards away, stood Birdie holding out her right hand to a yearling antelope. She raised her left hand and waved at Braden. He waved back.

Riding into the yard, he called out a hello. The door of the first shed opened, and Beryl stepped into the morning light. As on the previous visit, she was dressed in work clothes, but again they took nothing from her presence.

She said good morning and Braden returned the greeting, then swung down from his horse.

"Am I ever glad to see you!" she said, with an emphasis on the last word.

"Oh, really? For anything in particular?"

"Actually, yes. I had just gone into the shed to look for a shovel. There's a snake under the doorstep, and I want to get rid of him."

Braden looked around. "Let's see where I can tie up my horse. That rail where I tied him last time is a little too close to Mr. Snake."

"There's another rail over here," said Beryl, pointing at the second and larger shed. "I'll go get the shovel while you tie him up."

A minute later, Braden had the shovel in his hands and was headed toward the steps. "Is it a rattler?" he asked.

"I don't know. It's the first one I've seen this year, and whatever kind it is, I'd just as soon be rid of it."

"Well, I'll see what I can do."

He went to the right side of the steps and crouched against the house, trying not to block out all the sunlight. He could see the snake, wrapped in something like a figure eight, in the shadow of the lowest step. When he got over his first impulse to kill it just for being a snake, he peered into the dusky space and saw the pale green and dark brown markings.

"I think it's a bull snake," he said. "They're not bad to have around. They eat mice, and from what I've heard, they kill rattlers. I haven't seen it, but that's what they say."

Beryl had a tense look on her face. "I still don't care to have one around. Can you get rid of it for me?"

He understood that she meant for him to kill it regardless. "Well, I guess so. I'll see if

I can roust him out of there." He poked the head of the shovel into the recess, but the snake just rearranged its loops and hissed. "I think I've got him mad now." He poked a couple of more times, but the snake would not give up its hideout.

"Can you shoot it?"

Braden winced. "I've got a pistol in my saddlebag, but I don't like to touch off a forty-five in a little space like that."

"How about a shotgun?" she asked. "I've got one in the house."

Braden frowned. "That would still make quite a blast. But go ahead and get it. We might have to use it. I'll go get my six-gun just in case."

As Beryl went into the house, Braden walked across the yard to his horse. He went to the left side, unbuckled the saddlebag, and took out the gun and holster. He looked over toward the house and saw Beryl standing on the top step, holding a shotgun with the barrel pointed downward. Without any warning she let out a shriek and stepped back into the doorway.

"What's the matter?" he called out, stepping around the hind end of the horse and taking long strides across the yard.

"He's going over there," she said,

pointing at a chokecherry hedge on the west end of the house.

Braden turned and ran toward the bushes, just in time to see the snake slither into the cover. It would be hard to get at him with a shovel now, what with the way the chokecherry branches all grew out from ground level. He peered into the base of the hedge and could see the snake, its crooks and curves in the dappled shadow.

"I think I can try a shot now," he said. He pulled the six-shooter from its holster, clicked back the hammer and rotated a shell into place, sighted in on a dark brown stripe, and squeezed the trigger. The snake pulled into a tight mass and reared up, hissing. Braden thought that was impressive for a bull snake. He could see where he had knocked off a chunk of meat, but the snake was far from done for. Braden shot at the head and missed.

"Did you get it?" came her call from the porch.

"Yeah, but not good enough. I don't want to shoot at him all day. Maybe I should try the shotgun after all."

Beryl came down the steps carrying the shotgun. Braden saw that it was a break-down single-shot.

"Do you have any shells for it?"

"There's one in it. I always keep it loaded."

Braden felt his eyebrows go up as he took the shotgun and handed Beryl his gun and holster. He lined up the bead on the end of the gun barrel with the snake and followed it as it settled into a shifting heap. He put the bead on the snake's head, which had a background of loops, and pulled the trigger. The coils began to relax and then writhe.

"I think that did it," he said. "I'll see if I can pull him out with the shovel."

While Beryl took the shotgun back into the house, Braden put his six-shooter and holster back in his saddlebag. Then he fetched the shovel, and after a little maneuvering with the blade turned sideways, he managed to hook the snake and draw it toward him.

"It looks like it's still alive," said Beryl from a few feet back.

"It's hard to tell if he's all the way dead. Sometimes they still move like that as a reflex, I think. Like a lizard's tail that gets broken off. When I was a boy, I heard that a snake will keep wigglin' till sundown. They don't always, but they do keep turnin' and unwindin' for a while. Choppin' their head off doesn't seem to make any difference."

He made a couple of unsuccessful attempts at lifting the snake with the shovel, but each time the snake shifted and slid off the metal. "A lot of trouble just for a snake," he said. Taking out his pocketknife, he cut off a chokecherry branch about a quarter of an inch thick and two feet long, folded it, squeezed the V around the snake's neck, and stretched out the body. It was about four feet long and nearly two inches thick. Braden looked at Beryl, then dragged the snake a hundred yards off into the prairie.

When he got back to the yard, Beryl had regained her usual composure. "Well, I barely had time to say hello."

He smiled. "I guess I showed up at the right time. I thought I would drop by and see if there was any little thing you'd like me to do before I went away for a few weeks."

A half-smile played on her face. "That was the main job, I guess. And if you'd shown up an hour earlier, I wouldn't even have known to ask you to do that."

The sound of horse hooves on dry ground turned them both to the east. The palomino was trotting into the yard with Birdie on top, bareback, hunched forward and clutching the mane. When the horse stopped, she straightened up, brushed her hand across her face, and smiled.

"I heard some shots, so I thought I'd come and see."

Beryl, who was resting the shovel upright in front of her, used her free left hand to wave at the chokecherry bushes. "There was a snake under the doorstep, and he slipped over here into the bushes, where Mr. Braden killed him."

Birdie's face brightened. "Rattler?"

"Bull snake," said Braden. "But your aunt didn't want him around."

Birdie nodded. "Well, I just thought I'd come and see what it was." She pressed her right knee into the horse's side, and he started to turn.

Beryl's voice came out pleasant and assuring. "I'm glad you did, Birdie. Thank you."

As the palomino trotted away, Beryl turned to Braden and spoke. "Well, I hope you have time for a little visit. I've got some coffee on the back of the stove that's probably still warm."

"That sounds fine."

"Good. I'll be right out." She lifted the shovel and handed it toward him. "Would you be so kind?"

"It would be my pleasure." His eyes met hers as he reached his hand and placed it above hers on the shovel handle. Her gray-green eyes looked soft and deep, like a mountain pool in shadow. Her face relaxed into a smile.

"Thank you." She turned and walked to the house.

Within a few minutes they were seated on the bench, with the coffeepot and cups between them. Beryl looked out across the prairie, and Braden followed her gaze. Nearly a mile away to the southeast, Birdie's little bunch of animals was grazing. Beryl turned and looked at her visitor.

"There was something I thought I might tell you about."

Braden gave her his attention. "Sure. Go ahead."

She took a breath and exhaled. "A few days ago, not quite a week ago, I had a visit."

"Not a fellow named Rove, was it?"

She frowned. "No. I don't know anyone by that name. It was a man named Forbes, and he had Mr. Gundry with him."

"Oh. Uh-huh." Braden recalled the meeting he had with them, when he had the roan horse on a rope and the two men were headed in this direction. "I think that might have been the same day I was here."

"I believe it was." She paused with the cup in both hands.

Braden sensed an element of worry or hesitation. "Did he do something that was out of line?"

"No, not at all. And he had Mr. Gundry with him. What he did was offer to buy my place."

"Is that right?" Braden felt his eyes widen.

"Yes. I told him I didn't have any intention of selling it for the time being, but he just made his offer again, only in different words. He was very polite about it, but he left no doubt that he expected me to give in."

"I see." Braden looked around. There wasn't much to sell, as far as that went. The windmill would be worth something, as the water would give Forbes a foothold. What a cattleman liked to do was pick up parcels here and there, especially anything that had water, and then he could control the range in between.

"He told me he understood how hard it was for a woman to look out for her own interests and to make it on a place that had such little prospect for a profit."

"Like he was doing you a favor?"

She gave a wry smile. "Something like that. He said people had been losing cattle and perhaps I had, too. I told him I had sold all mine, so that cut off that part of his approach."

Braden shook his head. "They've got toadies in town that are telling everyone cattle losses are down, the calf crop is good, and all that. They say what they want when they want."

"I don't doubt it."

"But he seemed kind of pushy?"

"You could call it that."

Braden sipped on the warm coffee. "Well, it's your business. But I hope you don't feel pressured into selling when you don't want to. Anyone's got a right to hold on to their land." He looked at her.

Her eyes were neither soft nor hard. "When he repeated his offer, I repeated my answer. He told me I could think it over, and if I reconsidered, his offer would still be good."

"Which means he'll be back."

"I suppose so." Her subtle smile returned for a moment. "But if anything, he made me even more obstinate not to sell this place." She looked out across the prairie. "I do like it here, and so does Birdie. Even if it's not making us a living right now, it's the perfect place for her critters."

# Chapter Five

Braden and Beaumont sat with their backs to the wind as they ate their midday chuck. The breeze had come up after Lum had parked the wagons and gotten the horses un-hitched, and as he said, there was no point in moving the wagons to try to make a wind-break. The wind could blow in from the east, as it was doing now, and before the day was over it could be blowing just as strong from the west. So the wagons would stay where they were — the chuck wagon with its tongue pointed north, in the custom of the trail drives, and the bed wagon parallel with it but a few yards back. Now at midday the wagons stood on their own shadows, but as the afternoon wore on, the shadows would stretch out to the campsite.

The fire pit lay a few yards from the tailboard of the chuck wagon and straight east from the bed wagon. Braden and Beaumont and the half-dozen other punchers who sat cross-legged with their backs to the wind had an easy view of the whole camp — Lum's kitchen opened up and set out on the tail end of the wagon, two Dutch ovens hanging from the pot rack, orange flames and black smoke rising from the fire pit, and an occasional spark that rose on the wind and died before it reached the bed wagon. Out of habit, Braden watched one of the larger sparks make its passage and burn out just before it landed. With a little more life, it might have touched the sleeping figure beneath the wagon.

From the other side of the wagons, a couple of hundred yards away, came the bawling and mooing of the cattle that the men had gathered that morning. In the afternoon they would cut out the calves and brand and mark them, then put the day's gather in with the roundup herd, which was growing by the day. It was farther out and downwind, like the horse herd, which was also west of camp but within close walking distance. All three herds were kept or moved downwind so that the dust they raised would carry out onto the plains. Even with the wind blowing in the opposite direction, the cows and calves and steers that had been driven in and thrown together made plenty of noise.

"I don't know how he can sleep in the middle of the day like that," said Beaumont.

Braden shook his head. "Me neither." He glanced at the cook, who was tossing more wood on the fire. "I wouldn't be surprised if Lum does somethin' about it before long."

Beaumont chewed and swallowed, then spoke. "He's a different kind of night wrangler, that's for sure."

"That he is."

Braden dipped his biscuit in the bean juice. He didn't like the way things had turned out with the night wrangler, either. In addition to watching the horse herd at night, hitching up the wagon horses, and driving the bed wagon whenever the crew moved camp, the night hawk was supposed to be the cook's helper. That meant fetching water, gathering wood, cutting meat, or anything else the cook wanted. If the night wrangler got any sleep at all, he stole it when work slowed down and not just when he felt like it. His was the lowest job on the crew, but it was the way a fellow could get started and try to work his way up.

The man sleeping under the bed wagon, Engle, seemed to have no business being a roundup hand, but there he was, thanks to Forbes. Braden squinted at the thought. It seemed as if every time the owner of the

4BS put his spoon into the pot, something didn't smell right. On the first morning of roundup, Forbes had shown up with three riders instead of two, and the new man didn't look much like a cowpuncher. With a heavy build and a sallow complexion, he looked out of place in a company of men who were saddle-tough, windblown, and suntanned. After a brief council between Forbes and Gundry, word spread out that Engle would be the night wrangler. The kid from the MT would move up to try his hand at cowpunching, starting out as day herder and then moving in to be a circle rider when he learned to swing a rope. Braden could see that it made the kid happy, but he wondered how much trouble it would be to pull horses out of other men's strings to make up one for the kid. He wouldn't need but three or four for day herding, but he would need seven or eight if he became a full-time rider. There was no surplus of horses, as the Seven Arrow had come up a few head short in the horse gather, and the other outfits had brought the number they had originally spoken for.

Moreover, Braden wondered why Forbes had even brought along another man. Maybe he just liked to change things or to make others change. Braden knew some men were like that. But Forbes could have made a better choice, it seemed. If Engle had to start out as night wrangler, he was no more of a hand than he looked. And in the first few days of the roundup, he had not shown any great care about how things were supposed to be done. He had a sullen look about him, and a slow way of moving. He seemed indifferent about the work he did, whether it was cutting firewood or putting a halter on a horse. A chuck wagon cook might tolerate lethargy, but Braden didn't think Lum would put up with cheekiness for a whole season. Something in the way the cook had tossed the wood on the fire suggested irritation, displeasure.

A gust of wind blew up, and Braden caught his hat just in time. He settled it into place and tipped his head so that the wind went over and not under the brim. As he lifted his tin plate so that he could eat in that posture, he said to Beaumont, "What does it mean when the wind comes out of the east this early in the day?"

Beaumont looked at him and raised his eyebrows. "I don't know. Rain?"

Braden shrugged. "I don't know, either. Maybe it just means we're sittin' on the right side of the fire, to keep from gettin' ashes in our grub."

"That might be it," said Beaumont, clacking his spoon on the plate as he went back to his beef and beans.

Two riders from the MT, who had come into camp ahead of Braden and Beaumont and who had already helped themselves to seconds, now got up and carried their plates to the tailgate of the chuck wagon. The plates and spoons made a small rattle in the dishpan, and the MT riders each picked up a tin cup and moved to the fire, where the coffeepot sat on a rock inside the pit. Braden watched as Lum looked at the dishpan and then at the ground beneath the bed wagon.

*Here it comes,* he thought.

The MT riders poured their coffee and went back to sit down. When they had moved a few steps away from the fire, Lum picked up his pot hook, which was a metal rod a little over two feet long. Then he walked over to the bed wagon, leaned down, and jabbed Engle in the lower leg. Braden could hear him speak, but he couldn't make out the words. He saw Lum jab again, and he heard what he imagined were the same words. Then Lum jumped back, and Braden could see the hatless blond head as Engle raised himself up on his left elbow and settled his right hand back down on his hip. It looked as if he had begun to draw his six-gun.

Lum's voice was louder now. "Git up, damn you. There's work to do. You need to git some water and wash some dishes."

Engle rolled out from beneath the wagon and set his hat on his head, then pushed himself to his feet. He was shorter than average, with a belly that kept the sun from glinting off his belt buckle. He had blocky features that made him look Scandinavian, but he was nowhere as tall as most Swedes Braden had seen. After a quick look around the campsite, Engle went to the chuck wagon and lifted a tin bucket from where it hung on the sideboard. Then he turned and in his insolent manner walked past the bed wagon toward the creek.

Braden and Beaumont were spooning a second helping of grub into their plates when Engle came back into camp with the bucket about three-quarters full of water.

Lum, who stood by the right rear wheel of the chuck wagon, put a match to his pipe and said, "Pour it in the dishpan, and put the pan on the fire."

Braden glanced at Engle, saw the wart at the base of his left nostril, and noted the shine of perspiration on the now-florid face. Then he caught a glare of resentment in the blue eyes before the man averted his gaze and lifted the bucket to the level of the wagon. Braden heard the sound of splashing water and then Lum's voice again.

"We're gonna need some more firewood, too. You may have to go up the creek a ways to find it."

Braden could see only the back of Engle's head now. The man said nothing, but his hat moved as he nodded. Then he set the bucket on the ground and lifted the dishpan from the wagon. As Braden moved away from the fire pit, he caught a glimpse of Engle's stubby hands lowering the pan onto the coals.

Seated again on the grass, Braden looked at Lum, who still stood by the wagon wheel. It seemed as if the cook had picked his moment well. He had waited until the MT hands were out of the way when he started the confrontation, and then he laid on the second part when two men from his own outfit were present. From the glare he had seen in Engle's eyes, Braden imagined the effect was not lost on the surly man, either.

A moment later, Braden looked up as he

heard Lum's voice again.

"I wonder where the hell he's going."

Braden looked around the camp and then past the bed wagon, where Engle's squat figure was moving in the direction of the horse herd.

Beaumont rested his spoon on his plate. "I don't reckon we're rid of him that easy."

"No." Braden shook his head. "I don't think we'll be that lucky."

Braden turned out to be right. Two hours later, while he and Beaumont were helping to hold the herd that the crew was working, he saw Engle riding toward camp on the horse he had ridden the first morning. Behind him, on the end of a rope, two large tree branches dragged and bounced and sent up tiny clouds of dust. In spite of the tension that seemed to hover whenever Engle was in camp, Braden sensed an air of comedy as he watched the toadlike rider dragging firewood to the waiting camp cook. Engle might think he was showing others he could do as he pleased, but Braden was sure that Lum was not going to give up his authority.

From time to time throughout the afternoon, Braden glanced at the camp, fancying that he would hear an explosion or see a cloud of smoke. But he heard nothing, and through the silence he wondered if a confrontation had taken place. When he rode back to camp at the end of the day, everything seemed calm. Engle was chopping the last of the firewood, and Lum was peeling potatoes on the tailgate of the chuck wagon. Braden wondered how Engle had spent his time for the last four hours or so. Cutting up the firewood could not have taken more than an hour, so Lum must have saved him the dirty dishes and devised some other work, like sorting beans.

Engle tossed the last few lengths of firewood onto the woodpile, leaned the ax against the bed wagon, and went through a bit of work to get his shirt tucked in and his pants hitched up. Then he served himself a plate of leftover beans and sat off to one side to eat alone. The sun had not yet gone down when he tossed his plate and spoon into the wreck pan and set out toward the horse herd.

Other punchers came in and lounged around as Lum fried potatoes in two large cast-iron skillets. One of the two Dutch ovens sat at the edge of the fire, full of fried slices of salt pork. The wind had died down, and the smell of hot pork fat wafted on the air as the sliced potatoes sputtered in the grease. Lum looked around and beckoned toward Slack, who had just come into camp and had not taken a seat. Lum handed him the tin bucket and set the coffeepot on the tailgate.

Braden sat with the other three riders from the Seven Arrow as they all put away their grub. The hands from the other outfits sat in their groups, and the three owners sat together in yet another group. Braden looked around and realized that Wyndham and Farnsworth were not in camp. They would be riding their shift with the cattle herd. With them gone, and Engle as well, and the smell of coffee in the air, the cow camp seemed like a decent place.

Lum stood gazing at the fire, his narrow-brimmed hat set back on his head as the firelight played on his broad, shining forehead. He brought out his jackknife, opened it, and took to cleaning his fingernails. Then he put the knife away and set the coffeepot back from the fire.

One by one, the men finished eating and put their utensils in the dishpan. As Gundry made his way to the tailgate, Lum said something in a low voice and drew the boss into the dusk at the front of the wagon.

Again, Braden appreciated the cook's way of handling things. Lum had picked a moment when Forbes's outfit had a minimal presence in camp and when the roundup boss was well fed.

After several minutes, Gundry and Lum came back into the firelight. Gundry walked over to the spot where Forbes and Davis sat, and he said something that caused Forbes to look up. Then he spoke for almost a minute, with Forbes nodding every ten or fifteen seconds. After that, Gundry went to the fire and poured himself a cup of coffee.

In the morning, within the hearing of anyone who happened to be around, Gundry told Engle and the kid from the MT that they would be trading jobs. Engle shrugged, and the kid nodded. Braden felt sorry for the kid being sent back to night wrangling, but he thought there might be some justice in Engle having to go straight from night shift to a long, boring day of holding the herd. The kid, meanwhile, would have had a decent night's sleep and would be up to the task of driving the bed wagon to the next camp and getting set up.

When Braden rode into the new camp for noon dinner, the general tone had returned to normal. Greaves and Slack had already begun to eat, so Braden served himself a plate and sat down with them. Two of the MT riders came in and sat down to eat with two of the Davis hands. Then Engle showed up with Forbes, who spread his airy goodwill around camp. He patted the MT kid on the shoulder, asked Lum how he liked a nice day like this without any wind, sprinkled a greeting on the Seven Arrow riders, and then sat himself and his protégé down with the other four punchers.

Braden took a look at Engle, who was seated cross-legged on the ground like the rest of the hands and was shoveling in grub with the best of them. Try as he might to fit in, Engle was at least as much of an outsider as Forbes was, and he had less of an appearance of belonging in cattle country. Braden realized he could not place Engle; that was the problem as he looked at him now. The man was not a ranch hand, though he could get around on a horse all right, and he did not show any interest in becoming one. When a ranchman like Forbes hired a man who was not a cowpuncher, the average skeptic might think the man was a gunfighter. But Engle didn't fit that mold, either. It had looked as if he went for his gun when Lum riled him with the pot hook, but aside from that moment, he did not have the mannerisms of a gunman. A man who lived by the gun was dexterous — his hands seemed to have their own awareness wherever they glided, and the gun hand maintained a clear, open zone around the handle of the six-shooter. Engle, with pudgy hands and sausagelike fingers, did not have that touch. Braden had seen him crouched on his knees to split firewood for kindling, with the end of the ax handle tucked under his armpit, his right hand choked up on the haft so that he could wield the ax like a hatchet, and his stubby left hand holding the length of wood upright. He would raise the ax and firewood together and bring them down with a thud, and then the loose end of the ax would fall free, sometimes rattling against the butt of the six-gun. Engle had the surliness that might fit a gunfighter, but his ham-handedness would keep him from being much more than a bully or a thug.

Greaves and Slack got up to help themselves to a second serving. Braden flickered a glance toward Forbes and Engle, who seemed to pay no mind to the men who walked by. That was good enough, Braden thought. As the men came and went from camp, he had noticed the most uneasiness in Greaves when Wyndham and Farnsworth were around. No words crossed between them, and Braden had the impression that each side made an attempt to ignore the other.

After the midday meal, Braden roped out a fresh horse for his afternoon ride. When he had the saddle on tight and was walking the horse out a few yards prior to checking the cinch and climbing on, he glanced out at the country to his west. A low, gray cloud mass had begun to form, and he thought it might bring some rain.

The roundup had moved south for the first few days and would soon turn west, then veer northwest, making a broad half-circle around Black Hat Butte. Braden had seen the butte from time to time each day, and although he took pleasure in recalling the homestead that lay on the west side, he doubted that he would find an occasion to drop in for a visit. Gundry sent the riders out in pairs most of the time, and he usually sent Greaves and Slack to ride circles on the right while Braden and Beaumont rode out on the left. As Braden pictured the general sweep of the roundup, he saw himself on the outer edge, farthest from the butte and the mistress in the dell.

Pushing those thoughts to the edge of his mind, he kept his eye on the western sky, where the gray bank of clouds was moving in but not very fast.

When he rode back into camp at the end of the day, a slow rain had begun to fall. Lum had the wagons parked end to end, and with the help of ropes and poles he had put up an awning over the space between the two wagons. The day wrangler had set up a canvas lean-to for the saddles and blankets, so Braden stripped his horse, stowed his gear out of the weather, and hurried over to the canopy.

Once under the shelter, he glanced out at the sky and did not like the looks of it. He would much rather have an afternoon downpour than a slow rain that hung around for a day or more. That kind of rain did not improve the mood of a roundup crew. It meant wet clothes, wet blankets, slippery ground, stiff ropes, clumsy slickers. If the boss called a halt for a day or more, men would still have to ride out for their shifts on holding the herd, and the rest of them would stay bunched under the canvas with the low-hanging smoke from the campfire. That kind of arrangement had its own discomforts, especially if there were any abrasive personalities in the group.

As the evening wore on, the rain came drizzling down. The MT riders had a tent, which they set up for their sleeping quarters. Forbes and Gundry would have the privilege of sleeping in the bed wagon, and everyone else would stay out of the rain as best they could, under the awning or beneath the wagons.

It was a long, dreary night. Gundry divided the fifteen riders plus Davis into four-man shifts, each to stand one relief period of night-herding. Braden and Beaumont were assigned second relief, from ten to midnight, along with two of Davis's men. The four of them got their horses ready and tied them to the wagons, with slickers draped over the saddles. Then they sat by the fire until a little before ten, when they rode out to relieve Wyndham, Farnsworth, and two of the MT boys. After a couple of hours, Greaves and Slack showed up, so Braden went back to camp. Beaumont had lost no time getting in ahead of him and was standing by the fire. The area under the canopy was a mass of lumpy bedrolls, as rivulets of water ran under both wagons. Beaumont motioned with his head toward the spot on the other side of the fire where they had left their bedding, next to where Greaves and Slack had rolled out theirs. Braden nodded and took his place by the fire, to see if he might dry out a little before climbing into his bedroll. Looking around on the ground, he was able to identify all the sleeping men, including Forbes's two regular hands and the odd one, Engle, who slept with his mouth open.

Braden woke to the sound of a metal utensil clacking on the edge of cast iron. He poked his nose out into the cold, damp air and could tell from the odor of pork fat that Lum was frying breakfast. The cook had a lantern shining from the tail end of the chuck wagon, and smoke rose in narrow plumes from the fire pit. Braden rolled over and saw the first gray of morning beyond the eastern edge of the canopy, where water dripped to the ground. Then he propped himself up on his right elbow and looked around. Beaumont, Greaves, and Slack all lay still in their beds, as did Wyndham and Farnsworth. Engle, who had been assigned to fourth relief, was gone. A couple of other men were sitting up in their beds and pulling on their boots. Braden settled back into his blankets, hoping to steal a few more minutes of relative comfort before rolling out into the cold, damp world.

The camp began to stir, and the bed wagon creaked. Braden sat up in his bed and saw Gundry by the fire, a steaming tin cup in his hand.

"Up and at 'em, boys," said the boss. "This little bit of rain isn't going to stop anything."

Braden let out a long breath and reached for his hat. It would be just as well, he thought, to get away from all the close company.

The sky had lightened and Braden was just getting ready to go out into the drizzly morning when Engle came into camp. Wrapped in a wet slicker and topped with a dripping hat, he made a sloshy, whispering sound as he walked. Gundry, who sat next to Forbes near the fire, stood up and called his name. Engle moved close to the fire and, holding out his hands to the warmth, turned his wet face toward the boss.

"We're goin' to let you ride out with Vinch today," said Gundry, nodding toward the seated Forbes. "Do you know how to rope?"

"A little."

"Do you have a rope?"

Engle shook his head. "Not really."

Gundry turned down the corners of his mouth. "Well, just ride out today. We'll hunt up a rope for you when things dry out."

Braden shook out his coffee cup and set it in the dishpan, then caught up with Beaumont, who had left just ahead of him.

"Did you hear that?" he asked.

Beaumont gave him a sideways glance. "I sure did."

"Doesn't that beat all? You hire a man for the lowest job and he's no good at it, so you just move him up a couple of notches higher. Now they'll be meddlin' with the horses again, to fill out a string for him."

"Hell with 'em," said Beaumont. "Maybe after a few days of hard jigglin', he'll go away."

Braden kicked at an old white neck bone that had once been part of a deer or antelope. "Like I said before, I don't think we'll be that lucky. And even if we are, that's not the bigger half of the problem."

Beaumont gave him a full look. "I think I know what you mean. The *patrón*. His, you know."

"Uh-huh."

The rain drizzled through the day and began to let up at about an hour before dusk. Lum had moved the camp, and

Braden found the new place without any trouble. As he came into camp after putting away his horse, everything seemed drab. The ground was damp, as were the canvases and bedrolls that came back out of the wagon. The kid from the MT had "whooped up" a big fire, as he said, and half a dozen punchers stood close around it, with little wisps of steam rising from their damp, wrinkled clothing. Braden took his place by the fire and held out his arms.

"Lum said we'll be here two days," said the kid. "We can spread out everything on the bushes in the morning, and it can dry out during the day."

Braden could feel the warmth creeping into the sleeves of his jacket. He looked down at his soggy pants and muddy boots, where the slicker had not reached. "A little sunshine would be nice," he said.

The next day did bring sunshine and a light breeze, good drying conditions. When Braden rode in for midday chuck, he saw Black Hat Butte north of camp a few miles, sharp against a clear blue sky. He figured the wagon was at its southernmost point in the campaign. As they moved north and west, the country would get rougher. If they were going to have wet weather, it was just as well to have it here, where the land was smoother and the grass was thicker.

Gundry said they would brand in the morning, so after checking his clothes and bedroll and turning them over in the sun, Braden changed horses and rode out again to the south. It was a bright, cheerful afternoon, with the meadowlarks singing and the cattle hooves thudding on the soft earth. With the warm sun and a fresh breeze, and no dust, the world seemed like a much better place than it had the day before.

As the second gather from the same camp was a short one, most of the riders had gotten back to the wagon by late afternoon when Braden came in. Men were rolling up their blankets, folding clothes, and sorting through their war bags, so Braden went about the same business. When he had his things in order, he looked around the camp and saw Slack standing by himself. Braden walked over to make small talk.

As he got closer, he saw the familiar high-strung look on Slack's face, the close look in the dark eyes. "What's up?" he asked.

"Not much," said Slack. "But you'd

think Ed would've been back in by now." Slack's bushy mustache moved as he pursed his mouth.

Braden looked around to verify for himself. He saw Beaumont shaking out a pair of pants, but he did not see Greaves. "You'd think so," he said.

Slack turned to glance at the sun, then faced Braden again. "You think we should go look for him?"

Braden shrugged. He could feel Slack's worry. "I don't know. The boss isn't in yet, or we could ask him. He's probably countin' the gather. Let's see what Wes thinks."

The two of them walked over and had a short palaver with Beaumont, who didn't seem worried. But Slack shook his head.

"All I know is, Ed should be back by now. And he's seemed kinda jumpy these last few days. You just don't know if something's up."

Beaumont moved his head to either side, as if considering it. "Well, if you want to go out, I will, too."

Braden nodded. "So will I."

Within ten minutes they were saddled and headed out north of camp. Slack said he would take the middle, and he asked Braden to take the east side while Beaumont rode to the west. Braden thought of the little homestead over that way, but he didn't think a visit would fit in well, so he followed Slack's suggestion, which was to ride out until just before sundown and then loop back. If anyone ran into trouble, he was to fire a shot in the air, count to sixty, and fire another. The three riders split up, their horses' hooves drumming on the soft earth.

Gone was the broad, tranquil charm of a sunny spring afternoon. Shadows were starting to lengthen now, and the world lay in silence, except for the occasional whoof of a bullbat overhead. Braden saw no cattle at all, which was proper for a range that had just been combed. Nor did he see a horse or a deer or an antelope. He rode on until the sun almost touched the distant mountains, and he turned around. Now was the time of day when the sun sank fast.

Riding south again, he could see the dark silhouette of Black Hat Butte ahead and to his right. He nodded. Camp would lie straight south of there, so he had not gotten off course at all.

The sun slipped behind the mountains, and he let the horse slow into a fast, steady, walk. They would make it back before dark, or close to it, and there was no need to push the horse at this point. They had covered a lot of country, all of it empty, and the rest should be easy. For all he knew, Greaves was back in camp, irritated that his friends should go out looking for him.

Braden shook his head. He hoped Greaves was in camp, but he feared the opposite. Slack had been riding with Greaves, and he had sensed that something was not right. He had worried enough to put out a search. That said something. Braden looked across the broad country to the northwest, where the hills and bluffs cast shadows on a somber landscape.

Then he heard a shot. It came from the direction of Black Hat Butte, where Slack would be riding. Braden started counting — ten . . . twenty . . . thirty . . . forty . . . fifty. . . . Just short of sixty, he heard the second shot. Without hesitating, he turned the horse and kicked it into a lope, heading west across the darkling plain.

# Chapter Six

*Edwin Greaves.* Two words, the sum of a man who was gone. Braden had sounded the words in his mind a thousand times, trying to make sense of a man dying as he did. The cause of the death, a blow to the back of the head; the cause of the blow, unknown. Edwin Greaves, who had been brought back to camp tied across his saddle while Braden carried the dark, high-crowned hat, forever empty now — he was Ed to his friends, Greaves to others who knew him. Now the two full names together, *Edwin Greaves,* echoed in Braden's mind as if they were to give a full account of the man, such as one would find on a headstone, with dates of birth and death.

But the two words did not give a full account, not to Braden. Rather, they rose up as a reproach, posing questions: Would the man have died if Braden had done anything different? Did he have to die as he did? And would Braden have done better by him if he, Braden, had said more at the time of the investigation, what little there was?

He did not know the answer. He knew he had kept his mouth shut because it seemed like the smart thing to do. Braden did not believe for a moment that Greaves had died by accident, but to say as much would help the other side. It would sound a note of warning and put others on their guard. And, of course, there was the element of self-preservation. If a man had died for knowing too much, the next fellow would put himself in jeopardy by declaring that he, too, knew something. So Braden had kept his mouth shut and had ruminated on the problem, defending himself against his own implied accusation that to remain silent was to be a coward. In his defense, he reasoned it the other way, that he could do right by Greaves only if he stayed alive. If the man had died for knowing too much, then the chances were that someone was playing for high stakes. Greaves had probably known less than he was given credit for knowing, and anyone who admitted to sharing that knowledge might be describing himself as more of a threat than he was.

Nor had he mentioned Rove. As far as Braden knew, no one else on the roundup crew or in the immediate area had seen the stranger. When Braden checked with himself at the most basic level of his feelings, he did not suspect Rove. The man was eccentric, but Braden did not see him as malevolent. To mention Rove and to offer him up as a suspect would have misdirected the suspicion and given the guilty party a scapegoat to hang the blame on.

Braden had no doubt that there was a guilty party, but he knew he couldn't come out and accuse someone just on the basis of suspicion. From the moment he and Beaumont and Slack brought Greaves into camp, he could tell the deck was stacked. Forbes and Wyndham pronounced the death accidental and prejudiced any further investigation. Although Gundry sent for the sheriff, no one had any proof or evidence to sway the argument the other way. Braden could see that a counterargument would only amount to an accusation and make him vulnerable.

He had an image in his mind, derived from stories he had read about Robin Hood, Ivanhoe, and the like. The peasants were in revolt against the king but did not have a plan for storming the castle. One brave peasant rose up out of cover, ran to within thirty yards of the stronghold, and hurled his ax at the castle door. He made a good throw, sticking the blade in the timbers, but he got drilled by an arrow from a guard's crossbow.

He used that image to picture how he would fare if he rose up and hurled an accusation. By any definition, telling the sheriff what he had heard from Greaves would be the right thing to do. It would be right and it would be brave, but it would give him cause to think to himself, as perhaps the peasant did, that he had been very stupid. And moreover, he didn't know how the other peasants felt.

So he kept his mouth shut and did not show his hand. At least he thought he didn't; he could not tell how others read him. It seemed as if Forbes's men paid nobody any mind, as they went about their work with an outward indifference, but from time to time he felt he was being studied. And he knew he did not always have a good poker face. He found it repugnant that Engle now rode horses that had been in Greaves's string, and he imagined his feelings showed through.

Braden shook his head as he finished brushing the bay horse. He could feel the animal's energy on this cool morning; the horse was ready to go. Braden settled the blanket and pad into place, and then, swinging the saddle by its horn, he sailed it up and let it drop into place. The bay did not flinch. It stood still as Braden reached under its brisket for the cinch and then drew the latigo up tight. The words came to him again as he buckled the rear cinch. *Edwin Greaves*. It was like a job unfinished, and Braden did not know what the rest of the work consisted of.

A week had gone by, including half a day lost to the investigation and a full day lost to going to town for the burial. The roundup had settled back into its routine. The broad sweep had moved north and west of Black Hat Butte and was making slower progress now in the rougher country. Then this morning, before sending the riders out as usual, Gundry said they would not gather cattle until later in the day. They had a side errand to run, he said — a little job that would take Forbes's men and his own. He assigned shifts for day-herding and told the rest of the crew to make good use of a little rest time.

The sun had just cleared the eastern hills when Gundry and Forbes and their six men rode out of camp. Braden did not like the close association of the Seven Arrow riders with Forbes's men. Being on the roundup crew with them was distasteful enough, but at least the men from the other outfits would not see him as riding specifically with Engle or the others. On this little errand, however, he felt that an outsider would see him as part of a unified group.

When they had ridden west and a little south for about an hour, they came to a small creek, where they stopped to water the horses. All the men dismounted, and those who smoked rolled cigarettes. When the activity and the talk came to a lull, Gundry spoke. He said they were going to bring back some cattle from a fellow named Taylor, who lived a ways west of here and had just gotten back from repping at another roundup farther west.

Braden wondered how Gundry knew about Taylor's movements. No one from the outside had been to camp for a few days, so Gundry must have heard it from someone out on the range, or, more likely, from Forbes, who could have heard it from one of his men. It seemed to Braden a small thing to be suspicious about, but the circumstances called for a fellow to have his wits about him. Not only was he in the company of some suspect individuals, but the nature of today's errand still seemed a bit hazy.

Braden glanced around at the assortment of men and horses. He did not let his eye rest for long on Forbes or any of his men. Beaumont was checking the rigging on his horse, and Slack was gazing across the creek, his hard-set eyes squinting as the smoke curled up from his cigarette. Braden looked back around to his left, and as his eye traveled he noticed a patch of wild roses that had come into bloom. They looked bright and cheerful, as the first wild roses always did. But as he paused to appreciate the smiling pink blossoms, he thought of Greaves, who had sung the refrain of Beaumont's song as he went to check on the horses. It was a simple pleasure, singing. Greaves, a little shy about singing in the presence of others, often sang when he was off a ways. Now he would sing no more, just as he would never again see the new blossoms of the wild roses or watch the small trickle of a stream as it washed over a scattering of pebbles — pearl, jasper, and shiny blackstone — as the meadowlarks sang and the horses stamped and the cigarette smoke rose in tiny clouds on the morning air.

Braden shook his head and raised his eyebrows. The world went on, that was for certain. And a man who died for whatever reason would never see or hear any of it again. That was the way it would be, sooner or later, for all of the men here — himself included. A fellow could only hope for a fair deal, and when he saw where a man didn't get one, life didn't seem right. Greaves's hat lay on his bunk back at the ranch, next to his spurs and chaps where the boys had left them. Greaves was in the ground, while a snip like Farnsworth and a toad like Engle took in the new morning, with fried bacon and potatoes starting to work a progress through their guts. Braden kept himself from looking at any of Forbes's men. He knew his contempt would show.

After a few more minutes, Gundry mounted up and moved out. The rest of the men took the cue. There followed a small bustle of stomping out cigarettes, pulling cinches, leading horses clear of the others, and mounting up. The company moved in the same direction as before, west and a little south.

They rode for about three miles, and then a set of ranch buildings came into view. The house, barn, and outbuildings sat at the other end of a long swale, where they were pitched on a hillside that would give shelter from the strong winds out of the north and west. This morning the buildings showed a gray luster as they reflected the sunlight that poured from the east. Braden still wondered about the nature of this ride, as it had not been stated clearly whether the men were going for cattle that had been taken in on another roundup or whether they were getting cattle that had been held under some other circumstances. He looked at Beaumont and Slack, and he doubted that they had any clearer idea than he did.

Down the slope they rode and back up, until they came to the corrals at the edge of the ranch headquarters. Braden saw an assortment of cattle and horses, a few in each pen, but no bunch large enough to require a crew of eight men.

As they rode past the corrals, Braden thought he heard sounds coming from the barn, but he couldn't be sure amid the creaking, jingle, and clip-clop of eight riders. He kept his eye on the barn door, which was swung open, and within a minute, a man appeared in the dark doorway. The man seemed to hesitate, and then he stepped out into the sunlight. He called a greeting as the men rode forward.

Forbes and Gundry answered and then brought the horses to a halt within a few yards of the man. Braden waited for the bosses to dismount so that the rest of the riders could get down, but Forbes and Gundry stayed seated, looking down at the man.

Braden moved his horse to get a look at this fellow Taylor. The man had the appearance of a typical working cattleman — boots, denim pants, brown vest, gray shirt, brown hat. He was not very tall — maybe an inch or so below average — and he had a husky build. He looked to be about forty or so, as his face had filled out and his bushy mustache had streaks of gray.

"What can I do for you?" he asked, looking upward.

Forbes took the lead. "You're Taylor, aren't you?"

"Yes, I am."

"I think we've met before. I'm Vinch Forbes, and this is Patrick Gundry, from over my way."

Taylor looked from one to the other and nodded. Then, glancing at the rest of the riders, he said, "Looks like you're on your way to somewhere."

Forbes's light voice carried. "We came to see you."

Taylor gave a frown. "Is that right? What about?"

"About four little white-faced calves."

Taylor's face tightened. "I'm not sure I follow you."

Forbes's voice didn't sound quite so light and airy now. "I think you know what I'm talkin' about. Four calves that didn't have a brand on 'em and now they do."

Taylor shook his head. "No, not here."

Forbes came right back. "Yes, here. Four calves. They've been mavericked. You've got them here in a corral. If they were out on the range, they'd go back to their mothers."

Taylor spoke again, still in a firm voice. "You seem to know a lot, from a long ways away."

Braden stole a glance at Wyndham and Farnsworth, who both had wide-eyed, innocent looks on their faces. He imagined they felt his observation, as they seemed to be making an effort to freeze their expressions.

"I know what I know," said Forbes. "And you do, too. Don't make me call you something stronger than a mavericker."

Braden felt a chill. Calling a man a rustler, in front of other men, was as much as telling him to go for his gun.

Taylor looked around at the group of eight men. "If you know so much, then go take 'em if you think they're yours. But I'll remember this."

Gundry spoke for the first time. "That would be the best thing you could do."

Taylor gave him a sullen look but said nothing. Then, after giving a lingering look at the other mounted men, as if to say, "This is the way you are," he pivoted and walked back into the barn.

Forbes turned and nodded to Wyndham and Farnsworth, who turned their horses out to the left and back around toward the corrals. Engle followed. Then the rest of the company turned around as well.

Eight men for four calves, Braden thought. Forbes had set this up as a show of force, and Gundry had gone right along with him. It was not a new story to Braden. For years the big outfits had mavericked as they pleased, had even paid a bonus for men who branded a few head in the winter when they were not on the payroll. But if a little operator tried to do the same, the bigger cattlemen put pressure on him. He recalled how, several years back, they had gone so far as to lynch and shoot a few of the more independent and rebellious individuals. On slim evidence a group of men had hanged a woman, Cattle Kate, and her companion, James Averill. The lynchers went free. Three years later, an army of hired gunmen had killed two accused rustlers, Nate Champion and Nick Ray, and none of the attackers had to stand trial. Oh, there had been investigations and inquests, but no one in either case got punished. After those notorious events had settled down, Wyoming was supposed to be a more peaceful place to run cattle. Maybe it was, most of the time, but the attitude that might made right still prevailed.

Braden looked at Forbes and Gundry. They were no different from the others, he thought. Like the men who lynched Cattle Kate and the men who planned the extermination of alleged rustlers in Johnson County, they no doubt thought they were justified and had the right to do as they wished. On a very low level, these two had conspired. Braden recalled the more elaborate conspiracy of smearing Cattle Kate's reputation in the newspapers after she had been lynched; then he recalled the earlier and peculiar conspiracy of denying, in the newspapers, that the winter of 1886–87 was as bad as it was. Those were highly organized, as was the move against the list of men in Johnson County. That was all supposed to be in the past, but the old habit of thought remained. Men of power and influence, or even those who aspired to such things, felt that they could do things their way and gang up against individuals who resisted. So it was not a new story — not this show of power. What was new for Braden was his finding himself as part of it.

He would have felt petty if it were just a matter of eight men going after four calves. But more than that, he felt disgusted — at Forbes for setting up the move, at Gundry for going along with it, at Forbes's men for playing in, and at himself for being present. He looked at Beaumont and Slack. He couldn't blame them. They hadn't known what they were getting into, just as he hadn't, but he supposed they felt uncomfortable about the incident as well. Beaumont did not look up. He was checking the thong that tied his rope to the saddle. Slack was intent on rolling a cigarette.

Forbes's men brought the calves out of the corral. "Hee-yah!" called Farnsworth. He flung his rope and slapped a calf on the rump, then spurred his horse to cut the calf eastward with the other three.

As the calves fell in together and hit a fast walk, Forbes's three men took their places as herders — Wyndham on the left,

Farnsworth on the right, and Engle in the drag. Braden shook his head. Three men could drive ten times that many cattle, and there were still five men left over.

Half a mile out from Taylor's place, Gundry said, "We'll leave you three to handle this, and the rest of us will get back to work." He put his horse into a lope, and the other four riders did the same.

As Braden rode by, he did not look at Forbes's men. He had more contempt for them than before. He imagined they would carry on as if all of this were part of an honest job. They would probably vent the brand and put on the 4BS, then keep the calves close to home until Forbes found a handy way to sell them.

Back at the roundup, Gundry put his Seven Arrow riders and the kid from the MT on day herd while all the rest of the men, himself included, rode out to gather cattle. It was midmorning now, so the day's work was getting a late start, which would mean a late dinner. All of that, Braden thought, for the sake of helping Forbes push around another man.

On a day such as this, when the crew was not going to move camp, the roundup herd stayed in one place to graze. Unless a disturbance came up, day-herding was a slow job. A puncher rode around the outside of the herd until he met another rider, and after a brief chat he would turn around and ride back to meet the man coming from the other direction.

Braden rode along at a slow walk, glancing now at the herd and now at the surrounding country. It seemed all so peaceful and innocent, yet here he was on a range where a man had died from an unknown cause and where men took cattle by force. What he had seen in Gundry had soured him on the boss. A man rode for the brand, and he didn't have to like the boss. Although things worked better when he did, it was not imperative. But when the boss did something that ran crosswise with the way a man believed, the ride got rougher.

Braden thought that at least by some ways of looking at things, he should quit. He remembered the look Taylor had given them all, the look that had said that each of them was in it with the rest. Braden shook his head. He didn't want any part of Forbes, or a Forbes-Gundry alliance, or of pushing around other cattlemen. But he felt stuck. Even if he had justification, it would not be admirable, in the broader view of the world, to quit in the middle of the season. A man did his job. He didn't complain about the grub or about the company. If he didn't like things, he could move on, but if he valued his reputation, he waited until the work was all done in the fall.

He rode on. If things were way crooked, anyone could leave. But this incident was not downright dishonest — it was cheap, and unsavory, and demeaning, but it was not crooked, as far as Braden knew. If a fellow wanted to make a point of honor out of it, he would have to explain it a dozen times over.

The bay horse plodded on. Braden stopped to watch a little ruckus in the middle of the herd until the commotion settled down. He put the horse back into a walk, and after a few more minutes he saw Beaumont headed his way. As the distance between them closed, Braden saw that Beaumont had taken down his rope, a rawhide lariat, and was passing it between his thumb and fingers, inch by inch.

Braden was familiar with Beaumont's habit of handling his lariat, which he made himself. With long strings cut in circles from a scraped cowhide, then trimmed and beveled, Beaumont braided the strands into a lariat, keeping it pulled tight. Afterward he sanded it and oiled it and stretched it, and the end product was a work of beauty. Stronger than any grass rope, it was soft and pliant. A man who had such a rope took good care of it. Braden had come to imagine that Beaumont took pleasure in passing the lariat through his hand, as much to enjoy the feel as to check for any flaws or roughness.

When the riders were within a few yards of one another, Braden spoke. "What's up, Wes?"

"Not much." Beaumont did not look at him straight on.

"Did what's-his-name's men throw their big catch into the herd?"

"Not yet, I don't think." Beaumont's dark eyes came closer to meeting Braden's gaze.

"That was quite a little move, wasn't it?"

Beaumont nodded and gave him a direct look. "Almost dirty, but not quite."

"Uh-huh. And you wonder why we went along, except to show more force. I didn't like a bit of it."

"Neither did I. Surprised me about the boss." Beaumont rubbed his chin, which had a few days' worth of dark stubble on it.

Braden shook his head. "I think this fella

Forbes is bad medicine. Startin' with Engle, and now this."

Beaumont wrinkled his nose. "I'd go along with that. He's not like the Chinaman that wants to pee in his own soup. He wants to pee in everyone else's, too."

Thinking that the right opening had appeared, Braden said, "Yeh, he wants to get others tangled up into his problems, so they become their problems too, it seems like."

"I think you're right. I don't give a damn about someone else's four calves, and I can't see where Gundry should, either. But Forbes got him to buy into the venture."

"That's sure how it looked to me. I was just wonderin' if I was the only one."

"Nah. I could tell Slack didn't like any of it, either."

Braden let out a long breath. "Well, it hasn't been fun with these fellows to begin with, and I don't see where it's goin' to get any better."

"I try not to care too much, but I've got to admit I don't enjoy any of 'em very much, least of all that latecomer." Beaumont shook his head. "I still don't see why the boss buys into it."

Braden paused, then went ahead. "I

think what's-his-name is pretty slick. He wants others to be on his side, for one thing and maybe another."

Beaumont didn't seem to give much thought to the last part of Braden's comment. "Sure, he wants some of these fellas with a little pull to be on his side, but what's he got to offer them in return?"

"Oh, probably not much you could measure. There's not enough money in any of it to make that part matter enough. I imagine he's got the boss convinced that he's one of 'em."

"You mean that what's-his-name wants the boss to think he's one of the big boys."

"Uh-huh. And so he's got support to offer in return."

Beaumont seemed to be giving it more thought now. "That could be it. But you still wonder why in the hell any of it's worth it. A lot of trouble for damn little." He sniffed. "Life's too short as it is."

Braden had an image of a dark hat sitting on a bunk. "Isn't that the truth?" he said.

# Chapter Seven

When he got to the top of the last long slope, Braden stopped and dismounted to let the horses take a breather. The ranch was still a couple of miles off, and the horses had covered a lot of ground today. The stocky brown packhorse was holding up fine. He carried quite of bit of weight of his own, but he was plucky. He had started the day with two hundred pounds of salt blocks, and now the panniers were rolled up and tied to the sawbuck. Although he was breathing hard because of the long slow climb, he did not look tired. He looked cool and relaxed, like a day laborer who had gotten off work early.

The horse that Braden rode was a finer-boned animal, a sorrel with a wide blaze and three white socks. He looked a little tired, with sweat around the edges of the saddle blanket, as he had carried the same weight all day. The sorrel was a good riding horse. He had an energetic walk and a smooth lope, and he kept up a pace once he hit it. For that reason Braden had picked him for the day's riding and had picked the brown horse, which liked to slow down and loaf along, to follow on the other end of a lead rope. As lazy as the brown horse was, he picked it up when he had to, and he put in a day's work behind the sorrel horse without giving any trouble. Now as they paused for their rest they knew, as any ranch horse would, that they were on the homestretch. If horses could smile, the brown would smile like a farm boy who knew there was a pie in the oven; the sorrel would smile like a fellow who was going to see his girl in two weeks.

Some punchers judged a job by the quality of horses they got to ride. Braden had known men who would quit a job because they were given bum horses and who would feel they rose in status if they went to a place with better mounts. Braden didn't put quite that much value in his string, as he usually had a couple of horses he didn't care for very much anyway. But when he had a few good horses, like these two and the bay, he felt some pride in working for the Seven Arrow. The pay was fair and the grub was decent, but it was the work itself, and how a man was treated, in the jobs he was given and the horses he had to work with, that gave Braden a sense of worth. Now that spring roundup was over and the Forbes contingent was gone, Braden was able to settle into his own work. He wouldn't say of himself, as he would of Beaumont, that he was a top hand, but he thought he came close to that status, and he took pleasure in the thought.

As the horses caught their breath, he looked back over the country to the west, where he had ridden to put out the salt. Now as the day faded, the landscape lay in shadow. The lower buttes and ridges and bluffs cast a dark hue upon the grassland, now paling in midsummer. Farther to the west, the foothills and mountains lifted well above the plains and spread a bluish-purple haze across the lower-lying reaches.

Braden had learned to take in a moment like this, when he was alone on the land-scape with no sign of other humans. From where he stood he did not see a building, a windmill, or even a fence post. He knew that his own place lay a bit north and west of this spot, and Black Hat Butte, which he could see when he turned that way, sat a few miles south and west. But for the moment he could disregard his sense of benchmarks and property lines as he looked out over a landscape that seemed whole and constant. Something in him —

whether he should call it his heart, his soul, or his spirit, he did not know — seemed to flow from him at moments like this. He had the feeling that he spread out and hovered over the landscape, mingling with the energy that was latent in the land. At such a time he felt with more depth that life had promise and that the promise came from his merging with the rugged expanse of the land. Maybe he would never have a real ranch of his own, and maybe he would never share his life with a woman as fine as Beryl, but he trusted the indwelling power of the land and the potential of life lived in contact with the earth, its forms, and its forms of life. At least one line of Beaumont's song seemed to connect with that power, and Braden felt as if he heard the solitary verse floating in the dusk:

*"Yoodle-ooh, yoodle-ooh-hoo, so sings a lone cowboy."*

He did not know how many times he had sung parts of the song to himself before he realized he had taken it in and made it part of the words and thoughts and feelings that colored his inner life. Now, as he stood on the rim of his world, paused, in the company of two good horses, he gave soft utterance to both lines of the refrain:

*"Yoodle-ooh, yoodle-ooh-hoo, so sings a
  lone cowboy,
Who with the wild roses wants you to
  be free."*

Then he stepped into the saddle, picked up a happy gait with his two partners, and rode back to the ranch.

The next day, Gundry told Braden and Beaumont that he was sending them on a trip way over west to pick up three head of horses. He said a man named Wood had written him a letter saying that the horses had been running with his and were now in a fenced pasture where they could be caught. Gundry said he thought he would send two men, in case any of the horses had gotten too used to running free that far from home. Wood's place was a good twenty-five miles away, a long distance to bring back three horses on lead ropes. Gundry told his men he thought they could make it in one day over and one day back but they should use their own judgment, especially if it took any time to catch the horses. Braden and Beaumont said fine and were headed out of the ranch not long before sunup.

Braden had the location of the distant ranch printed in his mind — five miles almost due west of Shawnee, and north of the tracks. He and Beaumont headed their horses in that direction and moved at a fast walk. They wanted to cover as much ground as possible in the cool part of the day, but there was no sense in pushing the horses and tiring them too much the first day, as they would probably ride the same horses both days. For his own part, Braden did not count on getting a change of mounts from among the three runaways. Fighting a horse that had run far and free could make a long day much longer.

The two riders moved out without saying a great deal until they had left the ranch a good mile behind.

"Well, this should make the boss happy," said Beaumont. "There still might be one or two unaccounted for, but these three head'll bring us closer to a full herd."

Braden sniffed. "Uh-huh. He never did seem satisfied with what we gathered, even when we went back out and scoured the country."

"Well, you never know where they go. Just turn the horses out for the winter, and anything could happen — winter kill, runaway, or someone with a long rope."

"That's for sure. I think the old man's lucky to get back as many as he does. And that goes for cattle, too. Sooner or later he'll start fencin' in like this other fellow did, and he won't have so much trouble."

Beaumont cleared his throat. "That's what it's comin' to, all right. Everybody knows it, but they'll do things the old way for as long as they can. And it's not that bad. Maybe everyone loses a few head here and there — I'm talkin' mainly about cattle now — but it seems to come out even, and I'd hell of a lot rather hunt horses or round up cattle than build fences."

"Me, too. And if someone does want to lift a few head, a fence might make it a little harder, but it won't stop him."

"Oh, you bet. If it's worth money and it can walk away with a little nudgin', there'll always be someone lookin' over the fence and figurin' on how it can be done."

Braden thought there might be an opening in the conversation, so he gave it a try. "Of course, with no fences, it makes it all that much easier. With cattle, especially."

"Uh-huh."

Braden decided to try a little further. "Yeah, it's not too hard to get rid of a few head of cattle and not have to answer many questions."

Beaumont looked at him as if he wasn't sure where Braden was headed with his comments. "Well, that's up to whoever does it. I've never been too interested in it, myself."

"Oh, me neither. Not as somethin' to do. But it could be interesting to know about if someone else is up to it."

Beaumont poked his cheek out with his tongue as he gave Braden a sidelong look. "Depends, I guess."

"I'd say so. Maybe it depends on who does it, or how many head there are, or even who knows about it."

"Oh, uh-huh. You mean, if it was something bigger than one little incident, like you and me gettin' caught in a blizzard and preferrin' to shoot someone's steer rather than wait for one of us to die and turn into camp meat."

Braden laughed. "Somethin' like that. Or even if someone had to sell a head or two, just to make ends meet. You can look the other way."

"Sure. 'Specially if it's another puncher, like in the wintertime. It wouldn't be worth talkin' about."

"Right. In that case it wouldn't. But like you say, it depends."

Beaumont turned his head and gave

Braden a direct look. "I take it that you might have a little story that falls in a different category."

"Uh-huh. It might fall in the category of somethin' worth talkin' about."

Beaumont looked around. "Just you and me, and I can't even remember a good joke when I hear it, my memory's so bad."

"Well," said Braden, feeling a little hesitation. "I heard it from Greaves."

Beaumont did not smoke very often, especially out on the range, but when the two men stopped to water and rest the horses, he dug a curved-stem pipe out of his war bag, loaded it with tobacco, and lit it. Neither he nor Braden had said anything for the last half hour, and now he spoke.

"It's kind of one of those things that you don't know if you wish you'd never heard it, but you know it's somethin' that shouldn't be ignored."

"That's just about how I see it. But once he told me the first part, I was stuck. Then when he told me the rest I knew it was serious, and when he turned up dead — well, hell, you can't just turn your back on that."

"You sure can't. I still don't know what to make of him bein' in the room for so long that night, but as for whether what happened to him out on the range was accidental, I've had my doubts about that all along."

"I would think just about anyone should have at least some doubt. But if you say too much, all you do is make yourself a target."

Beaumont's teeth gleamed as he smiled with the pipe stem clenched in the left side of his mouth. "That's for damn sure. If you're goin' to do anything at all, you've got to stay alive to do it." He took the pipe out of his mouth. "What do you think you can do?"

Braden didn't like the use of "you." It sounded as if Beaumont was dumping it all back in his lap. "Well, the first thing is to try to get more of the goods on 'em. All we've got is hearsay and what may be coincidence. We need more to go on before we can take it to anyone else."

"Well, I doubt you can find an eyewitness, much less get a signed confession. This stuff is pretty well done and put away, it seems to me."

"Maybe so, but there are witnesses and evidence all over the place in the first part. Anything we can get there will help us in the main part."

"How do you propose to do that, without hangin' targets on ourselves? Go quiz the little girl in Shawnee? Not that I would object to stoppin' at a hog ranch, but anyone you talk to is gonna tell someone."

"Could be. Maybe it depends on who you ask and how you ask the question."

Beaumont grinned. "So the gal in Shawnee is out."

Braden smiled back. "Just for these purposes. You could talk to her about the price of hogs in Omaha."

"I think I'll save it. Even at that, somethin' could slip. Better we go about it the most careful way we know how."

"I agree." Braden liked the way Beaumont was talking now, including himself in the plan. But even that was fragile, so Braden didn't mention it. He just said, "Careful's the word."

They reached the Wood ranch, which was off in a land of rolling hills, by late afternoon. As they rode into the yard, they called out a greeting. When a door opened on their right, in the middle of a long, low building, they dismounted. A lean, red-eyed, white-haired man, who wore an apron and seemed to be in charge of the bunkhouse kitchen, told them they could find the boss in the barn. They walked across the yard, and just before they reached the barn, a man stepped around from the far end.

Taller than the cook but also lean and red-eyed, he said his name was Wood. The Seven Arrow horses had been around his place since March, he said, but he didn't know who owned them until he asked around during the roundup. When he found out, he put them in the pasture and wrote a letter. He said no one had ridden the horses or so much as put a rope on them. He gave the boys directions on how to get to the pasture, adding that he would ride out with them except he had the forge hot and was in the middle of a job.

Braden thought it looked as if both men had red eyes because they were sleeping off a drunk, and he wondered why he hadn't heard any of the clank and clang that came out of a blacksmith shop. Then he told himself none of it was any of his business, and he shrugged it off. He and Beaumont mounted up and rode out. They found the pasture without any trouble, and within a short while they roped the three horses they were after. Then they led the horses back to the ranch and penned them up for the night.

At Wood's invitation, they stayed to spend the night in the bunkhouse. Four other hands came in from haying, and the cook set out a pot of rice and two skillets of meat and gravy. The grub was edible enough, in spite of a burnt taste to the rice. No one spoke much, and not long after supper, everyone went to bed.

At breakfast the next morning, everyone was clear-eyed. Still no one talked much, so Braden and Beaumont rode out knowing not much more about the Wood ranch or the nearby country than they did when they came in. About a mile out from the buildings, Braden spoke.

"We're not in a hurry to get back if we don't want to be."

"Oh, I guess not," said Beaumont. "What have you got in mind?"

"Seems to me that we might stop at a place or two on the way back, maybe let on that we're wonderin' how these horses got over this way and what might have happened to the other three that are still out. Maybe, on an odd chance, we'll hear somethin' else."

Beaumont agreed it was worth a try, so when they got back to the other side of Shawnee, they stopped at one place after another. They heard plenty of stories

161

about traders and drifters and whatnot, but nothing about anyone driving half a dozen head of horses in March. That was fine with Braden and Beaumont, as they were more interested in the other stories anyway. In a couple of places they heard about a tinker who had no front teeth and traveled with a half-wit girl who neighed like a horse. At a couple of other ranches they learned that the foremen kept a record of travelers who stopped at their places. This was a practice carried over from a few years back, when cattlemen wanted to discourage cattle thieves from staying at their ranches. Braden and Beaumont did not ask to see their ledgers and they did not offer, but they made free mention of their practice of keeping track of all strangers and the brands on their horses.

Braden was beginning to grow weary of stopping in at so many places. By late afternoon they were barely halfway home. Then they struck what looked like color at a little out-of-the-way ranch run by a father and son who didn't seem to care much about barn and fence repair but who liked to drink coffee and talk a lot. At this place they heard about a couple of fellows who had to stop in for the night because of a late-spring snowstorm. In a sort of medley in which they took turns, the father and son told the story.

"It was in the last days of April, and the two of them were headed southwest. They come from somewhere over in the country where you boys say you're from. One fella, he was a little taller, and his hair runnin' to gray. The other, he was short and shifty-eyed. Didn't say what they was up to, or why they was this far off their range. They did bring in a bottle of whiskey, and the mousy fella drank damn near half of it himself, but neither of 'em said much. We like company as much as anyone, but we didn't get much news or gossip or whorehouse stories or tall tales from those two. Still, they didn't look like they was on the run. They said they worked for some newcomer over that way. Damn if I can remember the name, if they even mentioned it. And like I say, they didn't say much. Big and little, that's what they was. The little one drank most of the whiskey, like he wanted to make sure none of it went to waste. So that's it on them. Tell us about yourselves."

Well over an hour later, after giving a full account of themselves and then hearing all about the Rooshians and the Swedes and the plague of wheat farmers who, along with the railroads and sheepmen, were going to be the ruin of the little man who worked and scraped to try and run a cow outfit, Braden and Beaumont each managed to get a foot in the stirrup and mount up. The father and son had followed them out to where they had the horses tied.

"You can't ride all that far tonight," said the father. "You ought to stay here."

"That's right," said the son. "Put your horses away, and get some rest. Get an early start tomorrow."

"Thanks all the same," said Braden, "but we'd better make it a little farther tonight."

"Well, by God," said the father, "next time you pass by this way, be sure to drop in. You're no strangers now."

"We'll do that," said Beaumont with a broad smile. "And thanks again for the coffee."

"You bet," said the son. "And come again. We always like visitors."

Half a mile down the trail, Beaumont let out a long whistling breath. "That's workin' for it, isn't it?"

"It sure is, but I don't mind the work if you get somethin' for it. Big and little. Sounds like someone we might know."

"That it does. It's not much, but it fits in."

They stopped at another ranch several miles east, arriving at dusk and putting the horses in a corral as invited. Then, in accordance with cow country hospitality, they sat down to supper and settled in to relax for the night. They were close enough to home by now that they knew a couple of the hired men, so the evening passed with easy conversation until everyone turned in for the night.

When they got back to the ranch at noon the next day, they learned from Lum that Gundry had gone to town and had left word for them to help Slack on the fence project. Slack came in for noon dinner, and after the meal they all rode out to the spot where they were building a fence around a plot for haystacks. With few questions or comments on either side, Braden and Beaumont fell back into the routine at the Seven Arrow, and their trip to bring back the lost horses became just another job done.

Sunday rolled around, and as work was not pressing, Braden and his two fellow ranch hands got a day off. After breakfast and a leisurely cup of coffee, Braden shaved, cleaned up, put on a fresh shirt and clean pants, and went out to the horse corral. He had a mind to ride the sorrel horse, the one with the blaze and three white socks. As he looked over the horses, the one he had in mind caught his gaze and gave him a knowing look. The sorrel was a good horse, not the type that would bite or paw or kick, but like many a good-spirited horse, he would have his little game before he got led away for the day's work. Braden kept his eye on the animal as he went through the gate and closed it behind him. Still with his gaze fixed on the horse, he moved the coils of his rope to his left hand and shook out a loop with his right. The sorrel crowded in among the other horses, but Braden knew the game. He walked the horse down, one short way and then another, until he had it separated from all but a couple of others. Then he made his toss, and the sorrel knew the game was up for the day.

Braden rode south and west toward Black Hat Butte, which stood out clear in the morning sky. The day might well turn hot by afternoon, but for the present it was young and fresh. Braden could feel the energy of the horse as it moved in a brisk walk. A meadowlark tinkled, and a grasshopper clicked and whirred away with an orange fan of wings. Although life presented a couple of gloomy matters that he wasn't dead certain about how to handle, he had hope in his heart about the visit he was intending to make.

The sorrel horse covered the ground in good time, and the sun had not quite reached midmorning when Braden gave the horse a nudge to go up the slope at the base of the butte. This part of the landscape seemed spare today. The carpet flowers were long since gone, and the grass had begun to turn pale green and light brown. The sides of the butte itself had turned tan and dry. Braden looked around but saw no antelope, which he half expected to see. He wondered what had become of Rove and whether the pale rider would show up in these parts again, talking sense in riddles.

Up the slope and pausing at the crest, Braden gave a sweeping glance to the plain below. There, like magic, lay the little homestead with its buildings and windmill. Time and again in the last six weeks, he had thought about the place and what it looked like when it first came into view. It had not changed — not in location, of course, nor in appearance, nor in the feeling it evoked. It meant water and comfort, open friendship, and grace — a dark-haired woman with gray-green eyes, the touch of her hand, and the aura of a person secure in her own self.

As he rode down the slope toward the buildings, he looked around him as usual. He did not see Birdie and her critters or any other animal life in the grassland that stretched away on either side. Now closer to the homestead site, he could see into the yard itself, where two horses stood at a hitching rail and two people were brushing and combing the animals. Closer still, he saw Birdie working with the palomino and Beryl tending to the dark horse.

The sorrel let out a whinny, and an answer came from the yard. Sandy-haired Birdie looked around and waved; then dark-haired Beryl, in a blue work shirt and denim pants, stepped out from behind her horse and waved. Happy at the full sight of her, Braden waved back twice.

Into the yard and down from the saddle, he winked at Birdie and nodded to Beryl, tipping his hat. Then, as she stepped forward and lifted her hand, he took it, pressed the back of her fingers with his thumb, and released. With that sequence of motion he took a brushing glance at her, and the color of her shirt seemed to give a bluestone hue to her eyes.

"Nice to see you back," she said.

"Nice to be back." He motioned with his head toward the horses. "Were you getting ready to go somewhere?"

"Not really," she answered. "We thought we might take a ride, but we didn't have any real plans."

His eyes met hers for a longer moment now, and he saw them in their true color of gray-green. She gave him a clear, straight look — serious and almost cold. Then their gaze relaxed, and he admired her tan face and dark hair.

"I had a day off," he said, "so I thought I'd stop over."

"We're glad you did. It's been a while since we saw you."

He sensed she left something unsaid. "I wish I could have come sooner. Our roundup crew came right by here, as you no doubt know, but I was out working the other side." He paused and tried to think of the best wording, but nothing perfect came to him, so he just spoke. "Then, when our pal Ed had his accident, we all got tied up in that problem. Then, after that, we moved on and around, and this is the first time I've had a chance to come by on my own."

Her look softened a little, but it still

seemed troubled. "I thought as much, but when it happened, it didn't make things any easier to know that you were that close and couldn't come by. We would have felt better, I think, just to have heard your version."

"Did you hear it from the sheriff, then?"

"No, he didn't come by here."

Braden flinched. The death had taken place a mile away, and the sheriff hadn't taken the trouble to come this far to ask questions. "Who did?"

"Mr. Forbes." The corners of her mouth turned down for a second. "I couldn't avoid the impression that he was trying to scare us — dangers lurking about, you know — at the same time he was assuring us that it was an accident."

"Did it seem like he was trying too hard?"

"Something like that."

"Well, he's a thoughtful sort, isn't he?"

Her eyebrows tensed. "He would give that impression."

Braden took a deliberate breath. "Well, I'm sorry if it got you worried." He turned and took in Birdie as he spoke. "It was trouble for the roundup crew, sure enough, but it shouldn't have been for the two of you."

Beryl also took a deep breath. Glancing at Birdie and then back at him, she said, "Well, I suppose the trouble is past now."

He raised his eyebrows and tipped his head to the side. "I guess so."

She seemed as if she wanted to speak, but she hesitated for a moment. She flickered another glance at Birdie and then said, "The man who died — he worked with you, didn't he? That's what I understood."

"Right. We worked together. Not always partners, but for the same outfit. When we work in pairs, I usually work with a fellow named Beaumont. This fellow rode out more often with a puncher named Slack."

"I see. And his name was — ?"

"Greaves. Edwin Greaves. We called him Ed."

She gave a slow nod. "Yes, that was the name, of course. And what did he look like?"

Braden thought back. "Oh, a regular-looking fellow. I guess he had brown hair and brown eyes. The main thing about him, if he was out on a horse, was his hat. He wore a dark hat, with a high crown, that you could see a mile away."

Beryl looked at Birdie. "Does that sound like the man?"

All of the playfulness was gone from the girl's face as she nodded.

Beryl's eyes came back to meet Braden's. "On the day that it happened, Birdie saw a man up by the butte."

Braden looked at the girl, taking in her sandy hair and serious brown eyes. "Whereabouts?"

She pointed to the left of the butte. "He was riding from over there."

Braden followed her gesture. "Coming from the northwest?"

"Uh-huh."

"And which way did he go? Or, wait — where were you, first?"

She pointed at the butte itself. "I was up there, between the butte and that lower one."

He looked at the shadowed spot between the sugarloaf formation and the larger one. "Near where you were that day when I saw you with the antelope?"

She nodded.

"So he probably couldn't see you. And then what did he do? Did he ride on past the other side and out of your sight?"

"Uh-huh."

He looked at Beryl and then back at the girl. "You might have been the last one to see him alive. What time of day was it?"

"Late afternoon."

Braden gave a couple of slow nods as he tried to picture it. Then he looked at the girl. "Anything else you can remember?"

Birdie seemed to be holding her mouth closed as she moved her head down and up.

"Well, don't be afraid to tell me."

"She knows that," said Beryl, who smiled when Birdie looked at her.

Braden brought his eyes back to the girl and gave her a reassuring smile. "Go ahead," he said.

"I saw another man riding along behind him. At first I thought they were together, but then I saw the other man sort of hold back a couple of times. Then I figured he was following him."

Braden felt his face drawing together. "He might have been. Could you tell me what he looked like?"

The girl's brown eyes were steady. "He didn't look much like the rest of you. I could tell he was different."

"In what way?"

"He was round." She pronounced the word with a little bit of an "oi" sound in it.

"Short and stubby? Kinda look like a toad?"

Her mouth was open in a half-smile. "Yeah, like that."

Braden nodded. It would be Engle. But he would have had a hard time sneaking up close enough behind Greaves all by himself. "Did you see anyone else?"

Birdie shook her head. "No, just those two. The one in the dark hat, and then the fat one."

Braden let out a long breath. Then, squinting his right eye, he said, "I'm glad you told me this, Birdie. I don't know if I can do anything with it, but if I ever do, don't worry about any of it comin' back on you."

She smiled and nodded, then looked at Beryl. "Should I just go on a ride by myself, then?"

Beryl gave her a soft smile. "Is that what you feel like doing?"

"I think so."

"Well, go ahead. Mr. Braden and I will probably sit and talk for a while. Swing back and check in with me in a little while, and if it's not too late, maybe I'll ride out with you."

"All right." Birdie pulled loose the bow knot and drew the lead rope clear of the hitching rail. Then she led the horse away a few yards, sprang up onto its bare back, and rode away. At the edge of the yard, the horse went into a lope and carried the girl away in a smooth drumming of hooves.

Beryl watched the horse and rider for a few seconds and then turned to Braden. "She's been worried about it all this time, and we didn't know who to tell. Birdie's no fool, you know."

"I wouldn't think so." Braden moistened his lips. "I take it that you didn't say any of this to Forbes."

Beryl shook her head. "Not at all."

"Just as well you didn't. The little fat man works for him."

She caught her breath. "Do you think there was something — ?"

"I don't know. I've had my suspicions, and they've leaned in that direction. But by itself, this isn't enough to raise a fuss about. But it's more than I had before."

The gray-green eyes carried a steady look. "So you think there might be something."

He gave a slow nod as he looked past her and gazed across the empty grassland at the butte. More than before, the two strands seemed woven together. And the more certain it seemed, the more he saw the need for caution. He looked at Beryl. Here was a woman whose property Forbes wanted. It wouldn't do to give her too much to worry about for right now, but she needed to look out. "Yes. I think so," he said.

"If they had done such a thing," she said, bringing out the words with care, "what would be their purpose?"

His eyes met hers again, and he knew he couldn't withhold it all. "I think Greaves knew something, and they wanted to keep him quiet. That's probably about as much as I should say right now, but in a way it's quite a bit."

"Yes, it is. I don't think our having talked about it changes anything."

"What do you mean?"

"Well, if something really did happen, as it seems to be, it doesn't put us in any more danger now that we've talked about it than we were in before."

"Oh, no, not at all. You mean what Birdie told me."

"Well, that, but also what you just told me."

"Um, why would it?"

"I don't know. But knowing something could put a person in danger. You just said as much."

"More so when someone knows you know it." He smiled as he shook his head.

"We didn't tell each other anything."

She smiled back. "No, we didn't. And when you did, you didn't tell me enough to make it dangerous." She looked around. "But you're right. We didn't tell each other anything. Probably because no one knows anything to tell."

Braden felt as close to her then as he ever had, but an air of restraint still prevailed. He wanted to take her in his arms, ask her why she could make him feel such a degree of confidence, ask her what kind of a grass widow she really was. But it was too much all together, so he said, "I suppose it's good not to know everything at once."

Her look was calm and serious now. "I think you're right."

"But I hope things change."

"You mean, you hope you find out more?"

"That, and I hope I can tell you more, without, um —"

"Increasing the danger?"

"Yes, that."

"That would be fine."

He took his leap. "And then I would hope we could go on that way."

Her eyebrows drew together. "In what way?"

"Oh, I guess I mean we could go on sharing what we know." He took a deep breath. "I don't like to hold back when I trust someone, unless there's a danger like right now."

"I agree."

"And I would hope, maybe someday, I might be trusted, too."

Her face softened again in a half-smile. "I agree with you on that, too."

# Chapter Eight

The longest day of the summer had come and gone, but daylight still lingered late in the evening in the third week of July. As Braden rode into town with Beaumont and Slack, he noticed the trees that grew along the streets and in a few yards. Not a tree in town could be more than ten years old, as the railroad had come through just ten years earlier and the towns had formed after that. Trees did not grow fast this far north, so none of the trees in Carlin were big enough to host the crows that Rove had spoken of.

The three riders tied their horses to the hitching rail in front of the Lucky Chance and went inside. The place had not filled up yet, but at least a dozen men lounged along the bar and at a couple of tables. Braden glanced toward the back and did not see any girls. That was fine, he thought. He did not look forward to seeing the yellow-haired one named Emily, as he had uncertain feelings about her. He did not like to hold a grudge against someone, especially a woman, just on the basis of suspicion. But if she was thick with Forbes and had contributed to Greaves's ruin, she was part of the enemy. Braden did not like having enemies, but if he couldn't avoid them, he wanted to know who they were. So far, he was pretty sure of two of them — Forbes and Engle — and he had to assume that Wyndham and Farnsworth were in that camp. But even as sure as he was, he knew he needed to keep his judgment open.

Beaumont called for drinks at the bar as Slack cast a narrow look around the saloon. Braden wondered if he was looking for a girl or if he was just taking stock of the place. As Beaumont handed out the drinks, he suggested that they sit at a table. Braden called a greeting to Connors the barkeep and then sat down with his two friends.

Soon enough he became aware of a young fellow who sat at the next table with his back to them. The man wore a flat-crowned, flat-brimmed hat in the style of southerners, and it looked as if he wore a dark duster or a cape. Dressed as he was and sitting by himself, he gave a clear impression that he was a stranger.

Slack took out the makings and built himself a cigarette, while Beaumont went about stuffing tobacco into his pipe. The evening was young, and no one was in a hurry. Even if it were later in the evening, there wasn't much to be in a hurry about in the Lucky Chance unless a fellow got a late start and wanted to get falling-down drunk. Slack rolled his cigarette tight, licked the paper, tapped the seam, gave half a twist to the right end, stuck the other end in his mouth, and popped a match. After blowing away a small stream of smoke, he extended the match to Beaumont, who used it to light his pipe. Braden watched the shreds of tobacco rise in the bowl of the pipe; then Beaumont used the end of his jackknife to tamp the bowl, and with a timely puff he kept the tobacco burning. Braden yawned. For as much as a fellow had a hankerin' to go to town, he sure didn't have much to do once he got there.

Slack smoked his cigarette down to a snipe, then dropped it on the floor and twisted his heel on it. Beaumont smoked on his pipe a little longer and then knocked it against the leg of his chair.

As he put the pipe back into his vest pocket, he said, "I wish there was some music."

"It would liven things up," said Braden,

"even if it was one of those fellas that play to one tune and sing to another." He could venture such a comment because he knew Beaumont could sing better than most bar-room musicians he had heard; he also knew better than to suggest that Beaumont sing in a place like this.

The stranger at the next table turned halfway around and to his right and said, "Not much talent in these parts, then, I take it."

"Oh, do you sing?" asked Beaumont, who was sitting closest to him and made half a turn to face him.

"Not at all. I was just thinking the same thing, that's all. A little entertainment would help."

The young man stayed turned in his seat, giving Braden the impression that he had been waiting for a chance to work his way into the company at the next table. He looked at the three of them and said, "You fellas work around here, do you?"

Braden nodded. "We all work for the same outfit — the Seven Arrow, run by a man named Gundry."

The man nodded at each of the three. "Cowboys, huh?"

"Yep," said Beaumont. "That's all the brains we got."

The stranger hiked his right leg up over his left and brought into view a walking stick, which he rested against his right hip. The stick seemed out of place for a man no older than Braden and his two friends. "Is that all the kind of work there is around here?" he asked.

Beaumont answered. "Oh, there's that, and railroad work, and not too far from here there's coal mines. And of course there's a scarcity of musicians." He paused, and then with a light air he said, "Do I take it you're not a cowpuncher, then?"

The man shook his head. "I wouldn't be any good at it." He patted his right thigh. "This leg wouldn't hold up."

"Probably wouldn't do so well at railroadin' or coal-minin' either, then," said Beaumont, as if it were the stranger's good luck.

The man shook his head again and lowered it. "No, I'm afraid not."

Braden cocked his head. Because of the position of their chairs, he did not have more than a side view of the man, but even from that angle he thought the stranger was putting on a little show of self-pity.

"Well," said Beaumont, still not losing his cheery tone, "I suppose there's some kind of work for everyone. What's your line of work, when you can find it?"

The stranger turned in his chair to face the other three men with a direct pose. "I've had some experience as a financial manager. You might say I'm looking for an opportunity in that line."

Braden took a good look at the young man. He had long, dark hair that hung over his ears and down to his collar. It was shiny and not very clean. He had a rough, pitted complexion that seemed a natural companion to his stringy mustache, long nose, and beady eyes. Braden thought the man looked more like someone who would take money at rooster fights than someone who would be entrusted with the finances of a businessman or investor. From a front view, Braden could also see that the man's overgarment was indeed a cloak, fastened across his upper chest by a silver chain. What with the hat and the cloak, the man seemed to affect the image of a gentleman gambler or soldier of fortune, but with his comment about his preferred line of work, he seemed to be an opportunist in general. Braden imagined that a "financial manager" was someone who, at best, tried to put someone else's money to work for himself.

"It's hard to say," said Beaumont, taking

out his pipe again. Because he did not smoke very often, Braden imagined he was using the pipe as a diversion from having to say much more.

The stranger must have taken the hint, as he turned to Braden to keep the conversation going. "I didn't mean that I was lookin' to manage people's personal finances, you know."

"Oh, I didn't take it that way." Braden looked at his two fellow punchers. "I don't think any of us did."

Slack and Beaumont shook their heads without speaking.

"I might just as well have said I was an entrepreneur, but I didn't know if the word might sound a little hifalutin out this way."

Beaumont had a droll look on his face as he said, "Oh, don't worry about that. Braden knows a word or two of French."

Braden smiled. He could tell Beaumont was enjoying having pushed the stranger off on him. "Not many," he said, "but I do know that one."

"Well, you get the idea, then. I'm on the lookout for something where I can use my business sense. Not that I'm even askin' if you know of anything — just answerin' the question of what line of work I'm in."

Braden glanced at Beaumont and back at the stranger. "I think the question did come up in response to your own question, though, about what kind of work there was around here."

"Oh, of course," said the young man, holding up his hand. "Naturally, if someone had a tip, I'd be obliged."

Braden almost laughed. Here he had thought he was sticking up for Beaumont against the mild charge of being inquisitive, and he had allowed the man to get another grab on him, like a dog that wouldn't let go of his pants leg. "Hard to say," he quipped, in what he hoped was an echo of Beaumont's earlier remark. Then he had an idea that amused him. "But you know, wherever there's men workin', there's someone makin' money. And I don't mean the workin' man, of course. It's the railroad tycoon, the coal mine owner, the cattleman, the freighter, the hotel keeper — you know, the ones that are buyin' and sellin' and dealin'."

Beaumont, who had opened his knife and was scraping out the bowl of his pipe, paused and looked up. "You bet. Them's the type." Then he nodded and went back to his work.

The stranger sat up straight in his chair.

"And did I catch your name right? Is it Braden?"

"Yes, it is."

"Well, my name's Downs. Emery Downs. And pleased to meet you." He leaned forward, right hand outstretched, as he raised his eyebrows and nodded.

Braden thought the sincerity a little overdone, but he rose halfway from his chair to shake hands. Then he sat down as the newcomer learned the names of Beaumont and Slack. When they were all settled back in their chairs, Downs spoke again.

"So, has it been a good year for the cattle business?"

Braden shrugged. "Depends on who you ask, and on what day."

"Oh?"

"Sure. If it's in a man's interests to say that the prices are goin' to hell and the rustlers are bleedin' the range dry, that's what he'll say. But if the same fella has got a reason to say the herds are up, he'll say that, too — just not to the same person, you know." Braden glanced at his two companions. Beaumont seemed to be following his drift, but Slack wasn't paying attention. He was looking around the saloon again.

Downs nodded in a semblance of shared confidence. "Of course. Play everything close to the chest."

"That's it," said Braden. "So you see, we wouldn't know."

"But you work with the cattle."

Braden was starting to feel better now, as if he had dragged the conversation back to his own ground and could get free. "You bet we do. But we don't know anything about the business. Like Wes said, cowpunchin' is all we got the brains for."

Downs looked from Beaumont to Braden and then cast a glance at Slack, who had not humored him for a second. "Well, there's brains and there's brains," he said. "And the ones that're book-smart, they don't have it all. Some of them don't have a lick of common sense."

No one said anything for a long moment. Braden resisted the temptation to argue the last point in favor of a few book-smart people he had met who did have common sense. He thought Downs was trying to sidle up to the three cowpunchers with the tired old wisdom about educated people not having common sense, but he thought that if he argued back, he would get pulled in anyway. So he kept quiet.

Downs looked around the table again.

"So, what do you do for entertainment, then?"

Braden shrugged. "Sometimes there's music."

Beaumont tipped his head in Slack's general direction. "And sometimes there's girls."

Downs put on a smile. "That sounds good enough."

"Trouble is," said Beaumont, "you got to go to town for 'em, and they're not always there."

"You mean the girls, or the music too?"

"Both," said Beaumont. "There ain't no one in a bunkhouse can sing better'n a squeaky hinge."

"Oh, I guess it gets pretty dull out there, then."

"I should say so," Beaumont went on. "You damn near wear the spots off a deck of cards. Between that, and laggin' pennies, and cussin' contests, that's about it."

"Cussin' contests? That's a new one for me."

"Not around here. There's been cussin' contests since the first hands come up the trail from Texas with mules."

"Oh, what do the mules have to do with it?"

"They make the best judges."

Downs gave a forced laugh. "I bet they do."

Slack finally spoke up. "It's true. I've seen cussin' contests where they really did use mules for judges."

Downs looked at him. "Really?"

Slack gave a look in return that suggested Downs was the stupidest of all. "Of course. What the hell does it take to swear? And if both sides know all the same words, what's gonna be the difference? The tone, or the loudness, or whatever. And who's the best judge of that? Someone, or somethin', that doesn't know the words." Then, having said as much as Braden had known him to say in any one exchange, he lapsed back into a silence more sullen than before.

"That's right," said Beaumont. "You take a Chinaman that don't know any English, and you cuss him out in a real sweet voice, and how's he to know what the words mean?"

Downs sat back and pulled at his mustache. "I guess I understand the card games a little better. At least there's a point to them." He looked around the saloon, then at Braden. "Just about any place you go, you'll find someone playin' cards, maybe runnin' a game in a place like this."

Braden turned down the corners of his mouth. "Doesn't seem to be as much of an item in here, for as much as everyone plays cards out at the ranches." He rotated his whiskey glass on the tabletop in front of him, and as he did so he realized for the first time that Downs did not have a drink. "Of course," he went on, "if you're lookin' for some kind of an opportunity —"

"Oh, no, not really," said Downs, pushing up his lower lip and holding up both his hands, palms outward. "Nothing urgent. Just makin' conversation."

"No harm in that," said Beaumont, wiping off the blade of his knife with his right thumb and forefinger.

"Not at all," Braden added. "But if you wanted to get a better feelin' for the pulse of this town, there are others that know a lot more about what goes on in the business around here."

"Oh, is that right?" The eyebrows went up and down over the beady eyes, and then a casual expression crept over the man's face as he looked at the floor.

"Uh-huh. There's a couple of fellas that run the hotel and restaurant across the street, and they're pretty much in the know."

Downs still had a disinterested look on

his face as he brought his head up to look at Braden. "Oh. Uh-huh. I see."

"Sure," said Braden. "You could probably go over there right now, order a steak supper, and get to know 'em."

Downs hesitated, the tip of his tongue appearing beneath his mustache at the edge of his mouth. "Oh, it doesn't mean that much to me."

Braden made a waving motion with his left hand as he wrinkled his nose. "Ah, for all that, they'll probably be closin' in a little while. And they usually come in here when they do."

Downs shrugged. "Oh, if I see 'em, fine, and if I don't, no matter." He moved his walking stick into an upright position, then hauled himself up and out of his chair. He wavered for a second as he stood there, until he steadied. "I can't sit in one place all night," he said. "I've got to move around." Then, with what seemed like another artificial bit of courtesy, he touched the brim of his hat with his left hand and said, "It's been a pleasure, gentlemen."

The three cowpunchers returned the compliment with "You bet," "Likewise," and a nod. Downs turned and limped away toward the back of the saloon, where he disappeared into the dark hallway that led to the latrine and to the rooms where the girls did their work.

A few minutes later, Downs came back into the saloon and sat two tables away from the Seven Arrow riders. He sat again with his back to them, presenting a rear view of his dark cloak, long hair, and flat-crowned hat.

As Braden and his two companions had another drink, a few more men trickled into the saloon. A handful of railroad workers sat at the empty table where Downs had sat earlier, and soon enough their rowdy talk filled the air. After a while the tone underwent a change, and as Braden turned to get a look, he saw that Downs had introduced himself into the company of these fellows as well. Braden could not hear the comments, but every few minutes a curt laugh would go around the table, and it seemed as if the man sitting closest to Downs was baiting him. When Braden took another look about ten minutes later, he saw that Downs had turned back to his own table.

Not long after that, the trio from the Aster came sauntering in. First came chicken-necked Norman Dace, with his nose up and a little to his left. After him, threading his way among chairs and men, and patting a shoulder here and there, proceeded his colleague Varlett, leading with his head forward. Taking up the end of the short procession was Shadwell, who led with his stomach and had his hands in the front pockets of his pants. Braden watched the three as they got to the center of the saloon, paused, and looked around. The man in the dark cloak sat up straight, and the hat tilted upward. The three men from the Aster sat down at his table.

Well, thought Braden, the perfect little acquaintance was forming. To all appearances, Downs was watching his money and had not ordered a single drink, much less gone across the street to order a full meal. Instead, he had bided his time, and within a few minutes he would be confirming that these were men who might share his interests.

While Braden was looking toward the back part of the saloon, he noticed a splash of color and the flouncy shapes of women's sleeves and bodices and hats. The girls had arrived. Braden did not pause long enough to see whether any of them had yellow hair. Instead, he turned back to his own table, where a couple of the Davis riders stood talking to Beaumont and Slack. Braden lifted his head in greeting.

The other punchers talked on, but now Slack was casting full glances toward the back of the room. He stood up from his chair and moved around the table to stand by the chair next to Braden, all the time gesturing for the other two men to sit down. As they did, Slack set his drink on the table and withdrew with a nod. With a tug at his hat brim he sallied forth in the direction of the bright colors and dark hallway.

Beaumont and the two Davis riders had gotten into a conversation about fences and who was entitled to put them where. It was all very amiable, with no real disagreement, and Braden followed the commentary without joining in. After a while, he got up to go to the latrine. As he walked past the second table beyond his own, he saw an interesting arrangement.

Downs sat, as before, at the side of the table closest to the front of the saloon, except that he now sat sideways to the table, with his left elbow on the edge of the tabletop and his left thumb and fingers supporting his cocked head. His left leg was hiked over his right knee, and with his right hand he clutched the walking stick. Any designs he might have had for insinuating himself into the other men's company had clearly failed. Across the table from him, the other three men sat almost clustered, occupying about one third of the perimeter of the table. Dace had his back to Downs and his right elbow up on the edge of the table. Facing him, Varlett and Shadwell both sat sideways to the table, each with a left leg hiked up and a left elbow and forearm completing the barrier. Braden raised his eyebrows. It hadn't taken the men from the Aster long at all to snub the stranger, and in their collective pose he read a message that said, in effect, "We're members of a little group that runs things around here, and you aren't."

Braden shook his head. Maybe pushing Downs at the men from the Aster wasn't such a funny joke after all, if it gave those three the chance to act so smug. Braden almost felt sorry for Downs, until he remembered how much he wanted to get rid of the man himself.

When Braden came back into the main room of the saloon, he looked again at the table and saw a different arrangement. Engle sat, or rather squatted, in a chair that had been sitting empty between Downs and Shadwell. The man in the dark cloak was gone, and the other three had readjusted themselves in varying degrees to face the middle of the table. None of them looked up at Braden, but Engle did, raising his head enough for the overhead lantern light to fall on his sallow complexion for a brief instant, until he turned back to face the others.

When Braden sat down again at the table, Beaumont looked at him with a clever smile. "I thought maybe you'd gone in the same direction as Slack did."

Braden shook his head. "Nope." His glance caught Beaumont's, and he knew his friend was recognizing his caution with the crib girls. Then, for the sake of the Davis riders, he said, "Beaumont says you got to be careful in these places. They let the Chinamen in and out the back door."

The other fellows laughed.

"Ah, that's in those other places, where there's Chinamen," Beaumont said. "Minin' camps, and some of the railroad camps farther west. But it's true. I've seen it. They let 'em in and out the back door."

Beaumont fell back into his conversation with the other two men until Slack returned to the table. At that time, the two Davis riders finished their drinks, took leave, and left the saloon.

Beaumont looked at Slack and Braden. "Well, I saw our new friend leave. He must not have gotten too thick with the boys from across the street."

"Didn't look like it," said Braden. "When I got up to go out back, I caught a look at 'em. Looked like he fit in about like a potato in a box of peaches, from the way they were all givin' him the cold shoulder. Looked kinda funny."

"Well, they can't be all that picky," said Slack. "They got what's-his-name Dingle sittin' with 'em now." He took out his makin's and turned his attention on the prospect of a smoke.

"I saw that," said Braden. "Can't say I was surprised."

Within half an hour, the men from the Aster left, and not long after that, Engle made his departure with his six-gun swaying on his thigh. When Braden went up to the bar to order a round of drinks, he saw the chance to talk to Connors for the first time that evening.

"What do you know about that queer duck in the cape that was in here?" Braden asked.

The barkeep shrugged. "First time I've seen him."

"Seems like he's tryin' to strike up some kind of an opportunity to turn someone else's money into his."

"I wouldn't be surprised. He didn't seem to have that much of his own to spare. All the time he sat in here, he didn't buy a single drink."

"That's what it looked like to me, too." Braden glanced at the table where Downs had last sat. Then, looking back at Connors, he said, "Those other three snubbed him all the way. I was almost sorry I put him onto them."

Connors smiled. "Oh, did you?"

"Yeah, I thought it would be funny, but it just gave them a chance to act uppity."

"Oh, I think he would have given 'em a try anyway."

"Maybe so." Braden paused, giving Connors a direct look. "Those three seem to be pals of sorts with that would-be cowpuncher."

Connors held his lips together for a second and then spoke. "They do sit at the same table, but I couldn't say how good of friends they are." The blotches on his face gave it a clouded look.

"Oh?" Braden raised his eyebrows.

"I think his boss sends him in here to bully 'em around a little bit." Connors folded his bar rag and rested his left hand on it.

"Really? Just for the practice?"

"Oh, it could be. You know, I don't really know much. I know what I see. As for what I hear, I can't say I know that. And if I don't know it, maybe I didn't even hear it."

Braden nodded. "I know what you mean."

After a pause, Connors spoke again. "But where there's smoke, there's fire." He moved the rag a couple of inches to the left. "I remember a story I heard in Idaho one time."

"Oh, uh-huh. Long ways away."

"Sure is." Connors took a swipe at nothing on the bar. "But the story I heard, it was about a fella who was in cahoots with some tinhorns, and he beat 'em out of some of their cut, and when they complained, he sent a bully around to remind 'em to stay shut up."

"Huh. Isn't that just like someone in Idaho, to do something like that?"

"It sure is." Connors made a half-smile as he gave Braden a direct look with the coffee-colored eyes. "You ever been there?"

Braden looked again at the empty table where the local tinhorns had sat. "I think so," he said. Looking back at Connors, he said again, "I think so."

# Chapter Nine

Braden and his two fellow riders left the Lucky Chance at a little before midnight and hit the trail south toward the Seven Arrow. None of them spoke as they rode in the still night. Hoofbeats thudded, saddle leather creaked, and a jingle sounded now and then from a spur or a bit chain. Braden looked up more than once to see the quarter moon and the vast sky of stars. It was a clear night, not very bright, with no wind but a freshness on the air. He had not drunk all that much in the saloon, so he felt clearheaded and alert although a little tired. Sitting around in a barroom relaxed a fellow but did not restore any energy or give him the sense that he had accomplished anything. Rather, it gave him the feeling that he had had a little liberty and had taken the opportunity that presented itself.

He remembered other nights, here and in other places, when he had sought out the freedom of taking a tumble with a woman. Sometimes he had felt brimful of pleasure, but more often he had felt empty and let down, as if the mingling had been meaningless. Now as he rode along in the night, he did not feel he had missed much by passing up that pleasure this evening. He was satisfied with the neutral feeling of having put in his time and having enjoyed his simple privilege.

The quarter moon did not shed much light, but the horses as well as the riders knew the trail. The horses moved at a fast walk, and with the help of an occasional landmark or familiar object close to the trail, Braden maintained his sense of how much ground they were covering.

About two miles from town, Braden thought he smelled wood smoke. He mentioned it to the other two riders, and they agreed that it smelled like a campfire. A quarter mile later, Braden saw a flicker of light up ahead on the left.

"Whoa," he muttered, bringing his horse to a stop. The other two riders drew up as well. "Looks like a camp," he said in a low voice.

Then, before anyone could speak again, a voice carried on the night air. Braden could not make out the words, but it sounded like a song or a chant.

Beaumont spoke in muffled tones. "Wonder if someone's just up late singin'."

"I don't know," Braden said, still keeping his voice low. "I hate to be nosy, or bother anyone, but it sounds just strange enough that I think one of us should go take a peek."

Beaumont's voice had a note of caution as he whispered, "You don't know how many there are."

"I'll go on foot," Braden said, "if you fellas'll hold my horse for me." He swung down and crossed in front of the horse to hand his reins to Slack. Then he bent over, unbuckled his spurs, and put them in his saddlebag. "I'll be right back," he said as he turned and walked away.

Feeling with his feet as he moved along, he came up against cactus and low-lying growth such as rabbit brush, but he did not clunk against any rocks or stumble on sagebrush. As his path took a slight down-hill slant, he could see more of the camp-fire. It sat in an open area, with no trees or tall brush in view. With the quietest steps he could manage, Braden came within forty yards of the campsite.

A man stood facing the fire with his back to Braden and the trail. He was swaying back and forth, singing in some kind of a chant or loud hum that Braden still could not make out. But the outline of the man looked familiar, as the flat-crowned hat and long cape stood out in silhouette from the firelight.

The singing stopped, and the man's right elbow moved the cape outward. Then his head tilted up and held for a few seconds before it went back down. The right arm reached out straight ahead, and Braden could see that Downs had just taken a nip from a flask and was holding it out, perhaps to admire it in the firelight. He was not offering it to anyone else, because he was alone in the camp.

Now came the singing again, in sounds that did not make words. The melody reminded Braden of a hum he had heard porcupines make. A porcupine had a four-beat song that went "Hunh — hunh, hunh — hunh," over and over again. This song coming from Downs went "Hoynya, hoynya, hoynya, hoynya," then "Hey, hey, hey, hey," then back to "Hoynya, hoynya, hoynya, hoynya." The man swayed from side to side now, with a "Hey, hey, hey, hey" and "Hoynya, hoynya, hi-ya, hi-ya, kenji, benji, wenji, wenji," and on and on, going back to an earlier sound or varying it into a similar one, always four beats at a time. Then the sound changed to something like a measured snicker, with a sequence of "Heh-heh, heh-heh, ha-ha, ha-ha," which he ran through a few times before he went back to the "Hoynya," "Hi-ya," and "Kenji" sequences. Every once in a while the swaying would become more pronounced, with more of a lift on each side and then a hunching over to the left and right a couple of times each. Braden wondered if Downs thought he was working up some kind of a curse or voodoo, until the song changed to "Coony, coony, coony, coony; culi, culi, culi, culi," and the flask came out again.

*Hell,* thought Braden. *He's just makin' noise.* For that was the way it seemed — with the isolation and the darkness and the inspiration from the flask, Downs had no doubt shaken off his inhibitions and was just making sounds with his mouth. Braden himself had done it, when he was sure of his solitude, and he imagined that many another sane man had done the same thing, to give vent to things that needed to get out. All in a moment, the spell-like quality of the scene fell away, and although the antics still had a strange aura, Downs seemed as harmless as before.

Braden backed up a few steps, then turned and took soft steps to return to his friends. The chanting voice still carried on the air, and Braden imagined it would have taken a pretty loud noise for Downs to hear anything but himself.

"What is it?" whispered Beaumont.

"Oh, it's just that newcomer Downs, cavortin' around and makin' noise. Singin' to himself and gettin' drunk, it looked like."

"Is he loony?"

"Oh, I don't know. I think he just figgers there's no one around."

Braden took his reins from Slack and swung back onto his horse. He decided to ride the rest of the way without spurs, as he didn't expect to run the horses anyway.

As the men rode along, Braden had the four-beat melody humming in his head, and he found himself echoing some of the sounds. When the trio had ridden about a mile from the scene, Braden spoke out loud. "I tell ya, he sounded like a porcupine. Have you ever heard the little song they sing? I'm sure at one point he was goin', 'Coony, coony, coony, coony, culi, culi, culi, culi.' " As he spoke the sounds, he felt as if he was gratifying a compulsion to utter them.

Beaumont laughed. "He *is* loony."

"Loony, loony, loony, loony," said Braden, and all three men laughed.

★ ★ ★

In broad sunlight the next morning, as Braden rode toward Black Hat Butte, the incident of the night before seemed to shrink in proportion so that it became just an odd moment in the dark. It had been a strange spectacle, unreal but not quite grotesque, that emanated away from the campfire as if the darkness knew no boundaries. Now in the light of day, the familiar landmarks of hills and bluffs and buttes put the campsite and the firelight dance into place.

A wind blew from the west, mild and dry. The hot weather of midsummer had moved in for its yearly stay, and the afternoons had been heating up. In the thin air and light soil, the grass of the high plains went dry and hung on tight. Braden imagined the black roots of the shortgrass clutching the earth and not relaxing until a rainstorm built up. Under a warm wind such as today's, more of the thin blades of grass would turn from pale green to tan.

On the steeper hillsides, as on the sides of Black Hat Butte, the grass was brown. It ran greener in the low spots, in the swales and draws and little valleys. Now with his back to the Seven Arrow Ranch, the town of Carlin, and the scene of Downs's midnight dance, Braden could look out at the broad country and feel the freedom of the open range. He knew he could ride for days in any direction without having to get down to open a gate — across country where the cattle and loose horses moved at will, going where the grass was good and they could find water. The spirit of the open plains seemed to lie even deeper in the native animals — the deer and the antelope, now that most of the buffalo were gone. If a fellow saw a band of antelope on a promontory, he knew that in a matter of minutes they could sprint to another high spot a mile or two away and wheel around there. Even this pleasant buck he saw right now, off to his right in a pale green draw, might have traveled a few miles already this morning and might drift who knows where by afternoon.

Up and over the crest rode Braden, catching his first view of the homestead down below. Scanning the new countryside that came into view, he saw the distant reaches of the undulating grassland. Off to his left he noted Little Sister, then the hognosed butte, and beyond that the dark-turreted form of Castle Butte. Farther yet, in the distance, lay the blue-hazed Laramie Mountains. He found it always a comfort to see the landmarks as he expected to. Maybe the face of the country would change with the railroads and fences, and he had heard of whole little towns picking up and moving a mile or so, but he knew he could depend on the landscape itself and its constant features.

Bringing his view in closer, he saw a sprinkling of color off to his left and downslope. He recognized the larger shapes of the two horses and then the rest of Birdie's menagerie. Thinking he might see the girl, he focused his gaze as the bay horse moved beneath him in the direction of the homestead. After a few paces his perspective shifted, and Birdie appeared, rising up as if she had been sitting in the grass. Braden recalled her habit of watching what she called the "little people" — mouse trails, anthills, the laborious trek of dung beetles — and he imagined she had been drawn into some observation such as that. Now she stood straight up and waved. Braden waved back.

He rode into the yard and called out a greeting, then waited on his horse to see if someone might come out of one of the buildings. "Anybody home?" he called again.

His eye caught a movement from the

west end of the house, where Beryl stepped into view. She was dressed in a work shirt and trousers, as she often was, and in her left hand she held a book.

"Oh, hello," she said.

"Did I come at a bad time? Am I interrupting something?" The book didn't look like a Bible, but he was afraid he might have disturbed her reading of the Scriptures.

"Oh, no. I was just reading, over here in the shade where it's still cool." She began to walk forward. "Go ahead and get down. Can you stay awhile?"

"I thought I might, if it's no trouble."

"No, not at all. Let me put my book away, and I'll see what I can do about some coffee."

Braden dismounted and watched her go into the house. He stood in the yard for ten minutes, it seemed, during which time he caught a whiff of smoke from the stovepipe. At last she appeared at the door again. She held a spindle-back chair in front of her.

"If you wouldn't mind, you could set this one with the other one, around the end of the house where I was sitting. We haven't moved the bench back there yet. And we might not. We still use it in the afternoon."

He went up the steps to the top of the little porch and took the chair that she held forward. He felt assured by the relaxed look on her face and by the clear, open expression in her eyes. He also enjoyed, for that instant, putting his hands on the chair that she held in hers.

"Thanks," she said.

"A pleasure," he answered, with a smile and a nod.

He lingered in the shade at the end of the house, not far from the chokecherry hedge where he had killed the snake. The bushes provided something of a wind-break, but the warm breeze still passed through the foliage. No sounds came from the house, and he wondered if she would stay until the coffee was ready or if she would come out and then go back in. After a few minutes he heard a scuffing noise that sounded like the front door being closed, and then he heard light footsteps. He stood in expectation as she stepped into view.

"The coffee is under way," she said. "Shall we sit down?"

He stepped forward and held out his hand, which she accepted, pressed, and released. Then they sat down with their backs to the house and the chairs turned inward a little toward each other. Braden was sitting in the farther chair, on the right, while Beryl sat in the chair closest to her pending task.

"I was reading Parkman," she said.

"Oh?" Braden thought he had heard the name, but he wasn't sure.

"Yes. You know, he came through here in the early days."

"Oh. How early would that be?"

"Well, it's called *The Oregon Trail*, so it would be during that time. Fifty years ago, when he actually came through. Then the book was printed after that, of course."

"Uh-huh. I imagine it's pretty interesting."

"Yes, it is. He's no Arnold or Ruskin, much less a Thoreau, but he gives one an idea of what it was like." She paused for a moment and then said, "Anyway, it's a way to pass the time."

"Better than some." Braden looked at his boots.

"And yourself? Anything new?"

Braden reflected. "Nothing to speak of, I guess. The boys and I went to town last night. Everything was quiet. I didn't do much but turn my glass around and around on the tabletop. Met one fellow who was a little strange, but otherwise everything was as plain as could be." He looked at her. "How about yourself?"

She raised her eyebrows. "I had another visit from Mr. Forbes. I suppose that's noteworthy."

"Oh, when was that? Did he have Gundry with him again?"

"It was in the middle of the week, on Wednesday, I believe. Yes, that was it. And no, he didn't have Mr. Gundry this time. He had one of his men with him."

"Not Engle, the stout one?" Braden felt his pulse quicken.

"No. He was taller, and normal-looking. Name of Winslow or something like that. I just heard it once."

"Wyndham? Had some gray hair?" Braden used his left hand to make a brushing movement by the side of his head.

"I believe that was it. A plain-enough man, and he didn't say anything."

"Well, as far as I know, Forbes has just the three men working for him. This one would be one of the other two, the ones that Greaves might have known something about."

"I see."

Braden thought for a second about what he had just said, and he decided it would be just as well not to say any more on that point at the present, in view of the danger that came with that knowledge. He turned his thoughts to wording what he would say next. "I suppose he came on the same business as before — Forbes, that is."

"Yes, he did. He said he was hoping to acquire a couple of other parcels on either side of me and that this place would fit in just right with his other holdings."

Braden felt his stomach muscles tighten. "Did you get the feeling that he was saying, more or less, that he was going to have you hedged in?"

She had a calm look on her face as she nodded. "Something like that. He laid some stress on the idea that he would have land on either side of mine."

Braden recalled the episode at Taylor's place, when Forbes had appropriated the questionable calves. "I don't like his style. He likes to push people around and see if he can get 'em to give in."

"Well, he doesn't have anything that will work on me — not right now, anyway. I don't have any cattle to look after, or to be fenced in or out by him, and I'm not pinched for money."

Braden smiled. "So you can just sit tight."

She smiled back. "That's right. I'm not going to be pushed very easily by anything short of a buffalo herd."

*Or a prairie fire,* Braden thought, but he did not give voice to the words. Instead, he said, "That's a good way to be. I don't know how long he can last at his various games anyway."

As he said the words, he counted the strands to himself: There was the business of the stolen cattle with Wyndham and Farnsworth, the questionable presence of Engle at the time of Greaves's death, the show of force against Taylor, and the pressure being applied to Beryl and perhaps others. Maybe Beryl and Taylor were in the same strand. Nevertheless, whether there were three or four, or whether he tossed in the men from the Aster as well, Forbes's maneuvers all had a common element. He did what he pleased at others' expense, with the apparent assumption that he should get away with it.

"I don't know either," said Beryl. "Do you think he'll just keep on pushing?"

"Over here? Probably so, until he gets what he wants, or most of it. As for his other doin's, they're a little murkier, and maybe sooner or later someone can bring something against him. I just hate having to sit by and let him get away with it, but until I've got more to go on, I don't know how much I can do."

"Well, if anything else comes our way, I'll be sure to let you know. For the time being, though, I know what you mean about not being able to do something. It's sort of a paralyzed feeling, having to leave everything suspended."

From her look, he sensed that she was talking about herself as well as about him, but he could not think of a way to bring out any more. So he said, "You've been a great help with what you've told me so far. I appreciate the confidence."

Her eyes softened, and she gave him a warm smile. "The appreciation is mutual."

He wasn't sure of what to say next, so he sat silent for a moment until she spoke again.

"I think the coffee might be ready by now. If you'll excuse me, I'll be back in a few minutes."

"Certainly."

Left again to his own thoughts, Braden wondered about her comment regarding the inability to do something. It seemed as if she had more to say, and probably about her personal life, but he didn't have a clear sense of whether she wanted him to invite her to say it. He thought also that he could not expect her to tell him everything she knew about herself if he was still guarding information about Forbes's crooked deals. He winced as he felt the temptation to tell her more so that she would tell him something in return. It didn't feel right. If he wasn't quite ready to tell her everything he thought he knew about Forbes, he wasn't going to do it just for the sake of fishing something out of her. He would rather just ask her.

When she came back with the coffee, she also had a plate of cookies on the tray that held the cups. "I hope you like raisin cookies," she said.

"They're my favorites."

"Really?" She held the tray in front of him.

"Right now they are," he said, taking one.

She laughed. "Here, if you hold the tray for a moment, I'll pour the coffee. Then we can set the pot and the tray on the ground."

With his right hand he held the tray steady in his lap while with his left hand he held the cookie, which he had not yet bitten into. He wondered if she had even meant for him to take it. Maybe she had meant for him only to take the tray.

She stood close to him as she poured the coffee, and he enjoyed the tension of her presence. When she finished pouring, she set the coffeepot on the ground. Next she lifted the tray from his lap and handed him one of the cups. Then she set the tray on the ground and took a cookie for herself as she lifted her own cup.

"Don't be afraid to dip it in your coffee," she said as she took her seat. "I left them in the oven for a few minutes too long, and they came out rather dry."

He hesitated with the cookie in one hand and the cup in the other.

"Go ahead," she said. "There's no one for miles around, I'm sure."

He took a small bite from the cookie, and it was indeed hard. Nodding, he dipped the jagged edge into his coffee and put the moistened cookie into his mouth. "Just the way I like 'em," he said.

She laughed. "Good."

He ate the cookie and another one as he drank his coffee. Beryl poured him a second cup and filled up her own.

"You really don't talk much about yourself," she said.

"Oh, there's not much to me. I work, and when I have a little time off I try to relax. Like last night, I rode into town with the boys." He shrugged. "Nothin' really to speak of. And when I get a chance, I drop over here."

"Well, that's something."

"Seems like it to me. I like to think I, uh — well, I hope I would know if I shouldn't. Maybe I could say that better. I like to think I would know whether I was welcome or not."

She gave him the warm smile again. "Well, you are, and I think you're astute enough to know it."

He felt a flow spread through him. "It's what I hoped."

"I know it's not easy when you don't know things for sure."

A little spark lit up. "That's true." After a second or two of hesitation, he went on. "You say I'm astute, but sometimes I feel pretty stupid."

"You shouldn't, when it's not your fault."

"Well, I don't mean feeling stupid about things I don't know, but more about not knowing how to put things in the right words."

"Oh?" She sat back just a little.

"Well, yes. The last time I was here, I felt like coming right out and point-blank asking you a personal question, which wouldn't have been right. And here I am again, and I don't want to just blurt it out."

Her gray-green eyes had softened, but he saw more sympathy than affection in her expression. "I'm sorry," she said. "Maybe I can make it easier."

"Well, I don't know. If I'm still at this point, maybe you don't really want me to ask it."

"Don't worry about what I want. If you've got a question, it might be something you have a right to know. I don't know."

"Well, it's about your status." As soon as he said it, he knew he had asked too much, or more than she had been expecting. It should have been a question about how she felt about him rather than a question all about her. He could tell that just from hearing himself say what he said.

"You mean . . ."

He felt he was blundering on, but now it was the only way. "Well, your status. Whether you are or aren't — you know, spoken for."

She looked down at her coffee cup, which she held in both hands. Then she looked up with a pained expression on her face. "I think you have a right to ask that question, and it's my fault that I can't give you a clear answer right now."

"That's all right. I guess it has to be."

"It's not that there isn't an answer, but that I need to think about how to tell it."

Braden frowned. "I don't understand."

"I'm sorry," she said. "I'm sorry I can't make it clearer right now. I just need a little more time to think about it. But nothing is going to change between now and the time I tell you."

"You mean nothing is going to change in your circumstances, or in my being welcome to visit, or — ?"

"Either. Or both."

Braden felt his eyebrows go up. "Well, I suppose that's more of an answer than I had."

"It really is." She held out her right hand, palm up.

He placed his own hand palm downward upon hers. As he felt the hope racing within him, he tried to tell himself not to make too much of what he had just heard. But it would be hard not to interpret it as good news.

# Chapter Ten

Braden paused at the top of the slope, with Black Hat Butte on his left, and turned in the saddle to look back at the homestead. At such a distance he could not tell if Beryl was standing in the yard, but on the chance that she was, he took off his hat and waved with it. Then he rode up over the crest and headed down the other side, in the direction he had come earlier.

A hundred yards down the slope, as he was scanning the country around him, he saw a pale figure emerge out of a fold in the landscape. He could not have said why, but it did not surprise him to see Rove on the dun horse. Handling the reins with his left hand, the oncoming rider raised his right hand in greeting.

Braden drew rein and waited for the other man to come near. Rove looked as before, dressed in pale colors that kept tone with his long hair and drooping mustache. Braden saw again the saddle gun and grass rope on the right side, and he wondered if the man ever roped or shot anything. If he did, he probably made a neat job of it, for he was a graceful rider and had smooth movements with his hands. As he rode up to Braden, he handled the split reins between the fingers of his left hand while with his right he smoothed out a strand of his rope-colored hair.

"Friend Braden," he said. "How goes it?"

Braden turned his free right hand palm upward. "Oh, fair, I guess."

Rove lowered his right hand, brushed it along his right thigh, and patted his knee twice. Then, holding the hand up and pointing straight down with his index finger, he made a circular motion. "Not without trouble, of course. And not just wigs on the green."

Braden rubbed the side of his nose and then imitated the circular gesture. "You mean here?"

"Sawn doot. Sorry about your friend." The light brown eyes looked calm.

"So am I."

"Not a good thing."

"No, and I'm not satisfied with the way things worked out, as far as getting any answers."

"Four-bann. But not a sparrow falls."

Braden wondered if the code of the day was going to appear in the form of two-syllable words. "We like to think so," he said.

"Time will tell."

Braden looked at the ground around him. "Maybe time will have to. We can't get the grass and dirt to tell us a thing."

Rove's eyes brightened, and his mustache lifted in a faint smile. "You never know when there's a pigeon that hasn't been counted yet."

Braden sometimes wondered whether Rove actually ate and slept and made a living, or if he drifted with the wind. Whatever the case, the man seemed to know things and was willing to give a hint. So Braden asked, "Anyone I might know?"

"Comes a dark messenger." Rove made a wide flourish with his right hand and pointed over his left shoulder, to the northeast.

Braden narrowed his eyes. "Man in a cape?"

"He ain't no shitepoke." The words came out in a funny voice, like an impersonation of a southerner.

Braden felt as if he was groping a rock wall in the dark. "You mean he might have something to say?"

"Like the crows at dawn."

"I remembered your remark about that. I haven't been to a town that has trees big enough." Braden took another look at Rove. He wondered how much the man got around and whether he got his notions from talking to others or from covert eavesdropping. Strange as he was, Rove had a way of winning another man's confidence, and he might well have had a chat with the man in the cape. Downs, in turn, could have told him the names of the people he had met. That possibility gave Braden more comfort than the thought that Rove had been lurking in the background when Braden and Downs had chanced to cross paths.

Rove laughed. "Maybe the trees will come to them."

Braden laughed, too. It seemed like a good joke, as long as Rove was telling it. "Might be."

Rove lifted his head. "Stones have been known to move, and trees to speak."

"Oh, I imagine." Braden wondered where Rove came up with some of his lines. Sometimes he felt as if he were talking to the village idiot who had a streak of clarity to him — the old notion that some fools were touched by God — and at other times, such as the present, he thought the man had quite a bit under his hat but liked to give it out in code.

Rove nodded as he smiled again. "It's worth a thought."

Braden smiled back. "I believe you. And I thank you for the tip."

Rove made a rippling wave with his right fingers. "A small thing, but I hope useful."

"I hope so, too." Silence hung in the air for a moment until Braden said, "Something else?"

Rove shook his head.

"Well," said Braden, putting out his hand, "thanks, Rove. And I hope to see you again."

Rove nudged the dun horse around and put out his hand. "I hope so too, Braden."

They shook in a firm handshake. For as much as Rove seemed like an ethereal sort who nourished himself on rainbows, he was solid as a rock.

Braden did not look back until he was a mile away from the butte. However Rove came and went was his business, and Braden didn't want to give the man the impression of observing him, not any more than he wanted to ask questions about where he stayed or how he kept himself.

Braden looked at his shadow, then

around and up at the sun. It was a little past midday, and he was in no hurry to get back to the ranch. He could change his route and head more to the north. If he didn't catch Downs at his camp, he might be able to find him in town. Even at that, he could get back to the ranch before dark.

Veering north then, he rode across the country. He did not follow any given trail unless a cow path happened to be going his way for a while. It would have been easier to strike the main road north and then follow it, but he preferred not to run into anyone else on this particular mission. He didn't feel that he was up to anything secret, but he thought it would be just as well to keep things to himself until he found out more.

The day warmed up, and he could feel the sun on his back. Sweat trickled down his back. At one point he found a small dribble of a creek, where he stopped to let the bay horse drink and take a rest. Not a tree had appeared, nor any land formation abrupt enough to cast a shadow at this time of day. Braden dragged the cuff of his shirtsleeve across his forehead, then laid the back of his right fingers against the horse's neck. The bay had worked up a sweat but he had not overheated. A little rest was worth the while. Even if he missed Downs all the way around, it wasn't worth overworking a good horse. Braden loosened the front cinch and squatted in the shade of the animal.

He thought of Beryl, distant and cool. The shade would be gone from the west end of the house now, except for what came from the chokecherry bushes. Better shade would be starting to reach out from the east end by this time of the afternoon. He imagined Beryl, maybe sitting on the bench, and he had a sense of her firm presence and her sure way of handling herself. He didn't like the idea of Forbes coming around to lean on her, but she seemed capable, and Birdie's presence gave a little more protection.

Braden looked across the open plains to the north and west. There was a lot of country out there, with room for a thousand dirty little deeds. Most of the people he knew went about their business and did their work. Maybe they took out some time to go to town, or talk to visitors, or even read a book, but he didn't imagine that many of them spent much time planning and carrying out schemes. The country itself was indifferent; it didn't try to make things hard or easy for people who tried to make a living. On the other hand, it did invite a feeling of freedom, which sometimes translated into freedom from restraint. That was where the bad side of human nature came out in some schemes. Well, it sure wasn't the land's fault. Men like Forbes — and maybe Downs, for all he knew — would seek out places that offered that kind of freedom.

Back in the saddle and moving across the grassland again, Braden began to think about how he might approach a conversation with Downs. If he didn't have to, he would just as soon not disclose his prior knowledge of where the camp was, much less what he had observed there. That left him with the decision of saying that Rove sent him or of dropping in just as a matter of chance. The more he thought about it, the more he thought it would be better not to mention Rove unless Downs did. As he recalled the conversation with Rove, he realized Rove had made no mention of actually speaking with Downs, so it was possible at least that Rove had gotten his information through some indirect means. Then a thought occurred to Braden that made him laugh aloud. It was even possible that Rove hadn't been referring to Downs at all. Braden was sure he had, but he was also convinced that he would do well if he dropped in on Downs as if it were out of the blue.

He found the camp without much trouble. When he hit the main trail, he thought he was just a little north of the camp, so he doubled back, and in less than half a mile he saw where the ground sloped away on the left. He also saw hoofprints on the main trail, where Beaumont and Slack had held his horse and waited for him. He could smell wood smoke again, so he figured Downs might still be occupying the camp.

Braden turned off the trail and rode down the slope. When the camp came into view, he called out a greeting. He didn't see anyone around — not a man or a horse — but he saw a bedroll laid out on the ground and a tin cup sitting on a rock by the fire. A ways off from the fire, a saddle lay on the ground with a bridle draped across the seat. He called again, and then he saw movement farther off to his right. Downs, still wearing the cape in the warm of the late afternoon, came limping out of a clump of bushes.

Leaning for a moment on his stick, he called out. "What do you want?"

"Oh, nothin' in particular. I just smelled

your fire, so I thought I'd drop in, see who it was, and say hello."

"Well, I was sittin' over there out of the sun. There's not a hell of a lot of shade around here."

Braden looked around and yawned. "That's the truth." He still didn't see a horse, but he figured it was picketed somewhere nearby.

Closer now, the man on foot looked up, tilting the flat-crowned hat. "I met you last night, didn't I?"

"You sure did. My name's Braden."

"Well, go ahead and git down. I don't know what I've got to offer you."

"Oh, don't bother. I won't stay long anyway. I just stopped to say hello."

Downs gave him a close look. "Are you just now goin' home?"

"Oh, no. We went home last night. I've been out on a little ride, and when I leave here, I'll be on my way home again."

"Well, let's sit down. I don't like to stand for a long time." Downs walked to his bedroll, doubled it over twice, and sat on it with his right leg poked out straight. He laid the walking stick on the ground so that it lay parallel to his leg.

Braden sat on the ground and held the reins of his horse. "Well, did you get to meet a few people in town?"

Downs gave a short, sullen nod. "A few."

"Uh-huh. I don't suppose many business opportunities jumped right out at you."

"No, but that doesn't bother me any."

"Well, that's good."

"It doesn't bother me because I don't really care." Downs tipped his head toward the right a little, putting a fold in his dark, oily hair. "Those three you told me about, the hotel-keepers or whatever, they're real smug, aren't they?"

"I think they could earn that reputation fairly."

"And the fella that came in and more or less pushed me out — he's even worse, isn't he?"

"Well, I don't know. I was out back when that happened, so I didn't see him do any pushing. But I know who you mean, and if he didn't make a good impression, I would say it might not be the first time."

"I take it you're not friends, then."

"With him or with them?"

"Either one."

Braden shrugged. "I suppose you could say that. I don't have much to talk about with any of 'em."

Downs gave him a look that expressed

some satisfaction about himself and what he might know. "I'd say you're cut from different cloth."

Braden felt himself lapsing into his pose from the night before. "That might very well be. I come off the roll that they make cowpunchers with. I couldn't say that any of them fellas come of that same roll."

Downs had his eyes narrowed, and he lifted his mustache in a tight smile. "I bet I could tell you what they all four have in common."

Braden shrugged. "Anybody's guess." He waited for the answer.

"They all take a piss standin' up."

"Well, that's nothin' special. So do I. Fact is, that's what I was doin' when what's-his-name Engle came in and you left. That's a pretty wide loop, it takes in so many folks."

Downs kept up his clever look. "Should I draw it a little tighter, then?"

"If you want. It won't have much to do with me."

"Maybe not, but tell me if I'm wrong." Downs looked around, as if to ensure their privacy, and then he said, "What they have in common is a son of a bitch."

Braden's eyebrows went up. "Could be. I couldn't tell you you're wrong, at any rate."

"I suppose you know how to spell it."

"It shouldn't be so hard."

"No, not the way I spell it. It's got six letters, and it starts with an 'F.' "

Braden drew back. "I think that's a different word."

Downs moved his head from side to side and then pointed at Braden. "Not the way I spell it. When I think of a son of a bitch, I think of one in particular, and his name starts with an 'F.' "

"Could be."

"No 'could be' about it. If that's what I think, that's what I think."

"Well, like I said, it doesn't have much to do with me."

Downs gave his squinty smile again. "It might."

Braden turned down the corners of his mouth. "Like I say, I couldn't say."

"Let me put it this way. You're not friends with him."

"With who? With Eff?"

"Right. With Eff."

"Not in any particular way, no. I wouldn't have any reason to say I was."

"And you're not friends with his friends."

"No. We already covered that."

"But you might be interested if there was something to know."

Braden shrugged again. "Not neces-sarily. Knowledge isn't always a good thing to have."

Downs seemed to ignore the comment. "And you might even know that sooner or later, someone might find out something about him, and might want to know more."

Braden could hear a little warning voice inside. There was no point in letting Downs know what he thought he knew, and there could be danger in it. "That would be hard to say. I couldn't say I know anything along those lines."

Downs took a short, deep breath through his nose and exhaled the same way. "Let's suppose I had a golden goose."

"Well, all right. Let's suppose that."

"So, what would you think about it?"

Braden pursed his lips. "Oh, not havin' seen the goose, I guess it would be pretty general. I'd think you were a lucky fella, and I'd wish it did you some good."

"Well, what if it was a golden goose and I couldn't get much good out of it unless I gave it to someone else?"

"Sounds like a funny kind of a goose to me, but if it was gonna do you some good to give it to someone else, then I guess that would be the thing to do."

"That's right. But I wouldn't want to give it to just anyone. I'd want to give it to someone who could put it to good use."

"It would be better than givin' it to someone who would cook it."

"That's exactly right." Downs paused and gave his self-satisfied smile. "You're not the type that would kill the golden goose, are you?"

Braden held up his hand. "Let's not go too fast. I don't know what kind of a goose it is, or whether I'll have any use for it. And I sure don't have the means to pay for it."

Downs's expression turned cross. "Who said anything about that?"

"Well, last night you said you were lookin' for a business proposition, and this afternoon you're talkin' about turnin' a golden goose over to someone else. I can't imagine why you'd do that for free, if you follow me."

Downs gave him a hard look now. "This goose isn't worth a damn dime."

"I thought you were on the lookout for an opportunity."

"I am. I always am. But that's not what I'm talkin' about here, or why I'm here at all."

"Well, then, why are you here?"

"Because I hate Eff."

Time seemed to stand still until Braden came up with something to say. "So I don't understand what you were doing in the Lucky Chance."

Downs seemed to swagger from his seat atop the folded bedroll. "I was soundin' things out. Findin' out who his friends are or aren't. Don't think I'm stupid enough to think there's my kind of opportunity in a two-bit town like this."

Braden realized he still hadn't gotten an indication of whether Downs had had a prior interest in talking to him. "And so you want to give something to someone who isn't his friend?"

"That's right."

"Some information that someone might use at some point."

"Right again."

Braden gave him a square look. "Why would you want to do that? What's in it for you?"

Downs looked cross again. "I already told you. I hate the son of a bitch."

Braden thought it over for a few seconds. "Well, it sounds like the kind of goose that once you give it to someone, you can't take it back. But if you wanted to give it to someone else, you could still do that."

"I suppose so. But I'd just as soon give it to someone who was goin' to do somethin' with it, to begin with."

Braden poked the tip of his tongue against the inside of his cheek. "I couldn't guarantee anything."

"But you might be interested in hearing it."

After a deliberate breath, Braden said. "Go ahead. If there's some point where I think I've heard enough, I'll let you know."

Downs put the heels of his hands on the bedroll and readjusted his sitting position. "It's taken me a while to find him, but now I have. And before I leave, I want someone to know some things."

Braden nodded.

After a long moment, Downs began. "Well, the story starts down in Colorado — Colorado Springs, to be exact."

"Did you know him there?"

"He don't know me. And I'd just as soon keep it that way."

"I see." Braden cast a glance over the man, and he thought he understood him. Downs didn't have the guts to make any of this public, but he would dump it on someone else and hope it went somewhere.

Downs gave another look around and went on. "So he was in and out of a few crooked deals there. Mostly cattle and horses."

"I don't suppose he actually dirtied his hands with 'em."

"No. He had someone else do that. A fellow named . . . Walraven."

"Sort of a lackey, then."

Downs took on a defiant air. "A fellow who did work for him. We'll put it that way."

"All right. I follow you. Go ahead."

"Well, he had this fellow do the work, and then he wouldn't give him his fair share. So he complained."

"Walraven did."

"Um, yes. He said he didn't like it, and he had half a mind to tell someone."

"You mean he was goin' to blackmail him?"

Downs tightened his face. "He was just tryin' to get what he had comin' to him."

Braden thought he was starting to get the picture, until he remembered that Downs said the perpetrator didn't know him. Still, each time that Downs became defensive about Walraven, it seemed as if he was defending himself. "I see," he said. "Can't blame him for that."

"I don't." Downs narrowed his eyes. "Maybe it was crooked work. But it was work, you know? And the son of a bitch held out on him."

"Uh-huh. And then when he squawked, old what's-his-name, Eff, sent someone to bully him around?"

Down's rough face hardened into gray stone. "More than that."

"You mean he had him done in."

"That's what I mean."

Braden thought for a moment. "I wouldn't doubt that, and I 'specially wouldn't doubt how sure you are of it. But if there's not any proof, it's hard to stick anything on him."

"I know it as well as I know my own name."

"Like I say, I don't doubt that. But for anyone to do anything with it, he'd need somethin' more than say-so."

Downs raised his eyebrows a tight quarter of an inch. "Maybe we're gettin' to that."

"No hurry."

Downs adjusted himself on his seat again, reached for the walking stick, and set it back down. Then he gave a severe look at Braden but said nothing.

Braden waited a long moment, and, sensing that Downs might want to be coaxed, he said, "Anyway, this fellow spoke up, and then he seems to have died by foul play. Do I have that much right?"

"Yes, you do." Downs picked up the stick again, as if he wanted to wield it, and then he leaned it against the folded bedroll.

"And there's more to it?"

"There damn sure is. Jack Walraven had a wife." Downs paused.

"Uh-huh. Does it matter what kind of woman she was?"

"She was a married woman," Downs snapped. "Good enough to look at, but not perfect."

"You mean not perfect-lookin', or not perfect in the sense that she wouldn't be likely to be teachin' Sunday school?"

"Probably both. But she was his wife." Downs lifted his head. "And after he disappeared, she got a visit."

"From the man's boss."

"Exactly. He tried to have his way with her."

Braden flinched. It seemed to fit, but he wondered again how verifiable it was. "And she managed to keep him off?"

"She can be as mean as a coyote bitch, and he found out about it."

"Oh?"

"Yeah." Downs drew his left index finger

across his ribs. "Cut him a good one with a knife, right across the bottom of his ribs. Laid him open enough that he'd have a scar."

"On the left side?"

"That's right. She's right-handed, and she got in her dig that way."

"That slowed him down, I suppose."

"Damn sure did. He got the hell out of there, and left town not long after."

Braden sifted what he had just heard. "And that's what might work as proof. A scar."

Downs nodded.

Braden looked at the ground and then back at Downs. "How sure of this are you?"

"As sure as I can be."

"I mean, have you seen the scar? Or do you have it on her word?"

"She told me."

"And I assume you've got no reason to doubt her."

Downs shook his head. "None at all."

Braden twisted his mouth for a second and then spoke. "Does she still live down there?"

"Uh-huh."

"And what does she look like? Yella-haired? Red-haired? Dark-haired?"

"Oh, none of them, really. She's sort of mouse-haired." Downs gave him a close look. "Do you think you know her?"

"No, I'm sure I don't. I'm just tryin' to get a picture of her, that's all. But you can vouch for her, you say."

"That I can."

Braden hesitated and then took his leap. "You don't have to answer this if you don't want to. But do you know her as well as you know your own name?"

"I do. Jack Walraven was my brother."

# Chapter Eleven

On his way to the ranch, Braden's thoughts went back and forth between the story he had heard and the woman who lived on the other side of Black Hat Butte. Regardless of whatever kind of hellion the Walraven woman was, she was a woman, and an attack on her was the trademark of a coward. A man like that picked someone he thought was vulnerable, and then he made his play. Braden could only speculate on her terror, but he was sure she would have felt it, just as Beryl would if the man tried something there.

Braden had thought all along that it was ungallant of Forbes to be intimidating a woman. Up until now, Braden had seen Forbes's aggression, with Gundry's company on one occasion and with his alliance in general, as being similar to that of the otherwise respectable men who had hanged a woman on the Sweetwater; they banded together and did what they thought they could get away with. Now Braden saw it in terms that seemed to fit

Forbes in another way — getting leverage over a woman would bring him a sick satisfaction.

The attack on Mrs. Walraven, even if she was as brazen as Cattle Kate, also loomed as a personal affront. It was an attack on women, as Braden saw it, and he took it personally on behalf of a woman Forbes had made a different move against. It made Braden want to put a hole in Forbes, just on principle, but he knew he couldn't just go do it. Furthermore, he knew that whatever Forbes had done, here or elsewhere, needed to be answered on more than a personal level. If he, Braden, was going to do anything, it had to be justifiable and in the open.

A scar. There was supposed to be a scar. Even if there were, it would be proof of only one act. Braden did not doubt the story he had heard from Downs — or Walraven, as it turned out — and he did not doubt that Forbes had caused Greaves's death. But when a person couldn't know things for certain, even when he had no doubt in his own mind, it was hard to exact justice. He couldn't just say, "I am sure you did this thing, and I am going to make you pay." A person needed proof, incontrovertible proof. Without solid evidence, it could be disastrous to bring up an issue if the guilty party could dismiss it. A bungled accusation could encourage the perpetrator to go on believing he could get away with his maneuvers, and it could lead him to make another move in retaliation. Still, there was supposed to be a scar. If Braden could be sure there was no disproving that detail, he would have something to build a case on.

His thoughts looped back to the man in the flat-crowned hat, the limping figure in the dark cape. Call him by one name or the other — Downs or Walraven? Better to call him by the name he went by, Downs. Sleazy and vindictive, willing to be a snitch but not willing to face the man he accused, he had his justification all the same. Braden believed his story and gave credence to his motive, which was to dump the golden goose in someone else's lap and hope for the best. Braden wondered how many others the man had sounded out and if one of them had been Rove. It would have been an interesting scene, with Downs spewing his venom and Rove speaking in riddles. It might have taken place, or Rove might have had some other way of knowing that Downs needed someone to hear his story. However it happened, Downs had been ready to give his treasure to someone who was willing to take it.

As Braden sorted things out in the calm aftermath, he realized he had gone to Downs's camp with the hope of learning something about the stolen cattle or about Greaves's death and had gotten something quite different. Still, Downs's story had not taken him by surprise, for it matched everything he thought he knew about Forbes. He told himself he needed to be on his guard against accepting stories just because he wanted to believe them. Well enough. Until he could put it to the proof, the story was in the category of Birdie's observation or of the father and son's account of the two riders who spent the night. He was willing to believe it and it fit, but it was just say-so. But if there was a scar, there was proof.

When Saturday came around again, Braden was ready to go into town with Beaumont and Slack. He had told Beaumont about Birdie's account of Engle stalking Greaves, but he had not yet found the opportunity to tell him of the story he had heard from Downs. The ride into town, then, had a superficial, carefree air about it, as there was knowledge that Beaumont and Braden shared but could not discuss in front of Slack, and there was knowledge that Braden was keeping to himself so far.

When the three riders came to within a half mile of Downs's camp, Beaumont began to hum like a porcupine. When they were abreast of the camp, with no smell of wood smoke on the air, Braden asked the other two to wait for him for a couple of minutes. As dusk gathered, he rode down the slope and looked around. The camp was cleared out. A couple of tin cans and an empty pint bottle rested in the dead coals of the campfire, and half a dozen broken sticks lay in a small stack nearby. Braden rode over to the bushes where he had seen Downs emerge on his last visit, but he saw nothing there either.

Back on the road, he gave his news to the other two. "No one here."

"Must have hatted up," said Beaumont.

"Probably so." To himself, Braden thought, *That would be his style — get the hell gone before anything came back on him.*

The bar in the Lucky Chance had room along the rail, so the three riders from the Seven Arrow took their places. Braden stood on the right, Slack occupied the middle, and Beaumont took the space on the left. As Connors the barkeep poured the drinks, Braden asked him if he had seen any more of the stranger in the dark outfit.

"Nope. Not at all. And I haven't given him much thought. I saw him that one night, and I haven't seen him since."

"Must have moved on," said Braden. "To some place with more opportunity."

Connors glanced around the barroom and back at Braden. "I don't think he had much luck here. I don't recall that he succeeded at moochin' a single drink."

"Well, I hope he found a place where he gets a better reception."

"I hope so, too." Connors set the drinks in front of the three men.

Braden raised his glass in salute to the other two. After taking a sip, he spoke to Connors again. "Say, Lex, I ran into that other fellow I told you about, the one that has his funny phrases."

"Oh, yeah. The one that speaks trapper French. Or maybe pidgin French. You said he wasn't a trapper." Connors flicked his hand at a fly. "What did he come up with this time?"

"It sounded like 'sawn doot.'"

"Sawn doot?" Connors repeated it a

couple of times and then said, "Oh, it's probably *sans doute*. It means 'without a doubt.' "

"Well, that's not much."

"Nah, it's just one of those things that people toss in to flavor the soup."

"Uh-huh."

"Is that all?"

"Well, no. He said a couple of other odd things. One of 'em sounded like 'four-bann.' "

Connors put on a thoughtful look as he listened to himself say the sound four times. "Aw, hell," he said. "I think it's *forban*. It means 'pirate.' How did he use it?"

"I don't remember that he used it to refer to anything in particular. I just remember he said it. Damn if it doesn't sound familiar, though. I wonder if I've ever seen it written."

"Oh, you may have. It's not that rare of a word."

"How do you spell it?"

"F-O-R-B-A-N."

Braden drummed the bar with his right fingers. The first four letters did it. "I think it's some kind of a joke," he said, "or a clever way of referring to someone."

The coffee-colored eyes were steady.

"Someone we might know."

"Uh-huh." Braden let out a long breath. "This fellow seems to have no end to his riddles. There's one other that's been naggin' at me."

"Go ahead. Sound it out."

"Well, I think this one's English. It wasn't just a little dab by itself. He said, 'He ain't no shitepoke.'"

"You say 'shitepoke'?"

"I think that was it. What is it?"

"I'm pretty sure it's some kind of a bird, like a heron. There's a lot of those old-fashioned words about birds and such."

"Like 'rooks'?"

"Yeah."

"And 'daws'?"

"That, too. Did he saw 'rooks and daws' together?"

"I think so."

"He might get that from Shakespeare. This fellow sounds like a regular encyclopedia. Where do you run into him?"

"Oh, out on the range."

"Is he some kind of a hermit?"

"I don't really know, to tell you the truth. I just bump into him from time to time."

Connors shrugged. "There's all sorts." He tapped the bar with his left hand and moved away to tend to a couple of other patrons.

Braden wondered for a moment about Rove and the shitepoke. It wouldn't have anything to do with the wren. That was an accidental sound. But if Downs wasn't a shitepoke, then he was something else. Braden thought he remembered Rove saying something about a pigeon. Maybe that was it. Downs was a stool pigeon or a carrier pigeon. Or a raven, cousin to the crow. Braden shook his head and laughed to himself. There really was no end to it.

He turned to look around the room. Beaumont and Slack stood with their backs to the bar and watched a cow-puncher who was telling a card story. Braden had seen it done before, but it was always amusing if the fellow did it well at all. What he did was set up the deck and then deal off or turn over the cards to tell the story. In this one, Little Joe went down one, two, three doorways as the cards were dealt facedown and he knocked on the door. A lady, the queen of hearts, answered. Little Joe asked if she had a letter for his boss. She said one, and the ace of clubs showed. Little Joe went back one, two, three doorways and knocked on the door. A man answered. It was the king of spades. Little Joe said he had a letter. The man said, "Thank you, Little Joe. I'll tip you two bits," and the deuce of clubs showed. Then the man said, "Little Joe, I need some beer." So little Joe went down to the fourth doorway, bought the beer from the jack of diamonds, went back four doorways, and gave the beer to the king of clubs, who tipped him two bits with the deuce of spades. And on and on.

A few more men trickled into the saloon. Braden kept an eye out for Downs and for Forbes's men. He didn't expect to see Downs again, but if by chance the man showed up and crossed paths with any of Forbes's men, it would bear watching.

Eventually the three men from the Aster made an appearance. They stood by the table where the cowpuncher had told the story of Little Joe, done a few card tricks, and put away his deck. Some of the men who had been standing around had drifted away, but a couple of them had sat down, so there weren't enough seats for Dace, Varlett, and Shadwell. They stood by the table long enough to give someone the chance to get up, and then they took their places along the bar at Braden's right.

They seemed to be in good spirits as they ordered drinks, called out greetings, and took up their regular talk about other people's business. Braden wondered if they were talking loud for the sake of anyone other than themselves.

Shadwell, who stood closest to Braden, said it was good to see so many crews putting up hay.

Why, yes, indeed, said Varlett. Every haystack was that much insurance against a hard winter. Today's cattlemen weren't going to get caught again.

Shadwell responded by saying that things weren't the same anymore. Those cowboys who thought they would never have to get off a horse were goin' to find themselves out of work. These cattlemen didn't want a man who thought he didn't have to do anything but ride and rope. They wanted men who were willing to build fence, run a mowing machine, and stack hay.

Braden looked at Shadwell's stomach, which pressed against the bar, and he wondered how close the man had ever come to doing physical labor.

Varlett sent out a huge cloud of tobacco smoke as he lit his pipe. That was it, he said. For as much as some men didn't want to change, they were going to have to. They couldn't hang on to their old ways and expect the rest of cattle country to hold back for their sake. They needed to understand progress.

Dace, who seemed to subscribe to the theory that not saying much would increase the value of what he did say, gave a slow shake to his head. It wasn't easy, he said. Some men were so stuck in their ways.

Men were going to have to change with the times, Varlett went on. A hired man on horseback was fine, but he needed to understand that without the mowing machines and the freight cars, there wouldn't be beef to ship or a way to do it.

Shadwell took a drink of beer and set down his glass. Then he turned to Braden and showed his stubby lower teeth. "Are you-all puttin' up much hay?"

"Some."

"I guess everyone is."

"I don't know. I haven't checked on everyone."

Shadwell began licking a cigar preparatory to lighting it. He looked up with his pale blue eyes and said, "I've heard a lot of outfits say they were. Some of your neighbors."

"Well, that's good."

"And there's more 'n' more of 'em

growin' alfalfa." Shadwell stuck the cigar in his mouth and struck a match, then held it to light the end. "Doin' well," he said between puffs.

Varlett, with his head leaning forward, turned toward Braden. "I heard that the ones who put up the most hay had the best calf crops."

"Could be."

"But it's supposed to be a good year all over."

"I've heard that." *Right in here,* he thought.

"Should be a good year for shippin'," said Varlett.

Braden yawned. "We'll hope so."

Shadwell gave him the smile of the benevolent uncle. "Do you-all expect a good beef roundup?"

"I don't know."

"Well, I thought you could get an idea in the spring. That's what they say. You see the whole herd then. Of course, you don't really know until you're ready to ship. I guess that's what you mean."

"Something like that."

Varlett spoke through another large cloud of smoke. "I heard it's supposed to be a good year. Everyone expects good head counts and good weights."

"That's good to know."

Shadwell smiled at Braden again. "You always act like you don't know anything. I bet you know a lot."

"Not so much, I'd say. I don't talk to very many people, so I don't pick up much."

"Oh, everyone talks to someone." Shadwell's soft face, jowly and jaundiced, crinkled with his smile.

Braden turned down the corners of his mouth. "I don't run into that many people out where I work. And that's not all that bad."

"Oh, no," came the swift answer. "There's nothin' like peace and quiet." Shadwell rotated the cigar in his fingers as he rested his elbow on the bar. "But everyone talks to someone, even if it's just in town."

"Uh-huh."

"Like that stranger that was in here last week. He talked to everyone. He said he talked to you."

"I didn't learn much from him about the cattle market."

Shadwell took a puff on his cigar and squinted his eyes against the smoke. "Neither did I. But he talked a lot."

"As I recall, he mainly asked questions.

Seemed to want to know about any business opportunities. We couldn't help him much there, just bein' cowhands."

Shadwell tipped his cigar ash onto the floor. "I don't know," he said, "but there's something about you I like."

"If you put your finger on it, let me know."

"I think it's the way you let on that you don't know anything."

"It's not that hard to act that way, if it's so close to the truth."

"Aw, some of you cowboys are sly as an Indian." Shadwell opened his mouth as if he was going to say more, but he didn't.

"I know," said Braden.

Varlett, still with his head leaning forward, turned his chin and looked at Braden. "You're talkin' about that queer duck? I thought he was nosy."

Braden shrugged. "I don't recall him mentionin' any names. Did he ask about anyone in particular?"

"Oh, no," said Shadwell, straightening up and sticking his cigar in his mouth.

"No," Varlett added. "He just wanted to know who-all had the ranches here, and where the new money was."

"Well," said Braden, "he probably didn't get any satisfactory answers, and I'd guess he's long gone now."

Varlett palmed his pipe and puffed out a cloud of smoke. "I imagine so."

Shadwell scratched the top of his head, where his white hair was thinnest. Then he turned to Braden, and with his face relaxed into a smile again, he said, "You know what I miss? Pig's feet."

"Really?"

"Yeah. I haven't ate any since I was in Omaha. Have you ever had any?"

"You mean the pickled kind?"

"Yeah. They got a vinegar taste and come in a kind of jelly."

"I've tried 'em. They're all right, I guess. I get along without 'em."

Shadwell sipped on his beer and smiled again. "I don't know why, but I just like 'em." He turned to Varlett. "You know, you could order a big jar of 'em."

Varlett rotated his head toward Dace and then back to Shadwell. "They'd go better in a place like this. Then, when the jar was empty, they could put a rattlesnake in it."

Shadwell turned back to Braden. "Have you ever seen that? They say a man can't hold his hand against the outside of the glass and watch the snake strike at it."

"That's what I've heard," said Braden. "I've never played the game, though."

Slack spoke up at this point. "I never had much use for playin' with snakes. If I see one, I kill it."

"So do I," said Beaumont, "especially if it's a rattler."

Shadwell held out his cigar between the first two fingers of his right hand. "I don't care for 'em, either. But I've heard you can make a lot of money off of men who think they can hold their hand there."

"They won't make a nickel off of me," said Slack, who then craned his neck to look at the back of the saloon.

Shadwell took another drink of beer and turned to Varlett. "Maybe we could get Lex to order some," he said.

Varlett muttered something, and from that point onward the men from the Aster kept their conversation to themselves.

Braden followed Slack's gaze to the back of the room, where he saw the first flash of color for the evening. He imagined Slack would wander back there in a little while to find the redhead.

About five minutes later, Slack did just that. He crushed his cigarette butt on the floor and stepped away from the bar. Braden saw him approach the girls and then disappear into the dark hallway with the redhead. Beaumont paid no attention, as he took out his pipe and went about his laborious procedure of stuffing and lighting it. Braden glanced again at the other girls at the end of the bar, and he saw Emily with her head lifted. She had a sensuous look to her, as she exposed her throat and the upper part of her chest that the dress did not cover. She had very light skin, almost a gleaming white. At the same time that Braden found it stirring, he had another idea.

He stepped away from the bar and walked to the back of the saloon, where he gave the yellow-haired girl a glance as he passed her. When he came back into the saloon, he gave her another look, a more deliberate up-and-down gaze. Her eyes met his, and her eyebrows flickered. Then her forehead drew together and she nodded, in a gesture that beckoned him.

Braden changed his direction to go near her. She smiled, and her eyes danced. He felt a flicker of excitement, but he made himself remember what he knew and why he was flirting with her. Pausing next to her, he let her speak.

"What are you up to?"

"Not much," he said. "A reg'lar night on the town."

She smiled again. "You ought to make it complete."

He looked her up and down again. "Sometimes I think about it."

She took a breath and raised her bosom. "There's nothin' like the real thing."

He thought that was a good tease. "Oh, I know," he said. "It's a matter of bein' in the mood."

She stuck the tip of her tongue between her lips for a second and then said, "I thought boys like you were always in the mood."

He smiled and tried to look sheepish.

"Oh, c'mon," she said. "We both know about it."

"Oh, I know. It's just that — well, there's things to be shy about."

"There's a cure for that," she answered, with a twinkle in her eye. "Even the littlest soldier stands right up when we get the door closed and everything is soft and nice."

"It's not that," said Braden. "I've got a scar." He waved his left index finger back and forth above his belt on his left side.

"Oh, that's nothing."

"To me it is. It's new and pink and ugly, and I haven't let any girl see it."

"Is it clean?"

"Oh, yeah. It just makes me feel funny."

"Oh, hell, I've seen everything."

"Even big ugly scars?" He waved his finger below his ribs again.

"Honey, believe me. I've seen it all, and it doesn't make a bit of difference, as long as you're clean." She gave him a knowing look. "You know. In all ways."

"Well, there's not a problem there. I haven't been with a girl since before I got cut."

"How did you get hurt?"

"Damn horse tangled us up in a barb-wire fence."

She made a slow shake with her head. "You're lucky it wasn't some Mexican or Indian with a knife."

"I don't live that dangerous." He looked her up and down again. "I wish I was in the mood. I thought maybe I would get into it, but it didn't — well, you know."

She gave a rise and shift to her bosom. She had good moves, he thought, and he didn't doubt that she could fix things up when the door was closed.

"Come back when you feel like it, then," she said.

He gave a deliberate look at her bosom. "It's like dancin'," he said. "You need enough drinks to get the courage up, but not so many as to keep you from bein' any good at it."

She winked. "You're right about that," she said. "If you tip the balance the other way, come back and see me."

"I'll do that." Braden gave her a wink and then walked back to his place at the bar. He imagined she would very much like to get him into the room, and it wouldn't be to see his scar. She said she had seen scars like that before, and he believed her.

# Chapter Twelve

The next news Braden heard about the man who called himself Downs came from over by the Rawhide Buttes, five weeks later, just before fall roundup. A couple of riders for an outfit over that way found the body of a man with long dark hair and a dark cape. He had been dead for a while. The details were singular enough that the story traveled in a flash from Rawhide north to Lusk and then to all the towns both ways along the railroad. When it made its way through the Lucky Chance and the Aster, word went back to Lusk, by telegraph, that the dead person might be a man named Downs. The sheriff at Lusk wired back to ask for someone to come and make an identification of the body. Dace and Shadwell rode in the caboose of a freight train that same afternoon, and by nightfall, word came back that the corpse was indeed Downs.

Such was the story as it spread out to the ranches. Braden heard it at noon dinner when one of the MT riders dropped by with a delivery of mail. When everyone at the table had taken in the main details, some of the smaller points came out. The question of the cause of death arose, and the MT rider said he was certain he had heard it was a bullet wound. There followed a round of discussion about the Rawhide Buttes and the dark trails that passed through there. The route was favored by cattle rustlers and horse thieves moving through the country; it wouldn't take much for someone of that type to take a dislike to an inquisitive stranger like Downs. So went the commentary.

Braden thought the whole story sounded plausible, but he wondered about it. He didn't know what motive Downs would have had to be skulking around in that country. As Braden saw it, Downs had two items on his agenda: to dump the golden goose in someone's lap, and to go to a larger town where he could live off his wits. He might well have ended up in the Rawhide Buttes on his own hook, but he might have been escorted that way or even toted.

Braden imagined Dace and Shadwell in the caboose — one of them reading a newspaper and the other daydreaming of a large jar of pig's feet — on their way to identify the body. He thought also of how appropriate it was that the two of them should go. Dace would carry out the role of the somber dignitary and solid citizen, while Shadwell, with his earlier work as a jailer, would lend a small measure of authority by virtue of being familiar with legal processes. And if they wished, they could dress up any details about the deceased — such as his being nosy — that would solidify the theory that had been circulating. Even if Downs had ridden over there on his own initiative and had asked for trouble, Dace and Shadwell would do what they could to erase any doubt. Braden knew that the men from the Aster had taken a dislike to Downs. It might have been something explicit he had said, or it might have been something in his manner of hinting. At the very least, the stranger hadn't played his cards quite close enough to his chest, and he had aroused their suspicion. Braden had picked up that much, and from there it wasn't hard to imagine their passing the suspicion on to Engle.

As for Downs himself, Braden felt a little sympathy. Even if the man had a low-class, riffraff way about him, he had some justification for his bitterness. He had a brother, and the brother had been wronged. Call it malice or call it vengeance, Downs had gone on a mission to get even; and in his system of ethics he might well have thought that the golden goose served the interests of honor and justice. It was hard to know how much sympathy to have, when a fellow didn't know whether Downs had gone to look for trouble or if it had come to find him.

However it had happened, another life was ended, and early. Downs had never made mention of his own age, but from his appearance and from his air of easy familiarity, Braden figured him at about the same age as Beaumont, Slack, and himself — somewhere between twenty-five and thirty. His being close in age made his death, though distant, seem real. And for all that Downs was a drifter or confidence man, he was a human being. He no doubt had his hopes as well as his hatred. Maybe he had loved a woman, as his brother had. Now they were both dead, the two brothers, who lived in a rough and crooked world and died there. Maybe there was justice in the ways they died and maybe there wasn't, but Braden could not help thinking that they were treated like chaff. Life was cheap in their world, and the ones who lived at the lower levels were the most dispensable. That in itself did not seem fair, and Braden could not dismiss it with the easy notion that if a fellow hadn't been with the crows he wouldn't have been shot at.

The story about the dead man kicked around the bunkhouse as a conversational topic for a couple of days. Then one morning, as Braden and Beaumont went out to the corral to work with the horses and get them in order for fall roundup, Braden found a chance to bring it up. He had told Beaumont about Downs's story shortly after the dark stranger had disappeared, but he and Beaumont hadn't had any occasion to discuss it in the last few weeks. One week flowed into the next, and nothing new came up about Forbes's maneuvers, so it seemed to Braden that the case had gone underground. Now with the prospect of fall roundup and of the daily company of Forbes and his men, Braden expected something to surface. So when he found the chance to share impressions with Beaumont, he took it.

Beaumont had asked Braden to help him trim the hooves on a big sorrel. He said the horse was easier to work with if someone held the lead rope than if the horse was tied to a snubbing post, so Braden agreed to hold the horse while Beaumont did the trimming. They led the horse out of the corral and stopped in front of the gate. Braden had a good view of the yard and would see anyone approaching, so when Beaumont picked up the left front foot and bent over to work on it, he opened the topic.

"Kind of a curious story about the dead man at Rawhide Buttes, don't you think?"

Beaumont answered without looking around. "I thought so." He scraped the underside of the hoof with his hoof knife.

"Did it seem kind of — convenient?"

"Knowin' what you told me, yeah. But knowin' no more than anyone else knows, it just seems like one of those things that happen."

Braden heard the snap of the nippers as Beaumont clipped away the extra growth on the hoof wall. "Well," he said, "you don't know how many people he might have told, but you know he's damn sure not goin' to tell any more."

Beaumont straightened up and turned as he let the hoof down. "That's for sure. Even if he didn't want to stick around, there was the possibility that someone might be able to use him for a witness at some time. But that's all gone now."

"And it works to someone's advantage to have things that way, whether they were accidental or not."

Beaumont went under the horse's neck and turned to pick up the right front foot. "I don't know," he said. "One thing after another happens, and nothin' sticks."

Braden stepped forward and put his hand against the horse's neck. "I don't like it. And it seems to me that the longer things go on, the harder it'll be to prove anything."

Beaumont turned and looked at him. "I don't think there's anything a man could prove on this last one. They've got it all sewed up."

"They sure do. All we've got is a hunch. That, and the knowledge that no one else is goin' to do a thing about any of it. But I just can't stand the idea of lettin' things go by — the things that happened here. Not after what happened to Ed."

As Beaumont applied his strength to the nippers, Braden could feel the tension in the horse. When Beaumont finished with the hoof, he looked at Braden and nodded without saying anything.

"Well," Braden went on, "I don't like it. But if no one else is gonna do anything, I guess I'd better think about it good and hard and be on the lookout to see what I can do. If I can use anything that Downs told me to help get this fellow out in the open, it's worth a thought."

Beaumont nodded toward the bunkhouse, where Gundry had stepped outside and was putting on his hat. "You can't be too careful." He leaned over and picked up the right rear hoof and started scraping away the dead matter. "Nope, you can't be too careful. You can work around a horse a hundred times without a problem, and then one day out of the blue, he'll up and kick you."

"I know," said Braden. "I saw it once in Idaho."

The next day, Braden and his two fellow riders brought in the horses that had been in Greaves's string and had been ridden by Engle. During the middle and late summer, between spring and fall roundups, the Seven Arrow men had ridden and taken care of the horses in their own strings. Now, with fall roundup drawing near, Gundry told them to bring in the other string and get the horses ready. Beaumont asked Gundry if he was going to hire another hand, and he said no, that Forbes's man

Engle would fill in again.

Braden didn't like the idea of a man from one outfit riding all his horses from another. A man was supposed to ride for his outfit and be responsible for his own string for the whole season, but here they were, Braden and his pals, combing out manes and tails, trimming hooves, and getting the horses back under the saddle. Just more of the same, he thought — Forbes weaseling his way into arrangements that got other people tied up with him.

Braden took the loose horse hair from the manes and tails and stuffed it into the burlap bag that hung on the gatepost. Through the long winter, a man like Beaumont would sit by the wood-burning stove and weave the horsehair into hatbands, halters, saddle cinches, or even ropes. Beaumont had said he was going to try his hand at a *mecate,* a lead rope for a hackamore, pronounced "McCarty" by Slack and others. It would be long, slow work — good for the winter, when a fellow looked for ways to fill the time. Braden thought about a couple of fellows he had known of late who would not see another winter. For as much as braiding horsehair or working the long strands of rawhide seemed like a tedious way to spend the time, at least it was an option. Even men in the penitentiary, where some fine horsehair work got done, had that option; men in the ground didn't.

Connors the barkeep was in good form. He was telling a story about a man named Baker who had married a woman who ran a hotel. She had been widowed for a couple of years, and the man Baker, not having much to his name and seeing the opportunity, was pleased with himself for moving up a step or two in the world. When Baker and his new bride went to bed on their wedding night, he put his hand on her belly and felt something move.

"What's this?" he asked.

"A loaf in the oven," she said. "Why do you think I married a Baker?"

A ripple of laughter went up and down the bar as a couple of men repeated the turn of phrase. Then a man standing near the door called for a poem. Connors asked if he wanted something bawdy or something stately, and the puncher said he would like to hear something serious, as he could hear any of the other stuff from anyone he worked with. Connors lowered his head and closed his eyes; then after a moment he looked up and around at his audience and held the men with his steady voice:

> "Half a league, half a league,
> Half a league onward,
> All in the valley of Death
> Rode the six hundred."

He recited the poem all the way through, his voice rising and falling, rushing and pausing. When he finished, the audience applauded.

The bartender ceased to be the center of attention as he went about his work of serving drinks. Meanwhile, the flair for reciting poetry came out in the patrons. A man down the bar a couple of places to Beaumont's left chanted a twelve-line ditty that began:

> "Oh, she looked so fair in the
>    midnight air
> As the wind blew up her nightie —
> Her skin was fair beyond compare,
> And I swore like Gosh almighty."

When he was done and the murmur subsided, the man at his right delivered a single stanza, in a loud voice and with an upraised drink:

"Not drunk is he who on the floor
Has strength to rise and drink one
      more —
But drunk is he who flatly lies
Without the strength to drink or rise."

There followed a few scattered cheers, but not the applause of before. After a couple of more recitations along the same lines, the interest in poetry dwindled away, and the small groups of men took up their individual conversations. Slack left the bar to watch a card game, and Beaumont fell into a conversation with a man standing nearby. Braden kept his eye on the crowd and noticed that neither the men from the Aster nor any of Forbes's men had made an appearance.

When Connors paused in his work, Braden caught his eye. The barkeep meandered over and took to polishing the bar top in front of Braden. His face had color, as if it was flushed from his recent performance, and it looked full and open as the gray hair rippled back on the sides and top of his head.

"What do you think?" he asked.

"Oh, not much," said Braden.

"Same here. Not much call for it."

"I guess there has been a bit of news,

though, huh? Seems like we found out where the mysterious stranger ended up."

The coffee-colored eyes held steady as Connors nodded. "Still mysterious, you might say."

"Uh-huh. Reminds me of a story I once heard."

The eyebrows rose above the brown eyes. "From far away, no doubt."

"Sawn doot." Braden looked left and right, and then catching a confidential look from the bartender, went on. "But not from the fellow I heard that from. It was a story about a fellow who had the goods on someone else and then disappeared."

"I see. And then it was discovered that he had died?"

"That's right."

"So many of those stories are alike. You'd hope he did something with the goods before he wandered away."

"I think he did." Braden exchanged another knowing look. "This story happened so far away, I don't remember how it turned out. But the fellow gave the goods to someone else — I think it was a saddle that was all moldy. And the other man, he figured if he was goin' to get any use out of it, he needed to expose it to the sunlight."

"That's a good cure for mold, to get it

out in the open. I've seen it work."

"Over in Idaho?"

Connors made a deliberate forward motion with his head. "Not exactly, but it's the type of thing that could work there. You always want to be careful with mold, though, or any other kind of germs."

"Oh, you bet. I'm just tryin' to remember how that story turned out."

The bartender gave a short, confident nod. "He was probably real careful. Was he a cowpuncher?"

"I think so. Either that or a piano player in a whorehouse, I can't remember."

"Oh, they both learn to be real careful."

"I imagine."

"Oh, yeah. You take your average cowpuncher, and his big fear is gettin' a finger or two burned off when he wraps his rope around the saddle horn. And you know why he's so careful?"

"Why?"

"He figures it's a good chance he'll end up bein' a piano player, and he needs all his fingers for that."

Braden laughed.

"And your piano player, his big fear is that he'll get sent back to punchin' cows, so he's real careful about his fingers, too, so he can keep his easy job. Doesn't want to stick 'em in the meat grinder."

Braden held his right hand off the bar and wiggled his fingers. "Wanna keep 'em all."

"That's right. I bet the fellow in the story did just that."

A cold wind was blowing out of the northwest when the boys rode back to the Seven Arrow.

"Smells like a change in the weather," said Braden. "Cold and damp, like there's rain on the way."

"Sure does," said Beaumont. "Time to get out the gloves."

Braden wondered if Slack would say anything, but he didn't. The three of them rode on a while longer until Beaumont spoke again.

"Seems like weather comin', all right. What say we don't poke along too slow?"

The other two agreed, and they all put their horses into a trot, which they varied with a fast walk until they got back to the ranch. They put away the horses, and as they reached the bunkhouse door, Braden turned to look at the night. Away off to the northwest, a flicker of lightning showed in the sky. Clouds were visible in the light of a three-quarter moon, and the smell of moisture hung on the air.

In the morning, Braden put on gloves before he went out to the horse corral. The day being Sunday, and with fall roundup scheduled to begin on Tuesday, the boys had a day off before the nonstop work began again. Braden planned to make the best of the day by riding over to pay a visit on the other side of Black Hat Butte, so he roped out the bay horse and saddled him.

The wind that had come up the night before was still blowing, not very strong but cool and smelling of moisture. The morning sunlight came slanting in under a high cloud cover, reflecting on east-facing bluffs and paling their usual tan or sand color to a beige or bone-white. Beneath the blanket of clouds, the sky to the west and north was grayish blue, and the whole vast scene held the promise of slow rain. The cool air felt invigorating. It quickened the blood and spoke of colder times to come.

Up and over the slope by the butte, Braden saw nothing to catch his attention until he gazed on the homestead below. The sun had risen above the edge of the cloud cover and was not shining directly on the landscape anymore, so the buildings did not glare or reflect. Rather, they stood out in clear detail, with the gray of weathered lumber showing almost blue in contrast with the predominant tan-and-wheat tone of the grassland. Braden saw smoke threading out of the stovepipe, and the thought of Beryl snug in her house cheered him.

The bay took the last half-mile at a happy trot and then let out a whinny at the edge of the yard. A horse answered from the other side of the sheds, where Birdie kept the animals when she didn't have them turned out to pasture. Braden imagined, then, that the girl was still inside.

The door of the house opened, and Birdie stepped out onto the little porch. She was wearing a wool cap, a canvas jacket, denim trousers, and work shoes. She pulled a glove onto her right hand, waved, and pulled on the left glove.

"Mornin'," she said, her teeth gleaming as she smiled.

"Good morning. Are you goin' out to look after your critters?"

She gave a closemouthed smile. "Yeah. Gettin' a slow start. Didn't want to get up, it was so warm in bed, and then Beryl made hotcakes."

"Well, it's a nice morning, anyway."

She looked at the sky. "Do you think it'll snow?"

Braden looked up and around. "I don't think so. Not down this low. But I wouldn't be surprised if we got a little rain out of it."

"That's good. It'll make the grass quieter." She wrinkled her nose. "Just a minute, and I'll tell Beryl you're here." She opened the door, leaned in, and then turned back to Braden. "She says she'll be right out."

"Good enough." Braden dismounted and tied his horse at the rail as Birdie walked across the yard.

The door opened again, and there stood Beryl in a gray wool dress with her dark hair falling loose on her shoulders. The sight of her picked up his pulse and reminded him of why he had wanted to come visit.

"Hello," she said. "I was wondering when you might come again."

He felt himself smile. "First chance I got. I hope it's not a bad time of day."

"Not at all. Let me put on a shawl or something." She went inside and came back out a couple of minutes later wearing a dark blue wool jacket over the dress. "I put the coffee back on the stove to warm it up," she said. After a quick frown, she looked at him and asked, "Do you think it's too chilly to sit outside?"

"Not at all." He followed her to the east end of the house, where the bench sat close to the wall. He let her sit on the far end while he sat on the near end.

"The weather's changing," she said. "I suppose that's good. One gets so tired of the hot weather."

"Oh, it'll warm back up again until the real cold weather sets in. We can usually count on heat, wind, frost, rain, and snow in fall roundup. Maybe some sleet, too. Everything but hail."

"It's probably about time for that now, isn't it? The roundup, I mean."

"We'll be gettin' things together tomorrow, and then we're supposed to roll out the day after that."

She had a look of concern on her face as she said, "I hope it all goes well this time, without incident."

"I've got some worries there, of course. I don't like the company I'll have to keep for a month or more."

Her eyebrows made a perceptible move, though her gray-green eyes held steady. "You mean the person who would like to become a land baron?"

"Yeah, him and the fellows that work for him. Including the toad."

A grimace passed over her face. "Their whole presence just strikes me as so — unsavory. I wish he would leave and take his hired men with him, but it seems as if he's here to stay."

"He seems to have that intention." Braden looked at Beryl and admired her even temper. In spite of her firm demeanor, though, he saw her as vulnerable. She was a woman — quite an impressive woman, at that — and so she was a likely target for a man like Forbes. "I don't want to scare you," he went on, "but I think you want to be on your guard against him."

"Oh, I am. I don't like him."

Braden nodded. "I know. But what I mean is, I think you need to be on your guard even more."

She sat up straight and drew back. "Has something else happened?"

"I don't know for sure, but I think I know more about him than I did before, and even that wasn't good."

"I appreciate your warning, then."

He hesitated, wanting to touch her hand but fighting the impulse. "Beryl," he said.

"Yes?"

"I've gone around and around with myself on this, and I think I need to tell you more about what I know, or what I think I know."

"About the land baron."

"Yes, about him. You see, I shied away from telling you some of this before because it's kind of a . . . burden, I guess, to know something that's — well, what was the word you used?"

"Unsavory?"

"That's it. Anyway, I didn't want to weigh you down with it, but as time goes on, it seems I should tell you some of it so you'll have a better idea of what we're up against."

"I see. I can't imagine it doing anything but good."

"Thanks." He took a deep breath and exhaled. "Well, let me tell it in the order that I got it, or that it came my way."

She nodded, and her eyes gave him encouragement.

"Well, it starts with my friend Greaves — Ed, you know. He told me he heard about some illegal movement and sale of cattle, carried out by some gents who were in the pay of or in cahoots with the baron. Ed didn't go out of his way to hear this, but he did hear it, and the next thing he knew, he was gettin' real dirty looks from these other fellas. And then he turned up dead, and you know what theories we might have about that."

"This is a little more detailed than what you told me before, but it's not highly surprising."

Braden nodded. "So far, so good. Then, not too long after that, Gundry had us ride with Forbes and his men over to a place run by a man named Taylor. Over west of here. Well, Forbes rode roughshod over him, right in front of a whole crew of men, and took some calves from him." Braden paused and then went on. "This was about the time he started leaning on you a little more, too."

"Well, he didn't get anywhere, but he doesn't seem to have accepted it yet, either."

Braden took a deliberate breath and let it out. "Then I heard another story from someone who knew him, or said he knew him, down in Colorado." He waited for her nod and then continued. "This fellow said his brother had worked for Forbes in some kind of crooked deal and ended up dead when he complained."

Beryl shook her head. "This really is unsavory. It's so — cheap, I guess. Making so light of other people's property, not to mention lives."

"That's for sure." Braden held up his hand. "But there's a little more. The man who told me this story also turned up dead."

Her look narrowed. "Recently?"

"Yes. He's the one they found over by the Rawhide Buttes. I don't know if you heard that story."

"Not yet."

"Well, there's not much to it. A couple of riders found a dead man out on the range, and it turned out to be this same fellow. There's no way of proving he was done in, but it sounds fishy."

Beryl made three slow nods. "Regardless of how much of this you know for sure, it all points to the same thing. No regard for others."

"Exactly. And the general assumption that he can do what he wants and get away with it." Now he put his hand next to hers on the bench as their eyes met. "So I want to tell you, be careful. Among the things I heard from this last fellow, it seems that the friendly land baron might not be trusted around women." He gave her a full, knowing look, and she returned it.

"That's a good thing to know," she said. "But even that doesn't surprise me. Everything fits."

"That's the way it seems to me. On one hand, it's all hearsay and supposition, but on the other hand, it's as believable as can be."

She moved her hand and sat up straight again. "I'm sorry to interrupt our conversation, but I think I'll go for the coffee. Then we can continue."

He stood up as she did. "Go ahead," he said, wanting to touch her hand but still holding himself back. "I'll wait here."

She came back in a few minutes with the coffeepot and two blue cups. As she poured the coffee, she said, "I think what disturbs me about these stories you've told me is that this man hasn't been taken to account for any one of these things. However many of them he did, or caused, one would wonder why no one has done anything." Her eyes met his as she handed him the cup.

"Thanks." He took a sip and then spoke. "I think it's a combination of a couple of things. For one, it would be a lot of trouble for someone to bring up one of these things and press for an answer, especially knowin' how these mucky-mucks stick together. A man would have to go out of his way and risk some complications for himself. And the second thing is, if someone did want to take the trouble, he would need some solid evidence. Most of what I have is hearsay, like I said, and most of that came to me by way of a couple of fellows who aren't around anymore to vouch for it."

"But doesn't anybody care? About simple things like crime and justice?" She took her seat again on the bench and turned to look at him.

"Not very much, unless they've got something at stake or there's some hard-and-fast evidence." He looked at his coffee and then back at her. "It's been frustratin' as hell — excuse my language — knowing what I think I know, and not being able to do anything. If I'm going to do something, I need to see a clear way to do it. Otherwise, all I do is bring grief on myself, and that doesn't do any good. Just the opposite."

Her face softened, and her eyes looked like pools from a mountain stream. "I didn't mean that you didn't care."

"Oh, I didn't take it that way. I just figured you were saying what I'd been saying to myself all along. Of course, I've had more of it to chew on, so when I wonder why this fellow gets away with everything, I get a chance to try to figure out some of the reasons."

"Well, it would be good if someone could do something, but I wouldn't want you to put yourself in jeopardy."

Now he touched her hand with a couple of soft pats. "Thanks."

They lapsed into a silence for a minute or two. He waited for her to speak, and when she didn't, he did.

"You know, it'll probably be a few weeks before I get a chance to drop by again."

"Yes, you sort of touched upon that."

"Well, there was something I was wondering about, and I thought I should bring it up, rather than not say anything and then wish for the next month that I had."

She nodded. "Go ahead."

After a little hesitation, he made himself speak. "The last time I was here, I sort of touched upon — to use your words — I sort of touched upon a question. Somewhat of a personal one."

"About my status."

"Yes. I don't mean to be blunt, but I thought I could at least ask before I go away for a while."

"It's all right. And I'm sorry I've delayed so much."

He shrugged. "I gather that you've had your reasons."

"I have." She looked at the ground and

then back up at him. "You know I've been married, of course."

"Yes, I knew that much."

"And you knew that my husband — um — went away."

He nodded. "Yes, that's been sort of general knowledge, too."

She gave him a straight look. "I didn't marry very well, Noel. I married a man who seemed to want all this." She waved at the landscape with her right hand. "But he turned out to be the type that didn't want to work that hard." She looked at the ground again. "So he went out to raise some money."

"You mean, in a shady way?"

"Yes. He and a couple of . . . associates, you could say, did a poor job of stopping a train on the U.P."

"You mean they botched it?"

She had a cool, clear look on her face. "Yes, that's what they did."

Braden felt a pained look come onto his face as he squinted. "So they've had him locked up?"

She shook her head. "No, he was a casualty."

Braden felt as if everything inside him and outside him dropped with a force like gravity. "Then you're —"

"Yes, I'm a widow. But it's been a shame that I've been in no hurry to announce. And it's actually been to my advantage — not with you, but with others — not to change the public impression that someone was coming back."

"You mean, to help keep the wolf at a distance?" It made sense. If Birdie was one kind of sheepdog, a supposed husband was another.

"Something like that. But the main reason has been that I haven't cared to have it known that he ended up that way. It's been such a blight, or shadow."

Braden glanced away to the southeast. "And Birdie? Does she know?"

"All I told her was that he wouldn't be coming back. The less she knows, the less she has to carry around. But I had to tell her something, so she would know how our prospects stood around here, and so she wouldn't think it wrong of me to have a visitor." Her eyes met his again.

"That sounds right, all the way around. I mean, it sounds honest. And considerate." He shrugged. "I think you've treated me all right by letting me look decent to Birdie."

"It hasn't been an easy thing to manage," she said. "It's such a stigma, and it's been perhaps too easy to keep it in the dark and avoid talking about it. And I thank you for being tactful in the way you brought it up."

"Well, to some extent it was none of my business."

"Yes, but to some extent it was, and I appreciate your restraint — not just in asking that question, but in things in general."

"You mean, being a visitor."

"Yes, being a visitor and not pushing in any way. I knew you wanted to be a gentleman caller, and of course you were, but you've been good about not showing it."

"Well, I've been — um, I guess — interested in you all this time, and I don't think I hid it."

She lowered her eyelids and raised them again. "No, and I didn't mean that, of course. I think what I meant was that you didn't claim anything for yourself. You've been a gentleman caller, and you've been willing to pretend that you weren't."

"I guess I just did what seemed to be called for, if you know what I mean."

"You mean, appropriate to the circumstances?"

"Yes. That's well put."

The cloud cover was breaking up on its eastern fringe, and sunlight was beginning to straggle through. Beryl squinted as she looked at him. "I must say that I feel better about it all, now that it's out in the open — now that we've talked about it."

He nodded. "I know how it feels to have to keep things bottled up. It seems like we have to do too much of it, but sometimes it seems like the only way."

"Well, I have to admit it was convenient, too. And all this time that I've welcomed your attention, I haven't really felt free to recognize it."

"Because of this thing hanging over you?"

"That, and I think I just needed to live with things for a while and let them take their own course, to a certain extent." She gave him an inquisitive look. "Does that make sense?"

"Somewhat."

"Maybe I can say it in a different way. It's as if I had to live with two kinds of feelings, to grow out of one and sort of grow into another." She smiled. "So I still have to catch up with you."

Braden felt his eyes getting soft as he moved his head in agreement. He realized he had been part of the wolf she had been keeping at a distance, albeit a better part. "I'll try not to move too fast," he said.

"That way I won't be so hard to catch."

"I don't know how fast I'll be," she said, with a light laugh. "But I do feel I've been moving from one point to another."

He put his left hand on her right, and she turned her hand over to accept his. Without speaking or even thinking, he rose to his feet and, holding her hand, waited for her to rise and put her other hand in his. The sunlight fell on the unblemished complexion of her face, and she held her chin up. As they moved toward each other, she closed her eyes; in the instant before he closed his, he saw the beauty of her closed mouth, lovely as a redstone pebble in clear shallow water.

They separated, and then with a magic slow rush of willow-waving motion, they moved closer. He took her in his arms and felt her arms around him. He could feel the sun on his shoulder and on the side of his face. He could feel it with his right hand where he held it against her wool jacket. When he opened his eyes he saw the sunlight shine on her dark hair.

As they drew apart, her hands joined his once again, and their eyes met. "We were free to do that," she said.

"I'm glad." He saw the depth of her gray-green eyes, the luster of her hair, the light tan of her face. It all seemed softer now, as if she was no longer keeping up a line of defense. When he met her eyes once again, he felt the warmth and the freshness of the morning and within him the soft tone of a haunting, cooing song he had heard more than once on the cool, clear air of the plains.

# Chapter Thirteen

*"Yoodle-ooh, yoodle-ooh-hoo, so sings a
   lone cowboy,
Who with the wild roses wants you to
   be free."*

Braden swung easy in the saddle as the bay
horse trotted toward a small bunch of cattle.
The morning air, fresh and clear, brushed
against his face. The cool weather brought
up the energy level in a man, got the fires
burning. So did roundup, in its own way.
Braden felt an excitement at being out on a
big enterprise, working with a purpose. This
was the last part of the work season, the last
campaign before being laid off for the
weather; and a good cowpunch', as Slack
would say, wanted to wind things up in good
order.

He let the bay do what it knew how as it
went after the cattle. A good cow horse
knew what the rider wanted. He could tell
from the slightest indication if the rider
wanted to cut an animal out of a bunch or
if he wanted to herd the whole bunch

along. He also knew where to keep the cattle headed, which in this case was the center of a big circle made by riders who had fanned out and were closing in on a drive.

Braden kept an eye on the cattle as the horse went after them, cutting this way and that to keep them headed toward the main herd. One, two, three, four, five — he counted them for the tenth time in two minutes, noted the Seven Arrow brand on all of them each time. Three cows and two calves, the big ones jiggling along and the small ones trotting and rocking with their tails up. Three cows and two calves drumming the earth and raising dust. When a man didn't have much to think about, he counted the same things over and over. One, two, three, four, five. Three and two.

For a good part of fall roundup, the riders did not bring in cows with branded calves. They concentrated on animals that could be shipped for beef and on calves that had not yet been branded, for reasons of being missed in spring roundup or being born late. Therefore, on this roundup, most of the riders would pay little attention to cows and calves. As the crew was now four days south of the ranch, however, Gundry gave orders to bring in all the

Seven Arrow stock that had drifted that far. He wanted to push his own cattle back north toward his place. And so Braden found himself trailing three cows and two calves. He counted them again — one, two, three, four, five. Three and two. In spite of all the talk about the good calf crop, Braden had seen a little of this — a cow with no calf.

He told himself it was not his lookout. If Gundry wanted to be bosom friends with a man who was questionable, and if he kept close enough track to see that calves as well as butcher-weight animals disappeared a few at a time, he could decide for himself how far he wanted to scratch below the surface. For right now, Gundry seemed content to ride with Forbes, eat with him, confer with him, and even sleep in the same wagon with him when the weather turned cold and damp. When he thought about it, Braden found it puzzling that a man like Gundry, who was scrupulous about property, would cling to someone who was not. Braden was sure it had something to with their belonging to the Stock Growers' Association. When members of that organization formed their smaller alliances, they bought into each other in a deep way. And when a man like Gundry lent support to a man like Forbes, it strengthened the bond all the way around. Gundry could expect loyalty or commitment from other members as well as from Forbes. That seemed to be the code.

"Hee-yah," he called out, spurring the bay horse and giving the cattle another push. Then he turned to the right and rode to the top of a knoll to see what else he might find to drive back to the holding ground.

Facing west, he felt the sun warm on his back. The cool, damp spell had not brought much moisture, and although the mornings were cool, these days of late September grew warm and dry and dusty in the afternoon. That was fine. A man knew to enjoy the good weather while it lasted, because it was bound to change. He looked across the land, which seemed to lie under a hazy spell. Indian summer, they called it — the return of warm weather after the first frost. But the brisk mornings, and the turning colors in the leaves of chokecherry, box elder, and cottonwood, reminded a person that the easy weather would not last.

And change it did. On the fourth of October a cold wind blew in from the northwest, carrying rain, sleet, and a few flakes of snow. Out came the canvas shelter and the sleeping tents, the woolly chaps and the warm coats. By nightfall the snow was starting to stick, and by the next morning a couple of inches covered the ground. It melted off within a day, except in places where a cutbank, bluff, or butte threw a daylong shadow. The ground was soft, slick in the bare spots. Braden picked out the safer, more surefooted horses for a couple of days, and all of his movements were slow and cautious.

He liked the cool weather, and once he got back the touch of working in bulkier clothing, he enjoyed his work. He could feel a quickness in the air, which started with frost on the canvas in the morning and stayed sharp and clear all day long. He felt the energy that emanated from the horses and cattle; he even felt it from a prancing band of antelope a quarter of a mile away. On one morning he saw a mule deer buck, the antler tines gleaming in the sunlight as the animal grazed and then lifted his head. He was a husky fellow, out foraging to add to his reserves for the weather ahead. Braden had hunted a few deer in October, and he knew this one would have nice gobs of soft white fat in his body cavity, along the base of his ribs and around his kidneys. Braden took it slow, not wanting to spook the deer. Live and let live, he thought, until the time came to do otherwise.

The days rolled on, golden and fragile. The evening air chilled as soon as the sun went down, and in most camps the crew had two fires to crowd around. With the longer evenings and closer company came a gradual feeling of discomfort. Whenever Braden was in camp, he had Forbes or one of his men nearby. Engle was the most unpleasant, with his sullen demeanor and sour looks. Wyndham and Farnsworth went about their business with a nonchalance that seemed, to Braden at least, to cost some effort, for in spite of their easy manner, they kept their eyes open and didn't miss much. Forbes was more pleasant, on the surface, always ready with an affable greeting and a pat on the shoulder for any man on the crew. But Braden thought he was the worst, the most insidious, with his airy laugh and forced goodwill but a pair of blue eyes that never rested.

Knowing what he knew, Braden felt contempt for the man and had a hard time trying not to let his feelings show. He wanted to ask him what kind of a coward he was, trying to lord it over women and hiring out any dirty work he wanted done to men. But he said as little as he could.

When Forbes addressed hired hands with one of his yellow-daisy greetings, he always used the man's name. It would start with something like "And how are you today, Braden?"

"Good enough, I guess."

"Not sure, huh?" The smile would lift in the reddish-blond beard as the blue eyes flickered in the firelight.

"I guess not."

Then would come the pat on the shoulder, with maybe a parting comment like "Keep up the good work."

As the crew made its broad sweep across the country, the herd grew and the days shortened. It meant longer shifts for the night wrangler but more rest for the punchers. Braden went to bed early whenever he could, absorbing as much heat as he could from the campfire and then crawling into his bedroll in the chill of night. He had his blankets wrapped under and over by a good canvas tarp, with snaps along one edge. Once he was burrowed into his shell, the warmth gathered. He wore a knitted cap on the coldest nights and did not lift his nose out into the cold air until he had to ride a shift of night herding or until it was time to roll out in the dark of predawn.

The wagon crawled northward now, and Black Hat Butte lay well to the south and east. Braden looked in that direction now and then when he was on a high spot, and on some occasions he caught a glimpse of the flat top of the butte. He thought of smoke rising from a stovepipe, the warm interior of a house with the smell of coffee in the air — Beryl making hotcakes, or cookies, and Birdie putting on gloves and a cap before stepping out into the morning frost.

From time to time he also looked to the northeast. When the roundup was done, the crew would drive the beef herd to Carlin and the shipping pens. They would have a night or two with no night herding as they camped near town, and then they would disperse. When Braden looked in that direction, he could feel a tightening in his stomach. He recalled the conversation with Connors. Get it out in the open. Expose it. But watch your fingers. He knew he was going to have to do something in the last days of the season, or it would all be old hat by the time spring rolled around again and the right people were present.

In the afternoons he looked to the west, where the sun was moving southward. Time was passing, without a doubt. His beard had grown long enough that he could pull it now, even with a gloved hand. On the morning of the first snow, he could just catch a whisker with the nails of his thumb and forefinger. That was three weeks back, a long chain of burned-out campfires and digested meals. The time was coming for a confrontation, if it did not pass him by.

A low, gray cloud cover hung in the sky for two days, touching the hills in the east. Mist spread out below the clouds and reached down into the notches and draws. From the smell of the air, Braden thought it might rain or snow, either one. The day had started with a frost, but it had since melted, and the world was damp. Moisture beaded on the backs of the cattle and on the neck and haunches of the sorrel horse. Ropes were stiff, and men were curt.

Braden closed in with Beaumont, and between them they drove a half-dozen steers the last mile onto the flat where the day herders held the beef herd. The two riders turned the animals into the herd and rode together at a slow walk toward camp. Braden rode close so that he wouldn't have to shout above the lowing of the herd.

"A long drive tomorrow, and that'll be it," he said. "Then the roundup crew'll all drift apart."

"I won't miss some of these fellas."

"Me neither." Braden looked around. "I thought maybe something would have happened by now, but it hasn't."

"Uh-huh."

"For a while there I thought they might try to get me to show my hand, but things just went on, and now it looks as if I might have to do something or just let it all go away."

"You mean force someone else's hand?"

"Maybe. I don't know. But if something does happen, and it doesn't come to anything more than words, it might be best if you didn't come into the game right away."

"I can do that."

They rode their horses to the cavvy ground, where the day wrangler had set up a canvas shelter for the saddles and other tack. They stripped their horses, brushed them down, and turned them out into the herd. Then they stowed their gear and walked to camp.

Lum had set up the canvas canopy between the two wagons and had his cook fire going. Half a dozen men were standing around that fire, and the night wrangler was building another fire a few yards away, just outside the shelter.

Forbes, wearing a yellow slicker that covered him from his neck to below his knees, stood smiling as he watched the wrangler lay the firewood in place. After exchanging greetings with the two Seven Arrow riders, he said, "Long day, isn't it? Mike here is doin' somethin' about it. Aren't you, Mike?"

The kid grunted, then got up from his crouch and went to the live fire. He came back with a burning stick and poked the flaming end into the bottom of the little pile he had built. The flame grew and smoke rose.

Braden stood by the new fire as Beaumont drifted away. Braden glanced at Forbes, who was staring at the blaze. The silver streaks showed in his beard, and a hard look settled around his eyes. Then he turned to look at Braden. The smile came back, and the hard look went away.

"It's been a long season, hasn't it?"

"Regular, I guess."

"What I mean is, the weather makes it long." Forbes clapped his gloved hands together and held them to the fire. "Well, in a couple of days, we'll all be back sleepin' under a roof again. That'll be nice, won't it?"

"I suppose so."

"You almost forget how comfortable it is. I know I do."

Two of the MT riders came into camp and stood by the fire. As they took out the makin's to build cigarettes, Forbes started in on them with the same good fellowship. From their short responses, Braden gathered that maybe it had been a long season for others on the crew as well.

The next day started early. After a brief conference with Forbes, Davis, and the MT foreman, Gundry announced what everyone knew — that they would make a long drive and get the cattle into the shipping pens that evening. They would camp south of the railroad and town, and everyone was expected to stay in camp that night. After a general murmur of agreement, there followed a bustle of men finishing breakfast, rolling up their bedrolls, and hurrying off to saddle their horses. As Braden left the camp, he glanced back and saw Forbes and Gundry standing by the fire. Forbes, still in the yellow slicker, had his head up and was saying something in his lilting voice, while Gundry had his head lowered, as men did when they looked at nothing in order to hear better.

The crew made the drive as expected, making a short camp at midday. The men ate in quick shifts, changed horses, and went back to hold the herd until the whole outfit was ready to move on. The sun was just going down when the stock pens came into view on the west side of town. The men had allowed the herd to string out for about a mile so they would have less commotion as they penned up the steers. By the time they got the last animals into the corrals, night had closed in and the two fires were blazing at the campsite.

Braden felt an uneasiness as he moved into the firelight. Camp was full, with everyone there except the night wrangler. The men had a tired, relaxed look about them as they ate their chuck. Most of the work was over, but the spree was still a day out of reach, so the general feeling of jubilation was suspended. As men finished eating, they gathered around the fires. Braden, who had been one of the last to get served, tossed his utensils in the wreck pan and looked to see who stood at which fire. Seeing Forbes and Engle at the cook fire and Wyndham and Farnsworth at the other, he chose the one where he could be farthest from Engle. He took his place in the circle of warmth, across the blaze from Gundry and Davis, and out of what he thought was the main drift of the smoke.

A few minutes later, he saw a yellow shape beside him on the right and heard the nervous, airy voice.

"Well, how are you doing, Braden?"

"Well enough, I guess."

"Still not sure?"

Braden shrugged.

"Might be the weather."

"Might be."

"Don't you think this cold weather just seeps into a man?"

"If you say so." Braden felt a twinge, as if he had gone a little too far too soon. He looked around, and everyone seemed to be ignoring the conversation.

"That's a way with you, isn't it, Braden?" The voice was still light, with a tone of forced humor.

"How do you mean?" Braden looked at Forbes and saw the blue eyes, which had an expression of sincerity.

"You never say much, at least around me."

"I guess I don't have much to say."

"Maybe not." Forbes glanced at Gundry

and back at Braden. "But it seems you've been offish with me."

Braden looked straight at Forbes again, and as he did so he could feel the eyes of other men upon him. "I don't have much to say."

Forbes put a gloved hand on Braden's right shoulder. "You know, it's been that way since the spring. I've noticed it. If there's something wrong, I'd like to clear it up."

"There's nothing wrong." As soon as he said it, Braden realized he had played in. Forbes was getting him to say, in public, that there was nothing to talk about.

"Are you sure?" The hand went away.

"Actually, maybe there is something." A couple of more heads came up around the fire.

Forbes gave a look of concern. "Something I did?"

Braden shook his head. "Not that I could say."

"Well, what would it be, then?"

"Something that happened."

"Well, yes . . ." Forbes left the word suspended.

Braden took a deep breath and forged ahead. "A man died. And everyone here knows who I mean. Edwin Greaves."

Hearing his own voice, Braden knew there was no turning back now. The fat was in the fire. Other men were listening.

Forbes blinked a few times. "Well, we all felt that."

"Some more than others."

"Well, of course. He was your friend. You rode together."

Braden looked around the fire and saw the stonewall faces of Wyndham and Farnsworth among the attentive faces of the others. "Yes, he was. And he told me things."

"Oh, he did?" The question sounded like a good attempt at innocent curiosity.

"Yes, he did. He told me he was afraid somebody might do something to him." Braden could feel his heart pounding, and he tried to steady himself.

"And you think someone did?"

"I think someone might have."

Forbes waved his left hand. "Oh, come on, now, Braden. Why would someone want to? And how would they have done it? You were there. Anyone could see it was an accident."

"Maybe it was. People were quick to say so, anyway. But to answer your other question, as to why someone would want to, he told me something else."

"Oh. Uh-huh. And what would that have been?" Forbes's voice had a tinge of sarcasm now.

Braden glanced at the two stonefaces and picked his words with care. "He said he had heard about someone delivering some stolen cattle and that he was getting the feeling that someone wanted to shut him up." Braden did not look at anyone else, but he knew he had an audience.

"Oh, my God, Braden. Somebody told somebody something that somebody told him. That's gossip. Hearsay."

Braden took a breath and moistened his lips. "Maybe it is. But for one thing, even though your friends in town tell everyone what a good year it is for new calves and shippin' steers, anyone could tell there's some of both missin'." He looked at Gundry. "You keep track of your tally from one year to the next. You should know. And you should also know how many cows you've seen without calves."

Gundry spoke now. "Everyone loses cattle from one year to the next, and as long as there's an open range, there'll be rustlers. But before you go tellin' a man he's one of 'em, you'd better have proof. And until then, you'd be wiser not sayin' anything."

Forbes smiled. "Your boss is right,

Braden. Don't let your feelings about your friend get in the way of your judgment."

Braden could feel it — Forbes had tried to draw him out and now felt he had done it without any damage to himself. Braden hesitated for a moment, then cleared his throat. By now the men from the other fire were paying attention as well, so he spoke in a clear voice. "I haven't called anyone anything yet. I haven't named names. But it's not all hearsay, either."

Forbes gave him the hard look now but said nothing.

"I can verify that the men who were said to be moving cattle were off in that direction at the time."

Forbes relaxed his face. "And what does that prove?"

"Not that much, by itself." Braden took a breath and tried to keep himself calm. "But I can also show that someone saw a man sneakin' along behind Greaves just before he died."

Forbes kept his eyes trained on Braden, but his face had a worried look. "More hearsay, probably. And I still don't know what it has to do with me."

"Maybe nothing, but those witnesses can identify three men, and all three work for you."

Forbes's eyes shifted like those of a man on the run, but he kept up a good front. "Look, Braden, this is getting pretty serious. A man just doesn't say things like this without proof."

Braden shrugged. "I suppose you're saying you're not the type of man that would do that sort of thing."

The nod came fast. "That's exactly what I'm saying."

Braden looked around the campfire and back at Forbes. "What if I could prove you were?"

The face was impassive. "I'd say go ahead."

Braden felt he had his finger on the trigger. He wondered what it would do to Forbes, to his two hired men across the fire, to Gundry, to the rest of the gathered men, if he followed through. There was no way of knowing what would happen. He would just have to see. "Are you sure?" he asked.

"Sure. Why not? Let's get this foolish thing over with."

Braden's heart was beating hard now. He took a deep breath and then another. The others would know he was nervous, but he imagined they were on the edge as well. He glanced at Gundry and then back at

Forbes. Lifting his eyebrows, he said, "Why don't you show us the scar below your left ribs?"

Forbes paled, and his face sagged in a stricken look. "Go to hell. What would it prove even if I had one?"

"It would go along with another story. About a fellow named Walraven, who did some dirty work for a man. Then he complained about not getting paid, and the man had him done away with. Then the man made a mistake and tried something with Mrs. Walraven, and she cut him a good one. Left a big scar on his left side, just below the ribs."

Forbes was fighting for control now. "You've got a thousand ghost stories, Braden. Campfire stories." He looked around the fire. "But they're all just that. Stories."

"I suppose you'd like to know who told me that last one."

"Sure."

"Walraven did."

The blue eyes narrowed. "What do you mean?"

Braden held up his hand. "Oh, no. Not the Walraven you knew, and not his ghost." He looked around and saw Engle standing next to Farnsworth, but he still did not see

Beaumont. That was all right. Wes would not be far away. "I heard it from his brother. Some of you might have known him as Downs. The fellow who turned up dead over by the Rawhide Buttes not long after that."

Forbes shook his head. "Never heard of him."

"Never heard of the dead man they found over there?"

Forbes waved his hand. "Oh, I heard about that. But you're so far-fetched, it seems you're trying to pin that on me, too."

"Not necessarily, but I know what he told me. And it didn't reflect well on you."

"This is crazy. A ghost story and a dead man. Let's just drop it."

Braden thought he had him now. "Show us the scar, then. Or better yet, show us that there isn't one. Prove Downs a liar."

A flush came to the man's face. "Go to hell! You and that other snivelin' son of a bitch, whoever he was. I hope he's in hell already. Feeds you full of lies, and then you spread them all over. Try to ruin a man. You take what you heard from him, and you think it proves what you heard from someone else." His eyes flamed and his voice got louder. "There's nothing to any of it! Do you hear? NOTHING!" He looked around at the other men and shouted again, "NOTHING!"

Silence prevailed for a long, embarrassing moment. If Forbes had kept control with a bare-faced, brazen denial, it would have been bad enough. But the outburst was upsetting to anyone's sense of propriety, and Braden imagined that even Forbes's sympathizers had lost a little heart.

Gundry broke the silence. "I think we've had enough here, Braden. You've said way more than you needed to, and you've caused some trouble. In the morning you can roll your blankets, go back to the ranch, and wait there."

Braden nodded and walked away from the fire. At least he had done something. He had blown a hole in Forbes's façade. Even if he hadn't been able to prove anything or get definite satisfaction, he had gotten things out in the open. He had shown that Forbes deserved suspicion, and he had said in front of plenty of other men that there were witnesses out there if someone cared to investigate. This little incident would get around, he was sure, and someone was likely to follow up on it.

As Braden crawled into his blankets, he

wondered about that last point. Maybe, as Beryl had suggested, nobody would care enough. He felt a tinge of disappointment at not having resolved things better, but then he took heart at two other thoughts. For one thing, he was glad he had had something of a public audience, as it would lessen the chance of Forbes or his men coming right back at him. It would be too obvious. For another, the exposure had to have broken Forbes's power. A man like Gundry couldn't cling to him for very long after what they had all just seen.

# Chapter Fourteen

Braden spent a day and a night at the ranch by himself until some of the others returned. Beaumont and Slack showed up first, as they brought in the Seven Arrow horse herd at a faster pace than the wagon would travel. Beaumont said Gundry had bought a load of supplies the day before and was riding along with the wagon to keep Lum company.

Slack said he had gotten a hunk of bacon and a half-dozen potatoes from Lum, and he offered to rustle up some grub.

Braden said that sounded fine. He had foraged in the pantry for a couple of cans of tomatoes and a pound of rice, and he knew supplies were just about down to nothing. As he watched Slack go off to the kitchen still wearing his hat and spurs, he realized that in spite of the man's blunt way of acting and speaking, he must have had an inkling that the other two wanted to talk. Braden appreciated it.

As Slack rattled around in the kitchen, Beaumont and Braden sat at the mess table. Beaumont brought out his pipe and went about his process of stuffing tobacco into it.

"Things were pretty toned down yesterday morning when I left," said Braden.

"They stayed that way for a while. No one had much to say, you know, and of course no one was goin' to bring up you-know-what."

"Probably about what you could expect. How about the night before? What did it seem like to you?"

Beaumont gave him a direct look with the dark eyes. "Oh, I think you did as well as you could. He almost fell apart, but not quite."

"How about the others? How did they seem to take it? Did they believe it, or not want to, or what?"

"I think it was all believable, between what you said and how he acted, but you know that type of thing makes some men pretty uncomfortable, and maybe they'd prefer not to think about it very much." Beaumont lit his pipe.

Braden shrugged. "I guess that's just bound to happen. And what about Forbes? How did he act after I left? All hangdog, or brazen as hell?"

"More of the latter. Not too long after

you left, he stood by the fire and gave a little speech."

"Oh, really?"

"Yeah. I think he politicked Gundry and Davis into standing up with him, which they did. And then he went on for a good little while, sayin' he hadn't really done anything *here*, and really, nothin' wrong before, that anyone had any proof for. He said it was too bad that some people were willin' to tarnish a man's reputation, just from hearsay, and without presentin' any real proof. He harped on this whole proof thing quite a bit." Beaumont puffed on his pipe.

"And naturally, no one asked to see the scar, even if just about everyone was thinkin' about it."

"Of course. But for the most part, he talked about how he hadn't done anything here, and that was where someone needed proof."

Braden shook his head. "What a son of a bitch. I told him I had witnesses. But then he waits till I'm gone, and he gets in the last word. Puts everything in his terms."

"He must have figured that someone would think about the witnesses, and he sort of cut that off. He said Wyndham and Farnsworth had worked for him for a while now, and he didn't think they would do anything out of the way."

"As if they would have done it on their own if they had done something, and he wouldn't have had anything to do with it."

"That's the way it seemed. Then he went on to say he didn't know Engle as well, but if he got a chance to, he'd ask him some questions."

"What's holdin' him back?"

"Oh, I guess you didn't know that. Engle left sometime during the night. Took one of Forbes's horses."

"Well, that's handy. Let him sneak away, and then dump all the blame on him."

Beaumont nodded. "Seems like that's the way it worked. No tellin' where he went. I was hopin' he didn't come this way. But I imagine he hightailed it."

Braden opened his eyes wide. "I didn't even think about someone comin' after me. Especially this soon. But he would have known right where to find me."

Beaumont puffed on his pipe again. "If he's got any brains at all, he's long gone."

"Maybe so. And it's probably in Forbes's best interests to have him gone. Sort of shifts the blame and makes him look like the only guilty one." Braden thought for a second. "So, how did everyone seem to take his speech?"

"About the same. Not friendly, not hostile — just uncomfortable. After that, everyone got paid, got cleaned up, and went into town. In the afternoon, Forbes showed up and bought everyone drinks, and went on as if nothin' had ever happened."

"Damn. You'd think I'd have done a little more good than that."

"Well, you didn't get him locked up, if that's what you mean. That would have been best, but I don't know who would go to the trouble of turnin' him in or askin' for someone to look into it all. Still, I think he'll have to pull his horns in."

Braden shook his head. "Hard to say how much, if Gundry was still stickin' up for him."

"Well, you did something, anyway. He didn't get to sweep the whole thing away as if nothing had ever happened. He did have to answer to it, in a way."

The wagon rolled into the yard in the middle of the afternoon, and the boys went out to put the horses away and help unload the supplies. On one of Braden's trips from the kitchen to the wagon, he saw Gundry standing off to one side. The boss called his name, so he went over to face the music.

Gundry had shaved, trimmed his mustache, and put on a clean set of clothes, including a brown hat that was cleaner than his everyday work hat. His plain brown eyes had a clear expression, and he looked serious and businesslike. He did not speak right away but reached inside his coat and took out an envelope that had some figures written on it. "Here's your pay," he said.

Braden thanked him and took the envelope, which from the feel of it had several bills inside.

"You did good work all season," said Gundry, giving him a firm look. "But you caused some trouble there on that last night."

Braden nodded. "I won't say that he goaded me into it, but he asked what was troublin' me, and I told him. And I think I had some justification."

Gundry's neck turned red. "Think what you want, but it was more than anyone needed to say, or hear."

Braden looked him in the eye. "I can't say I'm sorry, because I'm not."

Gundry shook his head. "It wouldn't make any difference." He paused for what seemed like emphasis, and then he said, "I don't imagine you would expect to come back next season, but I wouldn't want there to be any doubt."

Braden flinched. He hadn't expected it to be so blunt. "I understand that," he said. He also understood that it meant he wasn't welcome to stay on for a while as the other hands were. "I'm on foot right now," he went on, "but I've got a place to stay. I'll leave as soon as I can."

Gundry's face showed a look of interest, as if he thought Braden meant a place where a grass widow lived. "I can lend you a horse, and when you get there, you can get another one to ride and bring mine back."

Braden cleared his throat. "Um, where I plan to go is my own little claim. But I need to buy a few things first, so I'd like to borrow two horses if I could, to get settled in. Then I could find a horse for myself."

Gundry hesitated. "I don't suppose it makes any difference, but —"

"Well, maybe I don't need two. I can get by with one, like you offered. I'll buy another one on my own, and then I'll get what I need, move it to my place, and bring your horse back. It's probably less complicated that way."

"Take what you need, and bring it back when you can." Gundry nodded, then turned and walked away.

"Thanks," said Braden, and then he was left to his own thoughts. Just for a moment, Gundry had relaxed into a decent ranchman, who trusted a hired hand and wouldn't put him on foot. But he must have felt himself weakening and then retreated into the code of the Stock Growers.

Braden went into the bunkhouse, rolled up his bed, and packed his war bag. He took his chaps from the wall and put them on, then went out to catch the bay horse. At least he had his own rope and saddle; there was some pride in that. He would have to buy everything else, and that would cut deep into the money he had thought to put into either a cabin or some cattle. *To hell with it*, he thought. If that was what he had to do, then he would do it.

He caught and saddled the bay horse, told Beaumont what was up, said so long to Slack and Lum, and then loaded his few possessions on the back of the horse and rode away. There was no point in going to his own place yet, as he didn't have so much as a tin can to boil water in. So he hit the trail north to town.

He looked back to his left and saw the top of the butte. Then he looked west across the dry-grass hills and imagined the spot where he would set his camp. There was nothing wrong with this land, he thought. It held promise. Men could make an honest living off of it. But some men abused it, corrupted the gifts. Someone like Forbes must have it in him to have to do things in crooked ways, while men like Gundry must have it in them to stick together and want to stay on top of the common men who worked and drank and scratched and rolled with whores.

Maybe that was all he was, part of the crawling mass of railroad workers, miners, ditch diggers, road graders, cowpunchers, and sheepherders. Some of them drank more, some of them stunk more — but they all worked for wages and lived hand to mouth, maybe more so than they realized when the boss or the company served up the grub. And here he was, Noel Braden, riding a borrowed horse and wondering how to pinch out his money to keep himself sheltered and fed.

Still, it was better than being a mucky-muck, from the looks of what it took to be one. He would rather not have a pot to piss in or a window to throw it out of than to have something to hide. He would rather be in the brotherhood of Beaumont and Slack — and Greaves — than in the tight group that thought they had to do things their way at any cost.

It surprised him to think how deep these fellows ran. He had to admit to himself that he had underestimated Forbes all along. To begin with, he hadn't thought the man posed that much of a threat. Then, later, he didn't expect him to hang on so tight to his own false position. The man could deny things so outright, maybe he believed some of his own lies. And he hung on when a wiser man would have counted his losses. It reminded Braden of the deep will of a hog that refused to die when its throat was cut. It heaved and gasped and sputtered through the slash in its throat, while a man standing by would wonder why it didn't know better and give up. Forbes should know that this country, cattle country, operated on trust, and his was in question. The word would get around and the doubts would hang in the air. Maybe someone would look into things, but even if they didn't, and even if he hung on, he should know he had taken a cannonball in the broadside.

He should know that, but maybe he could deny it to himself or hope the others would stand by him. These fellows stuck together. Braden nodded to himself. That was the other thing he had underestimated. He had thought Gundry would distance himself, cut himself loose, but he didn't. Maybe Gundry had a hoglike stubbornness, too. Maybe deep down he had the conviction that he couldn't let the hired men claim any authority at all, and even if it meant clinging to a rotten associate, he was sticking by one of his own kind. That could be it. It went against common sense, but it was the kind of mistake men made. Not without irony, Forbes had even touched upon it, when he sneered at Braden and told him not to let his feelings for a friend cloud his judgment.

Maybe there was a difference in the kinds of mistakes men made. A fellow like Greaves or Slack — and probably Braden himself, if it came to that — would be a fool for women. Others in their class would do it for drink, or a quick fistful of money. Looking at it in that way, Braden could see that he might be closer to Downs than he was to Forbes and Gundry and the others. The bosses made their mistakes, if they did, because they wanted to run things and have it all. Braden wondered if it would catch up with them or if, like the men on the Sweetwater and the men who took the hired killers up to Johnson County, they would prove they could do as they pleased.

He hoped Gundry had made a mistake, but whether he had or not, Braden had to admit he had made a couple himself, and not about drinks or women. He had underestimated the lengths that Forbes would go to, and he had thought Gundry would have to let go sooner. Yes, and there was another mistake that stood up now like a bear on the side of the trail. Uh-huh. He had thought that by exposing Forbes in public he was cutting down the risk of someone coming right back at him. It was a nice thought, that they wouldn't do to him what they did to Greaves, when it was all out in the open — but now it was a mere thought, when he didn't know where Engle was.

Braden figured he could make it to town by dusk, which in late October was early in the evening. He debated with himself as to whether he should go to the Lucky Chance and see how the wind blew, but as time went on, he grew less fond of that idea and of going to town at all. He couldn't pinpoint his feeling, but he had a sense of things not being right. He didn't know what it might be, but he had an aversion to going into town just before dark and keeping out of circulation. He wouldn't have gone to the Aster anyway — not to order a meal, nor to take a room. If he were to spend the night in town, he would probably sleep in the livery stable. He doubted that he would run any great risks by going into the saloon, but he thought it might be better to wait a few days for the gossip to get around and settle down before he tried to sound out public opinion. Also, he realized he would feel conspicuous if he went in by himself, after the other roundup hands had been there without him. So if he didn't go to the Lucky Chance or the Aster, he would find himself holed up in the livery stable for a good twelve hours or more. It didn't seem like a good plan. It would give him the feeling of hiding when he should have nothing to hide from.

Having decided not to go all the way into town, he kept an eye out for a likely place to camp. He passed by the site where Downs had had his camp, and a little ways farther on he found a spot that suited him. While he still had daylight he staked out the horse and gathered firewood; then he built a small fire and rolled out his bed. For his evening meal he ate a handful of dried apples and two pieces of jerky, parting gifts from Lum. He sat by the fire for a couple of hours, feeding it a few sticks at a time and keeping an ear tuned for noises. Nothing out of the ordinary presented itself — just the shifting of the horse and the occasional howl of a coyote. Braden enjoyed the wispy smell of wood smoke and the solitude of the dark night. The moon was down to a sliver, and the stars seemed tiny, distant, and cold. Braden recalled Forbes's comment about how soon they would be sleeping under a roof, and he didn't mind where he was. Life was trimmed down to the essentials, and he was free.

In the morning he blew the coals back into life, laid on some dry grass, and built up a fire with the remaining firewood. Frost lay on the ground, on his bedding and war bag, and on his saddle. He would have cherished a cup of hot coffee, but for the time being he would have to be satisfied with a slug of water and the warmth from the fire.

Soon enough he had his gear packed up and the horse saddled. The campfire had burned down to ashed-over coals, so he loaded up and led the horse out onto the trial. It was a crisp morning, slow to warm up at all, and he thought about the boys back at the bunkhouse. Lum would have served up breakfast by now. Braden shrugged off the thought. Things were going to be rough for him for a little while, but at least he had done something. That was worth a cold morning and an empty stomach.

About a mile from town, he met a rider coming his way. The man had the appearance and manner of a cowpuncher, and he was sociable enough to stop and talk. He said he had just finished work up in the Hat Creek area and was headed down to Hartville. He had spent the night in Carlin, in the hotel there. Quiet little town, it seemed like. One fellow got his nose broke in the saloon, but he asked for it. Got liquored up and then took to jawin' with a railroader. Kind of a little fella to be doin' that. But he'd been on a jag, they said. Name? Something like Arnfield. Farnsworth? That might have been it. Got pasted pretty good. Could have been worse, but his friend stepped in. Nice little town all the same. You expect a few drunks at the end of the season, when everyone gets paid. But the hotel was fine, clean and all, and they said it was rare they ever had any trouble at all in their town. Even the fella that got in the scrape, they said he worked for a good outfit and was a fine-enough chap when he was sober.

Braden rode into town, thinking about the story he had heard. It seemed as if he had done well to stay out of town the night before, and he wondered if the altercation between Farnsworth and the railroader would have had anything to do with Forbes and his dealings. That might be hoping for too much.

Once in town, Braden went to a little backstreet bakery and bought a loaf of bread. He rode out to the edge of town by the stock pens, empty now, and ate half of the loaf. He wrapped the other half in a clean handkerchief and stuffed it into his war bag.

After brushing the crumbs off his coat, he mounted up and headed to the livery stable. He knew the stable keeper kept a few head of his own and bought and sold when he felt like it. Braden thought it would be a good time to buy a horse, as they would be coming off the range, and any horse kept in a barn or corral would have to be fed through the winter. He looked over a few horses that the stable man had, and he tried out a couple. The first one was a switch tail, a little too nervous for Braden's tastes, but the second one, a plain sorrel, was calm enough that he would work for packing or riding. After fifteen minutes of haggling, Braden gave the man thirty dollars and got a halter thrown in as well.

Next he went to the mercantile store, where he bought a tent, a skillet, a Dutch oven, a coffeepot, and a few smaller cooking and eating utensils. He deliberated for a while on the question of whether to buy tent poles. They were good hardwood — two end poles and a ridgepole, each in sections held together with hinges and pins — but like everything else, they cost money. He thought about how long it would take him to go out and find poles straight and long enough, cut them, and bring them back. Even then, the milled hardwood was ten times better; the poles would last longer and be easier to pack. So he took them.

After that he bought his food supplies — coffee, bacon, flour, rice, beans, dried fruit, canned tomatoes and peaches, and a pound of cheese. Within a day or two the cheese would be gone, but before long, if the weather got colder, he might have to worry about the bacon and the canned goods freezing.

His purchases made three big piles on the counter, and he realized he needed a couple of sheets of canvas to wrap the items into bundles. His money was going so fast that he did not think he should buy a packsaddle. Rather, he could put his riding saddle on the new horse, tie the bundles onto it, and ride the bay horse bareback as far as his claim. With that decided, he paid for all the new gear and supplies, then hauled them in three trips to the livery stable. It took him more than another hour to get his packs into even weight, bundled up, and tied on, with the rolled-up tent balanced on top and in the middle. When he was ready to lead the horses out, the stable man passed by and stopped.

"If I'd'a known you were goin' to do it that-a-way, I'd'a offered you a packsaddle. You can still rent a ridin' saddle if you want."

Braden looked at the bay and then at the man. "Thanks, but I think I'll be all right. It would just mean another trip into town."

"Suit yourself."

Braden hoisted himself up onto the back of the bay, straightened out the lead rope, and got into motion. The sorrel fell into line, and with the exception of an occasional balk, he gave no trouble on the trip out of town.

As Braden rode along, tugging on the

lead rope and readjusting himself to keep from slipping to one side or another, he gave a little thought to his dealings in town. In addition to the liveryman and the storekeeper, he had met a couple of men on the street, and with all of them he had a passing acquaintance. None of them had treated him in any way he would have thought unusual, and none of them made mention of Forbes, Farnsworth, or anyone else connected with Braden's recent line of work. As he reviewed the incidents together, he realized he had gotten no indication of whether word had gotten around about the confrontation at the campfire, much less whether he had landed a cannonball in the hull of the pirate's ship. That was the way things seemed to be, he thought — a fellow never got to know anything for sure.

He rode on out to his homestead claim, arriving at a little after midday. After stripping the horses and setting them out to graze, he sat on the rolled-up tent and ate a lunch of bread and cheese. Life could be a lot worse, he thought. At least he had food, a camp outfit, and a horse of his own. As he looked at the various bundles of bedroll, war bag, supplies, and cookware, he remembered a detail he had thought of on the way out. Ever since leaving the Seven Arrow he had been wearing his six-gun beneath his coat, but it occurred to him that he might as well keep his extra gun on hand as well. In addition to the .45, he had a .38 that he kept in his war bag as a spare. He hadn't used it much since he bought the .45, but he figured it wasn't doing him any good at all where it was. So he dug it out of his bag, checked to see that he had five beans in the wheel and the hammer on an empty cylinder, and put the pistol in his right coat pocket. His was a canvas coat with heavy wool lining, and in cold weather he kept it buttoned up. Having the .38 closer at hand made him feel more prepared. Next he rolled out the tent, pegged it down, raised the center on the ridgepole, and stretched out the sides with guy ropes. He had the tent facing south, with the flap away from the prevailing winds that would come from the north and west. A southern exposure caught the sun at this time of year, and the front of his tent also faced in the direction of Black Hat Butte, which he had in clear view.

With the tent up and his gear stowed, he went about scraping out a fire pit. All he had for the task was the little hatchet from his war bag. He had used it to drive in the tent stakes, and now he turned the head sideways to drag dirt. It was a wonder he hadn't thought to buy a shovel, but he imagined he would find a need for other things as well before long, so he began a mental list as he scraped the earth. It was a slow job, and he could see also that it would take a while for him to find enough rocks to set around the edge. About all he had was dirt and grass — and sagebrush, which would do for firewood until he could ride out and drag back a few good branches.

He built a fire, cut a corner off the flitch of bacon, and went about heating up and greasing his new skillet and Dutch oven. The smell of melting bacon fat got him to thinking about basic things again. He was going to have to try to keep at least a week's supply of grub and firewood on hand, and to do that, sooner or later he was going to need an ax and a rifle. He put those on the list with the shovel. If he could shoot something, like a deer or an antelope, the meat would keep well in this weather. Thin black smoke was rising now from the skillet and the Dutch oven. He liked the smell of the bacon grease. It quickened his senses and reminded him that he was on his own for any grub that came to his pot.

The scrap of bacon had shriveled down to a curl of crisp fat with a sliver of meat in it. He let it cool on the tip of his knife blade and then put it in his mouth and enjoyed the salty taste. *Salt, damn fool.* He needed to put that on the list, too.

Before dark he took the horses a mile east for water, riding the bay bareback and leading the sorrel. Back at camp he staked them out again and built up the fire. Then he began to measure out flour and water for biscuits. *Saleratus, fool. Baking soda.*

The biscuits came out flat and heavy, like Slack's hotcakes. No matter. They were hot, and they were edible. They went down the hatch with the rest of the cheese.

In the morning he had coffee and a can of peaches as he burned up the last of his firewood. He huddled close to the small fire and thought: It was all up to him. Food, water, firewood. Keep a weather eye out for the enemy. Think about what to do when the winter came. Maybe build a dugout. Maybe go somewhere to get a job and stay warm. He looked to the south and saw the butte against the morning sky. He knew why he was staying around. That, and to see how things turned out with Forbes.

When the fire was gone, Braden saddled the sorrel horse and put the halter on the bay. Heading east, he stopped to water the horses where he had watered them the evening before. Then he let them move out, from a trot to a lope to a fast walk and back to a lope, until the headquarters of the Seven Arrow came into sight.

As he rode into the yard, the bunkhouse door opened. It was Lum, who said the boss and the other two boys had gone for a load of hay. Braden thanked him, said so long, put the bay in the big corral, and rode out to the southwest.

The sorrel horse covered the ground well enough, but he had a rough trot and lope. He would not have been Braden's first choice for a saddle horse, but he would do. Being in no hurry, Braden kept him at a fast walk and no more. As he rode farther from the ranch, he felt a pang of sadness, and he thought he could trace it back to leaving the bay horse. He had taken quite a liking to the animal, to it and to the little sorrel with three white socks, and now he would ride them no more. That realization hurt more than anything Gundry had said.

The sun rose in the sky and warmed the day somewhat. The country was going into its dormant season now, with the snakes denned up and the bugs dying off. It was a time for long hours by the stove, cleaning guns and oiling leather. He thought of Beryl's house up ahead. He was glad she had a snug haven. The thought crossed his mind that it wouldn't be a bad place to put up his feet for the winter, but he made himself think otherwise. If it came to that, fine, but it would have to come of its own accord.

He rode into the yard at about noon. Birdie's critters were grazing on the north side of the house, but the girl was not visible. Then, as he brought the horse to a stop, the door of the house opened. Birdie stepped out and smiled.

"Hello, Birdie."

"Hello, Noel. You're just in time to eat."

"Oh, don't say that. It makes me feel bad."

"Why?"

"It's like the old joke about the fellow that shows up with his whole family at dinnertime, and his little boy lets it out that he whipped the horses to get there."

Birdie's smile gleamed as she laughed. "Oh, don't be that way. Come on in."

"Well, I didn't come by to —"

"You don't want to make Beryl mad, do you?"

He smiled as he shook his head. "No, not at all."

Inside the house, he savored the warmth and the smell of food. Beryl gave him her hand, showed him where to hang his hat and coat, and went back to serving up dinner. Braden sat down to a bowl of potato soup and a slice of warm bread. He saw that the soup had little chips of ham in it.

"I feel like a mooch, getting here just at mealtime."

"No reason to," she said. "We're glad for the company, aren't we, Birdie?"

"Uh-huh."

Beryl turned back to look at him. "So, did everything go all right?"

"More or less."

Her face drew together. "No incidents, I hope."

Braden glanced at the girl and wondered how much to tell. "I had a little run-in with Mr. Forbes, but I don't know if anything will come of it. But I'm done workin' for the season, and I more or less wore out my welcome at the Seven Arrow."

Beryl paused before dipping her spoon into her soup. "Oh. You mean you got let go?"

He thought she might be thinking about

what he had already considered. The cattleman didn't have a formal blacklist anymore, but it still worked by word of mouth. "Nothing to worry about," he said. "As far as work goes, I'll see about that later. In the meanwhile, I got a few things to set up camp, and I'm staying on my own little place. You know where that is, don't you?"

Beryl said, "I think so," and Birdie moved her head up and down.

"Not very far, really. A couple of miles north of here, maybe a little more." His eyes met Beryl's. "If you think you need anything, just holler."

"I'll keep that in mind," she said. Then she looked at Birdie. "We both will, won't we?"

Birdie looked up and nodded. Braden expected her to put on a kid's smile, but she didn't. She was the girl who had told him about the fat man, and as Beryl had said at the time, Birdie was no fool.

# Chapter Fifteen

When he reached the crest of the slope,
Braden turned in the saddle and looked
back over the country. The homestead
looked snug as ever. Taking a broad view, he
saw Little Sister, the hog-nose butte, and
Castle Butte all in a line to the south and
west. Farther to the west lay the mountains,
dark and rugged as they rose above the lower
hills. Braden could have gone straight north
from Beryl's, but he chose to ride to a high
spot and get a panoramic view before he
headed home. The country never changed,
as far as the landmarks went, but he liked to
imprint it in his mind from time to time
throughout the year.

Looking to the north and a little west, at
the gap between Black Hat Butte and the
lower sugarloaf butte, he saw a band of
about a dozen antelope. They were moving
away from him, their white rumps
bouncing as they ran in their rocking
gallop. This was the time when the antelope bunched up. In a few more weeks they
would form even larger herds, and, skittish

in the November winds, they would be hard to get to. If he wanted to have one for camp meat, he had better be doing it pretty soon.

He turned to sit straight in the saddle and touched his spurs to the sorrel's flanks. Up and over the slope they went, trotting out to the edge of the butte's shadow before Braden turned the horse north. As he did so, he saw Rove ride up out of a dip in the landscape near the base of the butte.

Rove was riding the dun horse and wearing the same pale color of clothes as always. He raised a hand in greeting, and Braden returned the gesture as he rode forward. As they came closer to one another, Braden noticed that Rove was wearing the same lightweight coat he had worn in warmer weather, yet he did not look uncomfortable.

"Hello, Rove."

"And hello to you, friend Braden. What's on the wind?"

"Cold weather, I'd guess." Braden raised his free right hand and rubbed the back of his gloved fingers against his beard.

"That's a safe bet."

"Sawn doot."

Rove smiled. *"C'est vrai.* What else?"

Braden looked at Rove's dancing eyes

and said, "I guess I've been to see the critter."

"And did he bite?"

"Not really. But I ended up on my own." Braden pointed with his chin toward the north. "I've got my own piece of ground a couple of miles north of here, and I set up a camp there. If someone needed to find me, that's where I'll likely be."

"A stranger in a strange land?"

"Paddlin' my own canoe, anyway."

Rove nodded, then laid his gloved right forefinger against the side of his nose and, with a half-frown, gave a signal of caution. "A word to the wise."

Braden made a horizontal motion with his own forefinger but said nothing.

"We have scotched the snake but not killed it."

Braden stroked his bearded chin with his thumb and fingers. "Four-bann?"

*"Cochon."*

"Ko-shone?"

"Peeg."

Braden let out a little laugh. He supposed Forbes was that, too. "Not much else to mention on my part."

Rove made a waving motion with the fingers of his right hand, as some people did to simulate a bird flying, and he said, "You knew the raven came to grief."

"So I heard. He wasn't all that bad."

Rove made a somber up-and-down motion with his head. "That's true." Then he laid his finger against his nose again.

Braden imitated the gesture and followed it with a brief nod.

Rove drew up the reins with his left hand and smoothed out the loose strands with his right. "Not much else here either."

Braden met the gaze of the light brown eyes, and he had the feeling that he would see Rove again, so he said, "So long, Rove. See you later."

"Mighty fine," Rove answered in his imitation southern voice. Then he touched the brim of his hat.

Braden did likewise. "You know where to find me," he said. "Don't be a stranger."

Rove passed the flat of his hand downward in front of his face, then made a wry smile and said nothing.

Braden smiled back, and as he turned his horse away he thought, there was always a good joke with Rove, if he could just figure it out.

It took a lot of firewood to cook a pot of beans. Each time he rode the horse east to water him, Braden foraged up and down the little creek and dragged back a branch or two with his rope. He broke the thinner pieces against his knee or under his foot, and he hacked at the thicker pieces with his hatchet until he had it notched around enough that he could slam the branch against the ground and break off the piece. It was slow, primitive work, and it gave him time to think about such things as buying a rifle. It would take a good portion of the money he had left, but it was the one way he could keep himself in meat. With a rifle and an ax, he could keep his camp supplied and have time to go visiting.

He had just broken off a length of firewood and was beginning to chip away at another when he heard the rumble of hoofbeats to the west. Setting down the hatchet, he pushed himself to his feet and turned. Here came the palomino horse, with Birdie leaning forward and clamped on bareback. As the horse came to a jolting stop, Birdie bounced and slid off, landing on her feet. She was wearing a coat, a wool cap, and mittens.

"Someone comin'," she said between heavy breaths.

"Really? Who is it?"

"The fat man." Birdie fetched another breath of air.

"Comin' from the southeast?" That would be the direction of Forbes's place.

"Uh-huh. I saw him when he was over on the other side of the butte, and I thought he was comin' this way, so I took the long way around and rode hard."

"Are you sure he's comin' this way?"

"I took a peek about a half mile back, and he was pokin' along."

Braden looked at the girl. She didn't need to be around any of this, but he wasn't sure which way to send her. If Engle saw her riding away, he might figure out that she was the witness Braden had mentioned, and he might try something later on to keep her from ever talking. "We don't have much time," he said. "What do you think about hidin' in the tent?"

She bobbed her head up and down. "I can do that."

"Good. Give me that horse, and you get in the tent. Don't make a peep until I tell you it's all right."

"Okay." Birdie made a fast walk to the tent, untied the flap, and went in.

"You see that rope in there? How about handin' it out to me, so I can stake out this horse?"

She handed out the rope, and he took it. He led the horse east of camp a ways, slipped off the bridle, and tied the rope around the animal's neck. "This is just for a few minutes, I hope," he said to the horse as he patted its neck. Then he tied the other end of the rope to a clump of sagebrush and turned to go back to camp. As he turned, he saw Engle riding up on a brown horse he recognized as belonging to Forbes.

Braden's stomach kicked and his heart started pounding, but he wanted to show as much repose as he could, so he walked back to his campsite, unbuttoning his coat as he went. He heard the horse coming at a trot, and when he got to the edge of his fire pit, he turned around just in time to see Engle come storming in, wheel the horse around, dismount on the off side, and come up with a lever-action rifle in his hands. As Braden saw the menacing look on the fat man's face, he realized that this might have been the Peeg that Rove mentioned. It was too late to be funny; he heard the snickety-snick of the rifle as Engle levered in a shell.

Braden felt a sinking feeling inside. He hadn't expected things to happen quite like this. He had had the presence of mind to unbutton his coat, but he was still wearing his gloves. "What do you want?" he asked.

"Not much. You'll find out." Engle moved a couple of steps to his right, putting himself between Braden and the tent. "Just do as I say, and don't get too smart for yourself."

Braden said nothing. He remembered the .38 in his coat pocket, and he wondered if he would have a chance to get to it.

"Use your left hand to unbuckle your gun belt and drop it on the ground." Engle made a short waving motion with the rifle to reinforce his command.

Braden took off his gloves and stuffed them in his left coat pocket as Engle watched. That was good, he thought. The right pocket wouldn't look so conspicuous now. With his right hand he drew aside the front of his coat, and with his left he unbuckled the belt, let the buckle slip off, and swung out the belt, holster, and pistol.

"Drop it on the ground."

Braden didn't like to drop a gun in the dirt, but he had no choice. He kept his eyes on Engle's face, noting the sallow complexion and the wart by the left nostril, as he let go of the gunbelt. "What next?"

"We might go for a little ride."

"Over to the Rawhide Buttes?" Braden thought he saw the tent flap move, but rather than look beyond Engle, he trained his eyes on the man's hands and the rifle. He could feel his own hands getting cold.

"Don't you worry about —"

Engle's speech was cut off by a swinging blow of the skillet. Because he was not very tall, Birdie got the cast-iron pan up and around pretty well, heavy as it was. But she did not knock the man down. She staggered him and pushed his hat forward with the blow, and then she dropped the skillet and ran like a deer.

Engle pushed his hat back with his left hand, then got his hand back on the forearm of his rifle and swung around to his left. He was trying to pick up his target.

Braden had the .38 in his hand. It worked almost by itself as the hammer came back, the sights lined up, and the gun fired.

The shot hit Engle in the middle of his abdomen, below his chest and the level of the rifle. The impact of the shot jolted him loose from the rifle, which fell forward, and his hat, which fell backward.

Braden stood and looked at the man where he lay, flat on his back with his arms outstretched. His nose was up in the air, and his teeth showed. The sight reminded Braden of a garden mole that the cat had killed. He had seen a few, and they always looked the same — laid out flat, belly up, nose in the air.

Birdie's voice came across the thin air. "Did you get him?"

"Yes, I did. You can come on back."

When she had come within ten yards of the body, keeping it well to her right side, she stopped and looked straight at Braden. With a motion of her head, she said, "He was trying to get me, wasn't he?"

Braden nodded. "Uh-huh."

"I hit him as hard as I could, but I guess it wasn't hard enough."

"You did fine. It made the difference."

Birdie's eyebrows tightened. "What do you think we should do now?"

"I think you should go back and stay with your aunt, if you don't mind riding back by yourself. And I think I'd better go into town and report this." He looked at the pale sun. "I believe I've got just enough time before dark."

Braden sat in front of his tent after the wagon carrying the sheriff and Engle had creaked away. Almost twenty-four hours had passed since he had killed a man, and he still did not feel any great change. He had wondered a thousand times if he would ever kill someone and what it would feel like if he did, and here he was, not feeling anything at all. He did not feel guilty, victorious, or even satisfied. Maybe the reaction would come later, after the realization set in. He shook his head. He doubted even that. He knew he had killed a man, and he felt no remorse. Maybe the man had killed Greaves, or Downs, or both, but it didn't matter. Nor did it matter that the man probably intended to kill the man he held a rifle on. Braden didn't need justification or a sense of justice being brought into balance. Those things helped, but it didn't matter whether they were adequate. The man had aimed a rifle at a running girl, and Braden had seen a way to stop him. All other details were pertinent to his sense of what kind of a man he had killed, but when it came down to the question of justice, they remained incidental, as he had pulled the trigger for another reason.

Braden sat staring at the cold ashes of his campfire. He thought that for his next move he should talk to Beaumont and find out what news, if any, he had heard of Forbes. Although Braden had stayed overnight in the livery stable and had made himself scarce, he knew word of Engle's death had spread through town not long after he had reported it. The stable man had come around with his lantern before closing up for the night and had said, "I don't blame you. They said he was a bad pill." Braden imagined that by now, word might have rippled out to the ranches.

He tightened the cinch on the horse and rode to the Seven Arrow, stopping once for water and a dozen times to study the country behind him. Lum, who said he was alone at the ranch, asked him if he wanted something to eat. Braden said no, thanks, although he hadn't eaten since morning. He wasn't hungry, and he didn't want any of Gundry's grub. Lum said the boss and the two boys had gone out for another load of hay, and Braden should be able to find them at the fenced lot where they had stacked the hay in the summer. Braden thanked him and rode out in that direction.

On his way out, he met Gundry by himself. The boss was driving a wagonload of hay with three pitchforks stuck in the stack and lying flat across the top. He wore a brown wool coat and a winter cap of about the same color. He stopped the wagon long enough to tell Braden that he had sent Beaumont and Slack out to check cattle and that he expected them back at the ranch at about the time he got there.

Braden thanked him and rode on. He could not tell anything from Gundry's manner. The boss man had not conveyed arrogance, hostility, concession, or anything. Braden sensed that they had nothing to talk about, and that was it.

A couple of miles farther out, he saw Beaumont at a distance and waved him down. They met at the bottom of a long, broad draw. Beaumont had untied his rawhide lariat and was passing it through his right hand.

Braden spoke first. "I saw the boss, but he didn't say much. Just told me where I could find you."

"He's not very talkative today. I think he's wonderin' if his market value is goin' down."

"You mean his own?"

"Oh, yeah. He already got paid for the steers he shipped."

"I see. Then I guess word traveled."

Beaumont's dark eyes had a bit of a flash to them. "It sure did. Wyndham dropped by, and after a few words with the boss he took off."

"Goin' to town, or back to the ranch?"

"To the ranch, I'd say. I gathered he'd been to town."

"Huh. I'm surprised Lum didn't say anything."

"He might not know yet. The boss told us when we finished loadin' the wagon."

"What-all did he say?"

Beaumont took a breath and exhaled. "Well, he said Wyndham told him Engle had been out to your place and had got killed in a shootin' scrape."

"Did he say why?"

Beaumont shook his head. "Just that. Said no one knew Engle was back in the country." He looked down at the lariat, as if his fingers had found an imperfection.

"The hell. He came ridin' from Forbes's direction. That's what the girl told me."

"What girl?" Beaumont looked up.

"The one that lives with Beryl." Braden realized he hadn't referred to the grass widow in that way before, but rather than do anything about it, he added, "The one that saw Engle sneakin' along behind Ed."

"Oh."

"She came out to warn me he was on the way, and things got a little tight with him, and he went to take a shot at her, and that's when I did what I did."

"That's more than we heard, but who knows how much of the story Wyndham told."

Braden shrugged. "Well, that's the short version. He had already pulled a gun on me and wanted to take me for a ride. But when he aimed at the girl, that did it."

"I imagine." Beaumont moved his head from side to side as if mulling it over.

After a pause, Braden spoke again. "So, what about Forbes? Engle comin' back doesn't look too good for him."

"No, but from what the boss said, Forbes didn't know he was back. He's not even around. Went to Harrison, accordin' to Wyndham."

"I bet. Well, I hope this does somethin'."

"It should put a hole in his bucket, but you don't know. I think he should've given in earlier, but there's no tellin' how long he might hold out."

Braden shook his head. "I'm with you. That was a big pot of beans we spilled on him, and he faced down every part of it. So there's no tellin'."

Beaumont looked out over the country. "I guess we just wait and see."

"I guess so."

They said so long, and Beaumont said he would drop by in a week or so unless something came up in the meanwhile.

Braden rode on, no more satisfied than before. He needed to get over to Beryl's place, to see how Birdie was doing as well as to tell Beryl how things were sitting. He wished he had something more definite to report about Forbes, for Beryl's sake as well as for his own.

That was the trouble with this whole mess all along. He never knew anything for sure, he couldn't produce ironclad proof even when he knew it existed, and he couldn't get a definite resolution. Well, Engle being dead was definite, but not so far as it redressed any wrongs or answered any questions. Often of late it had seemed that not just his own life, but life in general, was plagued with uncertainty. The difference would lie in how people dealt with it. He doubted that Slack, for example, was troubled by it as much as he was. Both he and Slack, along with others, shared the question of how Greaves died, but Slack did not seem to be troubled by problems he couldn't solve. Then there were others, like Forbes, who did more than tolerate uncertainty. He seemed to thrive on it, even manufacture it; maybe he was comfortable with it because it troubled others, and that way he could use it to his advantage.

Braden shook his head, watching the ground as it passed beneath the horse's feet. He guessed there was no getting around it. Things weren't always clear-cut. Still, a fellow liked to know how things stood. Take this idea about hunting some meat. If he shot at a deer and knocked it down, he expected it to still be a deer when he got up next to it. It shouldn't have turned into an antelope. And if he shot a deer with a nice set of antlers, it should still have the headgear when he walked up to it. Things shouldn't change. If a fellow wanted to argue a point, the other man shouldn't be able to change what the argument was about. But people did. Braden wanted to argue about whether two men stole some cattle for Forbes, and as soon as his back was turned, Forbes turned it into a question of whether the two men would do something like that. And now this thing with Engle. He probably hadn't gone anywhere, but with the pretense that he had disappeared, Forbes could shift the issue.

At least a deer was honest. Shoot a nice buck with antlers, and he didn't turn into an old hag antelope just to be contrary. They said whores were honest, too. Braden didn't know about that. Maybe some of them were, the type that didn't pretend to be doing anything but business. Others, they were all smiles and smoldering talk, but when the time came they turned into a cold lump of . . .

Something split the air, and a wave of pressure whoofed against the left side of Braden's head. Following the concussion of air he heard the sharp crash of a rifle. Someone was shooting at him! He felt a jolt of fear in his upper body, from the pit of his stomach out to his arms. The sorrel horse had jumped and started trotting, so Braden kicked him into a gallop and leaned forward. Another shot sang through the air, first the whistle of air and then the boom of the rifle. Braden didn't know which direction the shots were coming from, but the second one seemed like a wider miss. A moving target was hard to hit, unless it was straight away, and he didn't think the shots were coming from behind him. From the corner of his eye he had noticed a little bluff a couple of hundred yards off to his left just before the first shot came, and it sounded as if both shots had come from there.

The sorrel horse was pounding the earth at a dead run, and Braden was dug in with his feet and knees as he bent low over the horse's neck. Another shot zinged behind him, it sounded like. He thought of turning the horse to get it to zigzag, but even at a run it had a rough gait, and he didn't want to risk any sharp turns that would leave him in the dirt.

Then he heard two more shots, but they sounded muffled as if they came from a different place and were not aimed in his direction. Maybe the sniper was shooting at something else now, or someone was shooting at him.

Braden slowed the horse to a gallop, then a trot, then a walk. Looking back, he was pretty sure he was out of rifle range from the source of the first shots; as he looked around from his position out on the open plain, he did not see where anyone else could get at him for the moment. Whatever was going on, he would like to know about it before he went any farther west.

Drawing the horse to a stop, he turned and studied the little bluff, which lay about three-quarters of a mile away. He should have been keeping a better eye on the country and not on the ground at his horse's feet. It all looked so evident now. He watched the bluff for a couple of minutes, until a pale horse and rider came out onto the plain and the man waved at him. Braden had no doubt that it was Rove. He wondered if Rove could have fired the shots at him, and he did not think it was possible. He thought it more likely that Rove had fired the second set of shots, or had drawn fire from the other person and had sent him running.

Rove continued to ride forward, waving. Braden did not think it was a trap. He had an instinctive trust in Rove, and even from the most skeptical point of view, he knew Rove could have gotten a lot closer for a shot if he had wanted it. Braden nudged his horse forward and rode back across the open country.

Rove was smiling as Braden rode up to him. "Let's go take a look," he said, making a circular, pointing motion with his left thumb.

As Rove turned the dun horse and headed for the bluff, Braden fell in alongside. He noticed the rifle and the grass rope as before, on the right side of Rove's saddle.

When they got to the bluff, the horses picked their way up a gentle rise of ground to get around to the back side. A hundred yards away, a saddled roan horse stood with its reins on the ground. Up on Braden's left, sprawled out at the base of an upthrust of white clay, the body of a man lay next to a rifle. Braden moved his horse forward enough to see what he expected — a reddish blond beard with a few streaks of silver.

Braden exhaled a long, slow breath. Gundry was going to have to let go now. He could cling to some of his earlier actions, but he was going to have to admit, to some extent, that he had bought into someone who was false.

Braden looked back at Rove, who had a mirthful look on his face as he reached back and patted the stock of his rifle.

"Got the weasel with my peep-sight."

Braden let out a quick breath and a short, nervous laugh. "I guess you did."

Rove, with his hands in front of him, rotated his pointing forefingers around one another, then gave Braden another wry look. "Didn't think anyone else was going to."

"Probably not, at least at the moment."

"And I guess you got the little woodchuck."

Braden had a flashing image of a man on his back like a garden mole. "I didn't have much choice."

"None of us do." Rove motioned with his head in the direction of the dead man. "He didn't. Not at the last, anyway."

"He sure enough chose to take a shot at me."

Rove made a back-and-forth horizontal movement with his right forefinger. "His mistake. And his last choice."

They both looked up and around at the sound of approaching hoofbeats. A half-minute later, Beaumont and Slack came into view around the northeast side of the bluff. They rode upslope to within five yards of Braden and Rove.

"We heard shots," said Beaumont.

"Rove here took care of someone who took a few shots at me." Braden pointed his head toward the dead man.

Slack craned his neck as Beaumont stood up in his stirrups. They both nodded and looked at Rove.

"Do you know each other?" Braden asked. When Beaumont and Slack said no, Braden introduced them around.

With that done, Rove made a hissing noise through his teeth and then spoke. "You can tell the sheriff he knows where to find me." Then he turned his horse and rode away to the southwest.

Beaumont tossed a glance in the direction of the body. "So much for his bein' in Harrison."

"That's what I thought," said Braden. "And so much for not knowin' Engle was around."

Braden looked back at Rove and watched until he disappeared into a fold in the landscape. Then he turned to the other two and said, "That's the fellow I mentioned before. The one with the funny words."

"Seemed like he thought there was something funny here, too," said Beaumont. "Where do you think the sheriff is supposed to find him?"

Braden shrugged. "I have no idea. But if you boys don't mind, I think it might be in the spirit of things if you passed this on to Gundry so he could report it. Oh, and if the sheriff wanted to, he could look for the scar."

Beaumont poked his cheek out with his tongue. "I suppose the undertaker'll notice anyway." Then he looked at Braden. "And you?"

Braden smiled. "You do know where to find me. I'll be in one of two places."

The other two nodded. "Good enough," said Beaumont. "We'll do 'er."

Braden turned his horse around and rode back out onto the plain in the direction he had been headed earlier. He still didn't have all the answers, but he knew as much as he was going to get to know for certain. And he had done something. He had a cool, clean feeling as he looked at the country around him.

When he was sure he was alone and well out of earshot, he sang the two lines he had borrowed from Beaumont:

*"Yoodle-ooh, yoodle-ooh-hoo, so sings a lone cowboy,*
*Who with the wild roses wants you to be free."*

He would be in one of two places, all right. If he wasn't at his own camp, he would be the gentleman caller at a little homestead over on the other side of Black Hat Butte.

# About the Author

*John D. Nesbitt* lives in the plains country of Wyoming, where he teaches English and Spanish at Eastern Wyoming College in Torrington. His Western stories have appeared in many magazines and anthologies. He has written many traditional Western novels, including *One-Eyed Cowboy Wild*, *Coyote Trail*, *Man from Wolf River*, and *For the Norden Boys*; more traditional Westerns are forthcoming. Two contemporary Western novels, *Keep the Wind in Your Face* and *A Good Man to Have in Camp*, keep company with *Antelope Sky* and *Seasons in the Fields*, two collections of contemporary Western short stories. Nesbitt has also brought out a collection of traditional Western short stories, *One Foot in the Stirrup*, and *Adventures of the Ramrod Rider*, a medley of parody, satire, poetry, and pristine romance. His fiction, nonfiction, book reviews, and poetry have been widely published. He has won many prizes and awards for his work, including a Wyoming Arts Council literary fellowship for his fiction writing, two awards from Wyoming

Writers for encouragement of and service to other writers, and two fiction awards from the Wyoming State Historical Society.

The employees of Thorndike Press hope you have enjoyed this Large Print book. All our Thorndike and Wheeler Large Print titles are designed for easy reading, and all our books are made to last. Other Thorndike Press Large Print books are available at your library, through selected bookstores, or directly from us.

For information about titles, please call:

(800) 223-1244

or visit our Web site at:

www.gale.com/thorndike
www.gale.com/wheeler

To share your comments, please write:

Publisher
Thorndike Press
295 Kennedy Memorial Drive
Waterville, ME    04901